The HEART'S CHOICE

Books by Tracie Peterson and Kimberley Woodhouse

All Things Hidden   *Beyond the Silence*   *The Heart's Choice*

The Heart of Alaska

In the Shadow of Denali

Out of the Ashes

Under the Midnight Sun

The Treasures of Nome

Forever Hidden

Endless Mercy

Ever Constant

Books by Tracie Peterson

Ladies of the Lake

Destined for You

Forever My Own

Waiting on Love

Brookstone Brides

When You Are Near

Wherever You Go

What Comes My Way

Willamette Brides

Secrets of My Heart

The Way of Love

Forever by Your Side

Golden Gate Secrets

In Places Hidden

In Dreams Forgotten

In Times Gone By

Heart of the Frontier

Treasured Grace

Beloved Hope

Cherished Mercy

For a complete list of titles, visit traciepeterson.com.

Books by Kimberley Woodhouse

Secrets of the Canyon

A Deep Divide

A Gem of Truth

A Mark of Grace

For a complete list of titles, visit kimberleywoodhouse.com.

The HEART'S CHOICE

TRACIE PETERSON
KIMBERLEY WOODHOUSE

BETHANYHOUSE
a division of Baker Publishing Group
Minneapolis, Minnesota

© 2023 by Peterson Ink, Inc. and Kimberley Woodhouse

Published by Bethany House Publishers
Minneapolis, Minnesota
www.bethanyhouse.com

Bethany House Publishers is a division of
Baker Publishing Group, Grand Rapids, Michigan

Printed in the United States of America

ISBN 978-0-7642-3897-0 (trade paper)
ISBN 978-0-7642-3898-7 (cloth)
ISBN 978-1-4934-4209-6 (ebook)

Library of Congress Cataloging-in-Publication Control Number: 2022053720

This is a work of historical reconstruction; the appearances of certain historical figures are therefore inevitable. All other characters, however, are products of the author's imagination, and any resemblance to actual persons, living or dead, is coincidental.

Scripture quotations are from the King James Version of the Bible.

Cover design by Dan Thornberg, Design Source Creative Services

Kimberley Woodhouse is represented by the Steve Laube Agency.

Baker Publishing Group publications use paper produced from sustainable forestry practices and post-consumer waste whenever possible.

23 24 25 26 27 28 29   7 6 5 4 3 2 1

To our friend Becca Whitham

Becca, you have given me much to smile about and I so appreciate your spirit and offer of prayers when things have been difficult. Thank you for being a friend.

—Tracie

Becca, what a ride we've been on, my friend! When we met twelve-plus years ago, I don't think either one of us could have ever imagined what God had planned for our families. It is a joy to share story and writing with you. The ups and downs of life have brought us closer together—thank you for being my friend. And now, we are family.

—Kimberley

Dear Reader,

We are so excited to start this new series with you. Tracie and I both have a love for Kalispell and when we lived in Montana less than two miles apart from each other, we spent lots of time brainstorming these stories and traveling to the locations. My husband and I moved east several months ago, but last fall, Tracie and I went back to the series locations together and did a ton of research. Check out my blog for fun pictures and historic tidbits: Kimberleywoodhouse .com/blog

This series will feature three beautiful historic landmarks in Kalispell. First, the Carnegie Library, which is now the Hockaday Museum of Art. Then the Great Northern Railway Depot, which is now the Chamber of Commerce. And finally the grand McIntosh Opera House, which is above what is now Western Outdoor on Main Street.

Though based on real locations and, at times, real people, this book is a work of fiction. We'd like to thank the Nineteenth-Century Club—a women's organization—that established the very first circulating library in the town in 1894 through their group the Ladies Library Association.

We thought it would be fun to have our heroine in *The Heart's Choice* be a trailblazer in her field, so we needed our hero to be chosen for the prestigious librarian position at the new Carnegie Library.

But with our fictional story, we wanted to give you some history. Since the 1930s, female librarians have been the majority. In fact, male librarians in 1930 made up only 8 percent. Prior to this time, however, male librarians were the norm. It wouldn't be difficult to see Mark vying for the position.

But in reality, Florence Madison served as the first librarian in Kalispell, followed by author Katherine Berry Judson, and then Janet Nunn. We don't wish to take away from what these women accomplished and did.

Since literature and reading is such a focal point of this story, we used several famous books as our characters' favorites, but the mysteries that our heroine, Rebecca, loves most are all made up in our minds.

Thank you again for reading *The Heart's Choice*.

We love to hear from our readers!

—Kimberley and Tracie

Prologue

A sharp jab to his ribcage jolted Mark Andrews out of the story world he'd been immersed in and back to the bumpy seat on the wagon. The fifteen-year-old frowned at the interruption and lifted his book higher.

Another elbow to his side made him grunt as he closed the book and narrowed his gaze at the offender—his older sister, Kate. She was always bossing him around, practically since the day he'd been born. "What? You were the one who said you wanted to drive the wagon. And now you won't let me read in peace?"

Couldn't she let him read for a bit more? *Around the World in Eighty Days* was the most exciting book he'd ever read.

Her huff preceded a giggle. "I was simply attempting to get your attention. For someone who's always loved mountains and water, it's ironic that your nose is stuck in a book when *this* is the view." A lift of her chin accentuated her

9

teasing words. "But far be it from me to interrupt your reading. Won't happen again." The wagon rumbled along.

Wait. What did she say? His gaze snapped forward. He'd been so perturbed at her—and so absorbed in the story—that he hadn't taken the moment to even look at his surroundings. Once again, she'd gotten the better of him. Of course, she would say that's what big sisters were for, right?

"Wow." The panorama before him was . . . awe-inspiring. Deep blue water edged by a line of mountains with peaks touched with the hint of winter snow stretched as far as his eye could see. "Where are we?"

"Flathead Lake." She released a sigh. "See? You wouldn't want to miss this because your nose was buried in a book, now would you?"

"You're right."

Another jab. A smile lifted Kate's lips, but she didn't say the dreaded words, *"I told you so."*

"The lake is much larger than I imagined." When Dad had told them about it, he hadn't mentioned the massive size, had he? Or maybe Mark hadn't been listening.

"The mountains are taller than I thought they'd be too." Kate slowed the horses a bit and shifted on the wagon seat. "I wonder if they're as tall as Pikes Peak?"

As gorgeous as the blue sky was, it paled in comparison to the deep shade of the water. "I don't think they could be that tall." The long line of carved, jagged mountains stretched north. "By the way, thanks for the bruises."

She didn't turn to look at him, but the side of her mouth turned up. "I am happy to take any opportunity to inflict pain." Relaxing her hands, she leaned back. The reins dipped in a slack line. "Now I understand why Dad chose this area.

It makes my heart happy just to sit and look at all of God's handiwork. The winters will no doubt be tough, but we've dealt with that before."

"No doubt." Though he didn't relish wrangling cattle through snowdrifts. The look on his sister's face told a different story. She'd always loved every last bit of ranching, no matter how dirty she got, how uncooperative the weather became, or how frustrating the work was. "You're excited about this new ranch, aren't you?"

She turned to him, light shining in her light blue eyes. Her smile grew. "Yes. Aren't you?"

He propped a foot up on the toeboard in front of him and shrugged. "Doesn't really matter to me. I wouldn't want to deny Dad his dreams. And you love it too, so that's good."

"One of these days, you're going to appreciate all the work we'll put into this new ranch. Once you're the proud owner." Her know-it-all glance nudged him as much as her elbow, but he didn't miss the half-second of uncertainty that she blinked away. Was that about her future or his lack of enthusiasm?

"Dad won't be handing anything over for a long time." Not for a couple decades, anyway. After all, in a few years, Mark hoped to go to college. He would prove to his father that there was a world of possibilities beyond ranching. Even if it took him a lifetime. But he couldn't let Kate know his thoughts for now. He shook his head. "I better finish my book before we get there. Dad will be along soon enough with the cattle." He craned his neck to look over his shoulder. The herd stretched out, dotting the green grass behind him in a wave of black lumps.

"Neither one of us will hear the end of it if we don't get

there in good time." Kate slapped the reins to urge the horses into a faster rhythm again.

Opening his book back to where he'd stopped, Mark tried to shake off what his sister's words had done to his heart. Was it wrong that he didn't love ranching like they did? Was it wrong to have other hopes and dreams for his future?

In Dad's mind, yes. Kate's too.

The few times he'd broached the subject at the dinner table, he'd been met with adamant declarations that he would have a different perspective soon enough. The responsibility and pride of ownership and hard work would be *his*. Owning land and cattle—ranching—was in his blood.

So they'd told him all his fifteen years of life.

But even gazing at the beautiful scene before him . . .

He wasn't convinced.

AUGUST 1890—CHICAGO, ILLINOIS

The throngs of people moving around her made ten-year-old Rebecca Whitman sway and shift as the crowd settled in for the parade. She squeezed her little sister's hand. Why did people get so pushy? Couldn't they follow the rules and have manners? Maybe they didn't know the rules or how to have manners.

Which was a little bit more likely, now that she thought about it. No wonder her mother was so insistent that she and her siblings learn those things, so *they* wouldn't be like the "uncouth of society" and would be able to make their way in this world. Whatever that meant.

Tipping her head back, Rebecca stared up at Momma,

whose new hat and dress had been a gift from Papa for her birthday. In her favorite color. Yellow. The woven hat with a wide brim boasted sunflowers and yellow ribbons. The dress was a simple material but boasted brocade cuffs. How Momma had oohed and aahed over those! And oh goodness, did she look pretty.

Rebecca sighed. Whatever *brocade* was, it was soft to touch and obviously meant something very good.

Maybe one day she would be as beautiful as her mother. Momma held her head high and had the best of posture and, of course, the best manners.

She straightened herself and pushed her shoulders back. When the man next to her bumped into her, she spoke in a clear voice. "Excuse me."

The man turned and grinned down at her. He tipped his bowler hat at her. "I am so sorry to have knocked you, miss. Please excuse *me*."

She smiled back. So this was how it felt to be grown-up. It was nice.

Momma squeezed her shoulder. "Stay close now and help me keep an eye on the younger ones. Keep using those good manners." She winked and then clapped her hands together along with the crowd.

Rebecca tried to do everything exactly like her mother. She clapped her gloved hands together too but stepped closer to Momma. Ebba and Kristina held onto Momma's skirts.

The crowd pressed in as it grew.

Parades were Rebecca's favorite, especially on Lake Street. The view was the prettiest here. When she was little, Papa used to place her on his shoulders, and she could see everything as it came down the street. She was too big for that now, but she still loved watching the parade up close. It was fun to get dressed up and see all the people, floats, and exciting new contraptions.

Papa stepped up to Momma's other side with Rebecca's younger brother Peter in tow. Papa shared a whispered conversation with Momma, and her cheeks tinged a lovely pink. The way they smiled at one another made Rebecca's heart sing.

"John and Lars are helping Mr. Littleton with his float." Her father grinned. "Who knows, maybe they will even get to ride on it."

Oh! To get to ride on a float in the parade! Wouldn't that be the best thing ever? One day—when she was older—maybe she could help with the floats too. The very thought gave her a shiver.

A giant float pulled behind six horses captured everyone's attention, but it was for the men's club and didn't have any flowers. Rebecca let out a huff. The only ones worth looking at were covered in flowers.

While the crowd cheered for the float, she glanced at the alley next to them. Who was moving over there? Oh, it was just a couple men. *Horsing around* as Papa would say.

She turned back, but then a shout pierced her senses. That wasn't a cheer. That sounded like someone in trouble. Where had the shout come from? Oh, if only the crowd would be more quiet—

Wait. There, in the alley. She peeked through the gap of arms and shoulders around her and frowned. What was going on? And why didn't anyone else seem to see it?

A well-dressed man clung to a black bag and shook his

head at a larger man who had his hands on the bag and tugged.

The big man punched the smaller man, but the smaller man held on.

Another punch.

Rebecca tried to cry out, but her voice caught in her throat.

The bigger man kept hitting and kicking the smaller man until he fell to his knees. Then with a horrible, final blow, the well-dressed man fell over and the big man kicked him one more time. Then he took off with the bag.

Tears stung Rebecca's eyes as she tugged at Momma's dress. *Someone* needed to help the man! But with all the chaos, her mother didn't acknowledge her.

With another tug at Momma's dress, she raised her voice. "We need to help him!"

Her mother turned toward her. "What's going on?"

Papa was at her side in an instant.

"I saw a big man hurt someone in the alley. We need to help him."

"Show me what you saw, my dear." Papa grabbed her hand and steered her through the crowd.

Darting her gaze back to the alley, Rebecca spied another man coming to the fallen man's rescue. She let out a long sigh, and tears streamed down her cheeks. Was the man on the ground all right?

Before Rebecca and her family could reach the alley, police officers ran in, blowing their whistles.

They grabbed the man bending over the fallen man.

"*No!*" Rebecca shook her head. "He's not the bad guy!"

The terror in the hero's eyes as he was dragged away

was enough to make her yank out of Papa's grasp and run forward. "He didn't do it!"

But the policemen didn't listen to her. Hadn't they heard her? She saw what happened!

The man on the ground wasn't moving.

More policemen moved in.

Pushing and shoving through the people who now swarmed the scene seemed to take forever, until she reached the alley.

She pointed. "That man didn't do it!"

But no one listened. They hauled the good man away.

While a pool of blood spread under the man on the ground.

January 12, 1904—Kalispell, Montana

The downright icy air around him burned his lungs as he inhaled, but it couldn't take away the sense of euphoria that filled him. After all these years of hard work, he'd gained the position of a lifetime!

The head of the brand-new Carnegie Library.

He, Mark Andrews, was the head of the Carnegie Library!

Of course, his father probably wouldn't be excited. Or impressed. Angus Andrews wanted Mark to love ranching. Plain and simple. But being a librarian had been Mark's dream. He'd gone after it and obtained it. Not only was he the librarian, but he was in charge of the whole place.

In the darkness of the early morning, he stared up at the large Second Renaissance Revival–style building in front of him. The deep, bracketed eaves above the pilastered entry made the dome above stand out.

From the domed, octagonal entry to the gray sandstone

from the Columbus quarries making up the base to the deep red of the brick exterior, the structure was beautiful.

"There's the cowboy."

Mark turned at the voice breaking the silence of the morning to hold out a hand to Judge Milton Ashbury. "Good morning, Judge."

No surprise that the man used his childhood nickname. Though he'd left the ranch, people around here would probably always call him Cowboy.

"Ready for the big ceremony? I know you haven't had much time to get settled."

True enough. Mark had arrived four days prior and had spent every waking hour with the books. "I'm looking forward to today, sir. Thank you."

A high-pitched *yip* diverted his attention downward.

"And who's this?" Mark crouched down to pet the white ball of fur.

The older man let out a long sigh. "Marvella's newest passion. His name is Sir Theophilus."

Mark raised his eyebrows, working hard to keep his amusement to himself.

It didn't work. A snicker escaped.

The little thing couldn't weigh more than a few pounds and seemed all fur. It bounced around on its tiny little paws, stabbing at the dirt and snow in the street, and then at the judge's pants.

Mark cleared his throat and gave his best effort to swipe the mirth off his face. "My apologies. It's a gallant name."

"Don't apologize. I think it's ridiculous as well, but you know my wife. Her group of church ladies named him. Apparently they are now working through the book of Luke, and it seemed apropos." The man's bushy white eyebrows, mustache, and beard all wiggled as he rolled his eyes. "And since my loving wife thinks I need more exercise, I've been declared the one to walk him in the mornings instead of 'pacing the halls,' as she puts it." With a shake of his head, he peered down at the little dog. "As long as no one thinks he belongs to me, I don't mind. I have a reputation to uphold, you know."

Mark chuckled. "Well, it *is* barely six a.m., sir. I think you're safe." He glanced around. "There aren't too many folks out at this time of day."

"Which is a godsend." The judge straightened his coat with the hand not holding the leash. "I wouldn't want to be seen with this little fluff ball too often."

And yet despite the man's gruff words, there was no denying the twinkle in Ashbury's eyes. If Mark wasn't mistaken, the good judge liked the little dog but wouldn't ever admit it. "He certainly is cute. How much will he grow?"

One bushy, wild eyebrow shot up. "This is it, young man. He's full grown, or so my wife informs me."

"Oh." Mark grinned. Maybe it was best to change the subject. "How are things with you? I know you were voted in as the district judge while I was in college. Are you enjoying the position?"

"Very much. All except for the travel. It's a large district to cover, and while most of the larger cases are transferred here to Kalispell, I still need to travel out to the other areas." He stuffed his left hand into his coat pocket. "At my age, it's beginning to be wearisome."

"I can imagine." Montana was a rugged land and not

always easily accessible. "Can you request that all cases be brought here?"

"As our great state keeps growing and more districts are added, yes, eventually. Until then, I'm afraid I will have to travel, which is much easier when the snow is no longer on the ground." Another yip from Sir Theophilus made the judge check his pocket watch. "I better head back, Marvella will be waiting."

"Please give her my love, sir."

Judge Ashbury laid a hand on Mark's shoulder and stepped a few inches closer. "We're all proud of you. It's wonderful to have you back home doing what you love— what you were called to do. I know things have been difficult with your father over the years but remember that he loves you. Marvella and I have been praying for the Lord's will to be done. You're family to us, and we're glad you're home." The man's eyes filled with a sheen of tears. He dipped his chin and cleared his throat. "I'll be back for the dedication ceremony later."

"Thank you, sir." Mark struggled to clear his own throat. He blinked several times as he watched the man and his tiny dog walk back toward the Ashbury mansion.

The judge and his wife understood Mark like no one else. They'd been like a doting aunt and uncle, filling the aching hole left in his life when his mother died. Mark had been a mere five years old. The Ashburys had poured into Mark from the time his family arrived in Kalispell to now. They clearly saw the passion in Mark for intellectual pursuits. They'd encouraged him and cheered him on. The judge had even lent Mark book after book from his own prized collection.

Mark straightened. Had he ever let the couple know how much they meant to him? How much he appreciated their belief in him?

The judge's words just now conveyed a lot. Soon Mark would make a point of sharing with them everything that was on his heart and mind, but it would need to wait until the library was up and running.

And after he had a long heart-to-heart with his father. Which was long overdue.

When Mark went out east for college a decade ago, Dad hadn't liked it but let him go. Probably hoped that time away from the ranch would prove Mark wrong—that he would miss the ranch and everything related to it. Instead it solidified Mark's love of words and books, his desire to earn the directorship of a large library, and his passion to share the love of books with people who hadn't had the chance to know the precious gift of reading. What doors reading could open. The dreams it could spark.

And yet . . .

Deep down, Mark sensed he'd failed. Oh, not his dreams or the Ashburys' hopes for him. However . . .

Had he failed his father? Dad's expectations had been high. Still were. And he and his father had let deep rifts develop in their relationship.

He could only pray that coming home and spending time with his father would allow mending to take place.

Enough. He needed to focus on the matters at hand. In the moonlight Mark glanced across Third Street and allowed the thrill of the coming day to take over. With swift strides, he crossed the road and walked up to the library's main entrance.

Andrew Carnegie, one of America's leading philanthropists, had given a generous donation of ten thousand dollars to the city for the library. The only provision was that the city had to provide the land and the funding to keep the library operating. So they purchased two lots here on the northeast corner of Third Street East and Second Avenue East.

Etched into the sandstone above the double doors was CARNEGIE, a testament to the wealthy man who didn't want to die rich. And in fact, Mark had heard that libraries were being built across the country thanks to Mr. Carnegie.

What an amazing thing to do.

Mark would be eternally grateful. Not just for the library, but for the opportunity of the job. He had high hopes and dreams for this place. For his home. To educate people. Help kids who, like Mark, wanted a life beyond ranching and farming. To have the opportunity for a college education.

Not that farming and ranching were bad. Not at all. But books and reading opened up doors to entire worlds beyond Kalispell.

It wasn't a bad town. No. In fact, he loved it here. That's one of the reasons he came back. But if he had the chance to impact the next generation, he wanted to take it. Especially with the age of machinery upon them. The world was changing at an alarming rate and their best option was to keep up with it the best they could.

They weren't living in the nineteenth century anymore.

Standing at the foot of the stairs, Mark smiled again. The entry was angled to the northeast corner of the block with the dome rising high in the pre-dawn sky. The tall wood doors welcomed him.

As he took the nine cement steps up to the front, his smile grew. Today was the day.

The dedication.

He slipped his key into the door, unlocked it, and opened it to the eight-sided entryway. The smell of lemon oil—which he'd used to detail and polish all the wood in the building—filled his nose.

The new construction was full of rich wood trim. From the hand-carved banisters on the multi-angled staircase that led to the daylight basement, to every window and door in the place, the craftsmanship was of the highest quality.

As he closed the door, he took a long slow breath and let the true aroma of the library take over.

The unmistakable smell of books.

Lots of books.

More than four thousand tomes filled the shelves. He'd cataloged, placed, and *knew* each one of them.

Breathing deep of the scents he loved and the satisfaction of a job well done, he filled his lungs and let his chest puff out. Just a bit. This moment was worth it. No one was around to see him anyway.

In a few hours, they would open the doors and hold the dedication ceremony. And in a couple weeks, the library would be open to the public. There were still furnishings and decorations to bring in and many little projects to do. Thankfully, he wasn't in charge of all that. The women of the Ladies Library Association were handling that side of things.

He strode toward the front circulation desk, where he would make his place every day. He turned on the light, then made a circle under the dome of the entry. Each window and door in the place had a beautiful, butted head casing with a hand-carved rope pattern in it. They drew the eye upward to the dome and high ceilings—the visualization of knowledge and higher learning. The oak floors shone in the light. He could imagine hearing footsteps throughout the library of those eager to read and learn.

He made his way to his desk, shed his coat and hat, and hesitated.

Kate.

Would his sister come today? He'd sent a note out to the ranch, but he hadn't heard back. It had been quite a surprise to come home and find Kate married. To a fellow Mark had never heard of. The man wasn't even from Kalispell.

But Harvey Monroe must be a decent guy if Dad had agreed to the wedding.

Dad . . .

Mark let out a deep sigh. Things hadn't been great between them lately. If he was honest, things hadn't been all that good since Mark left for college. Especially since he hadn't come home to the ranch after his schooling. But he was back now. He could make amends. Spend time with his family. And hopefully prove to his father that what he did was important.

A knock on the front door drew his gaze. He checked his watch. Wasn't even seven yet. Who could that be?

Mark strode to the door and unlocked it, then opened it a few inches.

"Mr. Andrews." The gangly kid handed him an envelope through the space. "Your father asked me to bring this by."

Mark took the envelope. "Thank you."

But it was no use, the kid was already loping down the stairs.

With a tear to the envelope, Mark then pulled out a piece of his dad's ranch stationery.

Mark,

I am calling a family meeting this evening. It is imperative that you be in attendance. 6:00 p.m. sharp.

Dad

Mark walked back to his desk and set the missive down. Just like Dad to demand an audience. So much for hoping that his family would come to the dedication today. He hadn't seen them since he returned—even though he'd sent several messages out to the ranch. Perhaps Kate would come. Clearly, he wouldn't see his father there.

Shaking his head against the negative thoughts, he refocused his attention on the excitement of the day.

He could deal with his father later.

River View Ranch—Andrews Family Ranch—Ten miles north of Kalispell

"I've come to a decision."

Angus Andrews placed his hands on the arms of his favorite leather wingback chair and narrowed his eyes. Even though they were clear and full of fire—as always—they couldn't hide the fact that Dad was aging. A lot.

More than Mark could have imagined.

He sent a glance to his sister. When Kate had answered the door, she'd hugged him tight and introduced him to her husband, but Dad hadn't given him as much as a how-are-you before insisting they all sit for the family meeting.

The man hadn't changed a bit. Whatever he said was law.

Kate took her seat next to Harvey and sent Mark a sympathetic look.

"This is how things will go. Kate and Harvey will continue running the ranch like they have been. All the day-to-day, hands-on work. Mark will take over the books and the management side of things. With all his college education, he must have some good insight into how we can grow. Kate and Mark will be equals in this endeavor. This is your ranch now. I'm getting too old and haven't been feeling all that great. I need to hand everything over to you two." Dad thrummed his fingers on his knee.

Mark had been expecting this from his father in the years to come, but not so soon. He'd hoped for some time to settle in and have a chance to prove himself. How was he supposed to answer his father honestly and honor him at the same time? "I'm not sure I will have time for all that, Dad. My work at the library will keep me busy."

His father grimaced. He waved off Mark's words. "After a time, I'm sure you'll be back here permanently, otherwise you wouldn't have come home. Get the library going, and then come back where you belong."

The man never listened. Never. As much as Mark hated the temper he'd inherited from his Scottish father, he let it seep to the surface. "I came back home, yes, but my job is the director of the library." There. At least he didn't allow it to boil over.

"Your *job* is to do what your father says." Dad's right hand pointed out the window. "I built all this for you. Don't be ungrateful."

Mark did a silent count to ten. "Kate is more than capable of running the business end and the physical end now that she has Harvey. You have plenty of hired ranch hands. She lives for this place. You know that."

"This ranch is for *both* of you. Now stop arguing with me." Red infused his father's face.

Enough. The ordering had to stop. "Dad, I'm the director of the library." Was he wrong to—in essence—tell his father no? Was he dishonoring the only parent he had left?

"Don't be so contrary, young man." His father pushed to his feet and shoved a finger at him.

Mark stood as well but kept his tone low. Forceful, but low. "You never listen. I thought after all these years things would be different." He stepped toward his sister and leaned down to give her a hug. "Come see me soon?"

"Of course." Unshed tears glistened in her eyes.

He turned his gaze to his new brother-in-law. "It was nice to meet you. I'm sorry for the circumstances, but perhaps we could chat at the library sometime?"

Harvey gave him a sympathetic smile. "Nice to meet you too. Next time I'm in town, I'll look you up."

Mark headed toward the door without another glance at his father. It was for the best.

"Don't you walk out on me, Cowboy!"

The words halted his feet. He couldn't—wouldn't—look back. His face toward the door, he kept his words calm. "I'm not walking out, Dad. I'm giving us both some space so I don't lose my temper and say things I will regret. My mind is made up. I never wanted to run the ranch. I appreciate all you put into this place, I do. But you know I don't love it like Kate does."

"Always choosing books over your family, aren't you?"

As silly as the words were, they still stung. Mark spun around. "I'm not choosing *anything* over you, Dad. I thought you would be happy and *proud*. I've worked hard for this. I've been given an incredible opportunity. And I'm back home where I can spend time with all of you." As his gaze spanned the room, from Dad's fury to Kate's anguish to Harvey's discomfort, his heart twinged.

Dad fisted his hands. "Proud? When you've wasted ten years gallivanting around doing whatever you pleased. I allowed it, but now it's time to come home and do your duty. I didn't raise a quitter."

No. He would not let the words that sprang to mind have their entrance to his heart. Dad didn't mean it. The heat of the moment always brought out the worst in him and he said things for dramatic effect. How often had he and Kate joked about their father's bluster?

Kate held up a hand toward each of them. "I think we all need to sit back down. Perhaps have some dinner and cool our tempers."

Dad shook his head. "No. I'm not sitting down to dinner with him. Is that still your answer, Mark? You gonna tell me no again?"

Mark took a long breath and then exhaled. "I'm sorry, Dad. But my answer is no."

"*Fine!*" His father's roar echoed off the walls of the room. "Do whatever you want. Kate will inherit the ranch. From this day forward, you're disowned. You hear me?"

"I heard you. I'm guessing all of Kalispell heard you." As

much as Mark tried to keep his voice under control, the words burst out of his mouth in equal volume to his father's. He stomped out of the room.

Why had he ever come home?

He couldn't sleep. He kept getting up to pace the room while the events of the evening replayed in his mind. Why couldn't Dad see Kate's passion for the ranch and be grateful? Especially now that she was married to a husband who seemed to love the ranch too.

Mark pulled back the drapes and gazed out into the darkness. There was so little sunlight these days. Winter had brought its long, dark nights. At least the dedication ceremony had gone well. The people of Kalispell seemed more than pleased to have the new library in place. A crowd had waited outside in the cold, they'd been so excited. Two schoolteachers from the local high school even made arrangements to bring their classes over to learn about the Dewey decimal system.

He let the curtains fall into place and went back to the bed. Sat on the edge. Mark prayed. For wisdom. For healing. He didn't want to hurt his dad or dishonor him, but he'd made a commitment to the town—and to God—regarding the library.

"Lord, I need wisdom to deal with this matter. I love my father, but I love my work at the library as well. Since Dad paid for me to go to college, I thought he understood my passion and the plans I had for the future. Plans I feel certain are ones that You have ordained for me. If I'm in the wrong, please help me to see that and be willing to acknowledge it. Please show me what to do."

Every last bit of anger he'd held onto from the evening dissipated. The whole ride home, he'd muttered under his breath about his father's outburst and how the older man was clearly in the wrong. What a waste of time and energy.

And what irony to accuse his father when he'd been equally wrong in his response.

"God, I'm ashamed of my behavior toward my dad, but he brings out the worst in me. Help me to bite my tongue when I need to. Which is probably a lot more than I think." He blew out his breath between his lips.

Why was his relationship with his father so full of conflict? Why couldn't they understand and accept each other? Was the only way to rectify that to give up everything he'd worked for—his hopes and dreams . . . ?

Mark's throat tightened. Could it be? He bowed his head, but his heart hurt as he prayed, "Is that what You want me to do, God?"

2

Sucking in a gasp, Rebecca Whitman put a gloved hand to her throat. She bit her lip and gaped at the envelope one more time. Could it be?

With a glance around the small lobby, she spotted several ladies from the neighborhood huddled in a group. Watching her.

Ready to gossip about whatever they saw.

Well, they'd have no fodder from her today. She tucked the letter in her reticule and pretended that nothing of consequence had arrived. With steady steps, she headed for the door as if this were any other day.

Keeping that attitude proved harder the farther she walked. The missive she hid seemed to scream for her attention. But those eyes were still on her. She could practically feel them on her back.

Once she passed the mercantile, she couldn't resist any longer. She pulled out the cream envelope and studied it.

It was from the court system in Montana.

31

Montana!

She ripped open the envelope, pulled out a paper, and then started walking again.

Perhaps it was rude to read and walk at the same time and ignore the passersby, but it couldn't be helped. She'd been waiting for a response—from several states—for longer than she cared to admit.

Unfolding the sheet, she held her breath and read.

Dear Miss Whitman,

Judge Milton Ashbury, of the 11th Judicial District of Montana, hereby requests your services as Court Stenographer for the Kalispell Court. The offered salary is $700 per year which will be paid weekly in a sum of $13.46.

Rebecca gulped at the number. No. That couldn't be correct. She blinked several times and read it again.

Seven hundred dollars per year. Right there in print. Unbelievable!

Judge Ashbury requests your arrival by the first of February. Please respond via telegraph with your answer as soon as possible so that your tickets may be provided for you.

> *Sincerely,*
> *Samuel Marvin Tuttle*
> *Secretary to the 11th Judicial*
> *District Court, Montana*

Her first job offer outside of Chicago! And for quite a sum.

Oh, to jump up and down right then and there! But her vow of no fodder for the women stopped her. Instead, she smoothed the front of her shirtwaist and grinned. February first didn't give her much time. She'd have to check the train schedule so she knew how many days to leave open for travel, pack everything she owned, and say goodbye to everyone she knew.

That is, *if* she wanted to take the job.

She bit her lip.

She did. Oh yes, she *did*.

For years she'd wanted to get out of Chicago. Heavens, the farthest she'd ever traveled had been up the shore of Lake Michigan. Maybe fifty miles from home.

There simply hadn't been time nor money to do any traveling.

And now? Seven. Hundred. Dollars. A year. The amount was more than she could imagine.

Her parents had sacrificed so much for her and her siblings. Papa's job at the barrel factory had provided well enough until his accident a few years ago. Ever since, the owner had taken pity and given him a small job that he could do while seated, but her older brothers had worked to help support the family. Until they got married and left home. During that time, Rebecca finished high school— something her parents insisted on for every one of their children. Then she took court stenography classes while working at the post office.

For the past two years, since receiving her certification, she'd worked in the lower courts in Chicago, hoping for the day when she could apply for a higher position and obtain it.

Now that day was here.

Her parents would be so proud! She loved them with all her heart and would miss them something terrible. But Momma and Papa didn't need her help anymore.

It was time. She'd longed to spread her wings ever since John and Lars left home. Peter was still at home to help the family out. His job at the barrel factory was a good one. Ebba and Kristina worked for one of the top seamstresses in Chicago.

Yes. Rebecca *would* take the job.

Her brisk steps took her down the street toward home and she refolded the paper and shoved it back into the envelope.

Wait . . . what was that? Another sheet of paper was inside.

Rebecca pulled it out and unfolded the small piece of stationery.

Miss Rebecca Whitman,

Allow me to introduce myself. I am Marvella Ashbury of the Kalispell Women's Club, the Ladies Library Association, and the Montana Woman's Suffrage Association.

I do hope you accept my husband's request to become the first female court stenographer in all of Montana. That is quite an accomplishment, my dear! Rest assured, you have my full support, and I will be here if you need anything. Allow me to offer you one of our apartments that we own as your living quarters. It is safe, clean, and an appropriate place for a young single woman to live. I look forward to meeting you in person.

Please come visit as soon as you arrive. I can arrange for the furnishing of your living quarters, and we can get to know one another properly. We women must stick together if we are to accomplish all our goals. Kalispell won't run itself, as I'm sure you are well aware.

Godspeed and best wishes,
Marvella Ashbury

Rebecca couldn't help but smile. The first female court stenographer in all of Montana. How exciting was *that*?

An incredible salary. Her travel paid for. *And* a place to live!

As she tucked the envelope back into her reticule, she let it all wash over her. Then her mind couldn't stop the whirlwind of questions, what ifs, and lists that needed making.

What would her family say? God's provision was too magnanimous to even put into words.

Her steps quickened until she wanted to break out into a jog.

Oh, bother with societal conventions! She lifted her skirt an inch or two and took off at a full run. Who cared what anyone said? She wouldn't be here much longer anyway.

Many a look was shot her way as she raced around the picket fence of her home. She took the front steps two at a time and burst through the front door. "Momma!"

"In the parlor, dear." Her mother's singsong voice greeted her.

Out of breath, Rebecca put a hand to her chest and raced to the parlor. "I've been offered a job!" The words rushed out as she held up the envelope.

"Isn't that wonderful news?" Momma looked up from

her embroidery and set it down beside her. "Come tell me all about it. Is it close by?"

She hated to douse the jubilation on her mother's face, but it couldn't be helped. "Well . . . no. It's in Montana. But it's a wonderful job. I'd be the very first female stenographer in the whole state, and they want to pay me seven hundred dollars a year."

Momma gasped, her eyes as wide as her teacup. "Gracious, heavenly days"—she sputtered for several seconds until she took a sip of water—"that's a small fortune for a single young lady!"

"I know." Rebecca pressed the letter to her chest. "I'm dumbfounded."

Momma took several breaths and then laid a hand on Rebecca's knee. "Is this a reputable place, my dear?"

Pulling out the sheets of paper, she showed her mother the letter from the judge's secretary and the other from his wife.

Reading the letters aloud, Momma made several comments to herself, raised her eyebrows a few times, and then shook her head almost as if she couldn't believe it. "I'm certainly excited for you. Especially with the judge's wife wanting to take you under her wing. That makes my mother-heart feel more comfortable with the situation." She tapped the papers against her chin. "Perhaps we could ask the reverend to check into this judge and town. Just to make sure?"

"If that would make you more comfortable, Momma, I will gladly go over there now and ask."

"I think your father would appreciate it, too."

"All right," Rebecca stood, "I'll go right now."

Momma's hand on her arm stopped her. "Wait. Before you go, and while we still have a moment of quiet . . ." She let the words fall as she glanced down at her lap.

What was this about? She sat back down beside her mother.

"If you're going to head off into the wild west, you need to understand that there will be many a man looking to find a wife. Promise me you won't fall in love and marry the first man that you meet. Not like I did."

For a moment, her world froze. Her parents had been the epitome of everything good and decent in her life. "But Momma, I thought you loved Papa!"

"Hush, now." Momma's stern words were whisper-soft. "Of course, I love your father. Very much. But I was much too young. We married for all the wrong reasons. We both admit that. God took our blunders and turned it into something beautiful, but I've always wanted so much more for you."

More than a good marriage full of love and family? Rebecca blinked, and not a single word came to mind.

"Don't look at me like that, Rebecca. What your father and I have has been wonderful. But it has also been a very hard life. We've endured a great deal of loss and sorrow. So many things we wanted to give to you children, but couldn't."

"But life isn't all about money. You taught us that. Over and over again you told us God would provide. Love was what mattered." Why did it feel like the rug had been yanked out from underneath her feet?

"All true words. But you're an adult now. About to venture out on your own." Her bottom lip trembled. "I knew this day would come, but I was unprepared all the same. You are our eldest daughter. It's different for you than for the boys."

Didn't she know it. She'd been faced with that fact her whole life.

"Are you certain you want to take this job?"

After the last few moments . . . she wasn't sure what to feel anymore. But she straightened her shoulders and looked her mother in the eye. "Yes. I've worked hard for this. Montana is beautiful country, I hear."

"Hm." Momma didn't sound convinced. "Go speak to the reverend and have him check into it. If he approves, then I give my hearty approval as well."

She hadn't come seeking her mother's approval, but now she longed for it. "Thank you."

After a long walk to the reverend's home—and a stern lecture from him and his wife about venturing into the West on her own, and a promise from the good reverend to speak to clergymen in Montana and report back to her parents—Rebecca was spent.

But that didn't stop her future plans from swirling in her mind. Oh, what she wouldn't give to be able to share all this with someone who didn't rain on her parade with words of doom and gloom.

Her feet ached as she made the trip home one more time. Had she known when she dressed this morning what was going to transpire, she would have worn different shoes.

The fact of the matter was, she had been offered a very prestigious position. At least, as long as it was confirmed to be true. And why wouldn't it be? She'd applied for the position in Montana. The court system had responded. The stationery had been authentic looking. The verbiage just like that of the letters she transcribed every day. It must be the real thing.

Then there was the note from Judge Ashbury's wife. A note of such a personal nature couldn't have been forged. The woman seemed influential and highly self-confident. Exactly what Rebecca hoped to be in her maturity.

All these years of study and hard work had paid off.

Letting a smile stretch across her face, she walked up the steps to her home again.

The door opened and Papa greeted her with a wide grin. "I hear you had a job offer today."

"I did."

He hugged her. "Care to go for a walk?"

While her feet screamed that it was the last thing she wanted to do, she shrugged. "I'd love to."

She waited for him to work his way down the steps with his cane and then took his free arm. "How was your day?"

"About the same as usual. An honest day of work." He limped beside her. "Your mother told me all about the job and that you've requested the reverend to check into things?"

"Yes, he hoped to get back to us within a day or two. He was sending telegrams." She fidgeted with the sash around her waist. "I'd be the first female stenographer in Montana."

"So I've heard." He kept a steady pace, despite his injury. "Montana is a good distance. Across the country to be sure."

She bit her lip at the hitch in his voice. She'd always been under her father's protection and love. Was she ready for that to change? Her excitement about the opportunity overruled everything else. She swallowed. "I'll try to get home as often as I can. Depending on the days I'm allowed to leave my position."

He stopped and turned toward her. Since they were at the end of their quiet street with nothing but a field in front of them, it afforded them a bit of privacy. He patted her hand. "I would love nothing more than to keep you here, but it's time for you to spread your wings. Perhaps your mother and I could come visit you. She has longed to travel and see the Rocky Mountains." His brow crinkled. A sure sign that a serious subject was about to be broached. "My dear girl, might I offer some words of wisdom as your father?"

"Of course." Hopefully he wouldn't make this more difficult with a lengthy list of cautions. With a lift of her shoulders, she folded her hands in front of her and prepared herself.

"The West is full of men looking for wives to help them settle and work the land. Don't be in a rush to marry like your mother and I were. Don't fall for a bunch of flowery words and promises. Men are all too accomplished at that. You're going to have a good job and if you're wise with your money, you can have a prosperous life without marrying the first man who promises you the moon."

Tipping her head to the side, she studied him. "Do you regret marrying Mother?"

"Heavens, no, Rebecca. I regret that she has had such a hard life. Being married to me, she never had a chance to do any of the things she dreamed of. I did my best in the early years to give her a treat here and there, and bought her a new dress every year for her birthday, but ever since the accident, well, things have been more difficult. And we'd hoped that if we worked hard, the latter years of life would be a bit easier." He tapped her nose like he used to do when she was a little girl. "Your mother is the best thing that ever happened to me. God was good to bless us even in our hasty decision-making. We were young and in love. Your mother and I simply want you to have a better life than we have. I think most parents want that for their children."

If her parents had such a wonderful love and family even with their hasty decision, she could still hope for the same. She wouldn't make any reckless decisions about men, but she was ready to venture out on her own. "You would still make the same choice? To marry Momma?"

"Of course, I would—"

"Well then"—she cleared her throat—"respectfully, I'd like to ask you to allow me to make my own choices. But I will also take your words to heart."

Papa's eyes crinkled at the corners and his lips wiggled as if he was trying to keep from laughing. He tipped her chin up with his finger.

"You'll do just fine, Rebecca."

Five days later, Rebecca gazed out the train window with tears streaming down her cheeks as she waved to everyone she held dear. She hadn't known how difficult it would be to say goodbye to her family. If she had, she might not have made the decision to leave.

But everyone had now been hugged. Her valise was overflowing with gifts from each of her siblings. Momma had packed her a basket full of enough food to get her to Montana and back. Papa had winked at her and told her to take Montana—as the proverbial bull—by the horns.

The train began to move.

Her heart skipped a beat and she swallowed back the tears that clogged her throat.

Once Reverend Montgomery had brought the news of the respectable Judge Ashbury and his wife, Rebecca had scurried around with all that needed to be done. All the preparation kept her busier than ever before. Which helped with her nerves.

Now . . .

She had days to ponder over each of the notes from her family, and the dream of her future.

One thing was for certain: she would *not* fall for the first man she met.

With the last swallow of his whiskey, he wiped his mouth with his sleeve. Kalispell was such a boring little town.

A man of his intellect and brilliance needed more . . . *inspiration* to keep him entertained. But at least with the way things were going, it should only take a few more months to get what he needed.

He'd invested so much time already, might as well see it through.

He got up from his stool and stretched. The saloon was crowded and noisy. Which was why he chose this place. Easier to go unnoticed.

Walking out into the cold night air, he shoved a peppermint candy into his mouth. No sense in letting the wife know that he used them to cover up his indiscretions. He'd asked her to make them for him saying it was because he had a weak spot for peppermint sweets, and it helped cover up the smell of manure.

As a loving and doting wife, she'd believed him and obliged.

Now she made a new batch every couple weeks. He kept it in an old Hignett's tobacco tin a friend from Liverpool had given him years ago.

Shoving his hands into his pockets, he walked to where he kept his horse tied up down the street. The animal snorted at him.

"Need another peppermint, eh?"

The horse's head bobbed up and down. He pulled the candy from his mouth and palmed it for the horse to take. The gelding wasted no time.

"Fine." After he climbed up and situated himself in the saddle, he drew out another peppermint for himself. "Happy?" He pulled the collar of his coat up to his ears and nudged the horse into a canter.

Why he talked to his horse, he didn't know. But he was bored. Whenever that happened, it was usually time to move on.

No matter, it wouldn't be too long now. By summer, the old man would be dead, and he'd be on his way to parts unknown.

3

What a day. After the dedication ceremony a couple weeks ago, Mark had scrambled to finish everything that needed to be done to get the library fully operational. Once the town, and a good deal of the Flathead Valley, had seen what the new library had to offer, excitement built and he fielded dozens of questions a day.

Exactly what he'd hoped and prayed would happen. Yesterday was opening day and he couldn't be more pleased. The ladies of the Library Association had done a beautiful job with the interior, and patrons the past couple days ventured in and out in a steady stream.

As he straightened his desk, he picked up his list of ideas for the future. The potential of what the library could offer was astounding. Lectures, dramatic readings, educational seminars . . . he could even have a special day for the children to come and he could read to them. Perhaps a chapter at a time of an exciting story that would keep them returning. Might get them more excited about reading. Wouldn't that be incredible? But as much as he'd love to implement everything right now, he'd have to wait and be content with planning ahead.

He tucked the list along with another to-do list into his briefcase, as well as several books he hoped to read in the next few days. Never stop learning. That was his motto. And he intended to stick by it and show the people of this town how important it was to educate the youth and adults alike.

A note from his sister, Kate, sat on top of his calendar. She'd been good to keep him up to date on what was happening back at the ranch since the family meeting. Over time, he would prove the value of his work to Dad. Despite the man's negativity and hardheaded, stubborn, unforgiving opinion.

Mark winced. Not very honoring to allow thoughts like that. His attitude needed adjusting. He would do an excellent job running the library. The town would thrive. It wasn't profitable for him to worry about pleasing everyone. His focus should be on pleasing the Lord. No one else.

Besides, Dad had always been rash with his words and then after he had time to cool down, he would be a bit more rational.

Kate's note attested to that fact. Their father was no longer spouting off about disowning his son and had asked after Mark several times. She was convinced a visit from Mark would be welcome. Especially since Dad's health seemed to be in serious decline.

Mark paused. That wasn't good. Tomorrow, he would venture out to the ranch and check on him. Pretend nothing had happened and be available for the man who'd raised him. Just because he didn't want to run the ranch didn't mean he couldn't offer to help out a little. This was family after all.

Gathering the last of his things, he checked his desk one more time. He pulled the chain on the lamp to turn it off then put on his overcoat and hat. The chill outside would surely help keep his pace brisk on the way back to the hotel.

He closed up the building and took a long look at the front doors. Every day he was filled with a sense of awe at this place. And the fact that he had been chosen as director.

He hoped that feeling never went away. *Lord, don't let me lose appreciation for all You've blessed me with.*

A gust of wind whipped at his face and he headed down the front steps. Gracious, it was cold!

"Just the man I wanted to see."

Mark turned at the voice and smiled. "Judge, good evening. What a pleasure to see you. How may I help you?"

"I hear you're not living at the ranch—although I can't blame you, that would be quite the trek into town each day. I came to see if you were in need of a place to stay."

After his father's rejection, this older couple's affection warmed his heart. Gave him hope that someone believed in him—his dreams. "I've been so focused on getting the library up and running that I've been content to board at the hotel. Mrs. Carver has been very generous in her care of me, but I think it's time to find a place of my own. It appears you might have a suggestion?" The thought of the dear older couple inviting him to live with them was a bit far-fetched, but it wouldn't be unwelcome.

"I do in fact. Mrs. Ashbury and I would like to offer you one of our apartments to rent."

"I didn't know you owned apartments." How providential.

"Another of Marvella's ideas. Six of them. Downtown in a large brick building." The judge's bushy eyebrows wiggled over his twinkling brown eyes.

Once when Mark was just a scrawny lad and new to Kalispell, he'd been convinced the man was Santa Claus. The white hair, the glowing smile, the generosity all matched. "That wouldn't be far to walk." Even better to not have the expense of a conveyance.

"Not at all. A few blocks at most. They have been quite profitable. I've put some thought into building another six or more if the need arises. Since we have an opening, we'd like to offer it to you first. It's a much better use of our gifts if we can help you out."

"It is much appreciated. Any chance I could see the apartment? If it's suitable—which I'm sure it will be—I would love to get moved in as soon as possible. Would probably help me feel more settled now that I'm back home." What an answer to prayer. If this worked out, he could continue to walk to the library and then hire a horse from the livery whenever he needed to head out to the ranch. That would help him save money for his own horse and carriage. Perhaps even a horseless carriage one day.

"Of course." Judge Ashbury stroked his thick white mustache. "Why don't we head over there now? I don't know why I didn't think of it earlier. Since you have family here, I'm guessing we simply didn't put two and two together." Huge snowflakes started to fall from the sky.

Mark lifted his collar a bit higher. "I noticed your little friend is absent this evening."

The older man grunted and Mark worked to keep his laughter at bay. "Sir Theophilus, wasn't it?"

The judge pointed a finger at him. "Watch out, son, or walking that little fluff ball will become your daily chore." As much as the man groused over the little dog, Mark had seen him walking Sir Theophilus in the early hours, carrying on quite a discussion and appearing to enjoy every minute.

They took swift steps a few blocks toward downtown. When they reached a red brick building, the older man walked up the steps and unlocked the outside door. They stepped into the vestibule.

"There are three apartments here on the first floor and three upstairs. The one available is just over here. Number two." Searching through the keys on the large ring, he found the correct one and opened the door.

"Have a look, son." The judge lifted his chin in the direction of his home. "Then why don't you join us for dinner this evening and we can hash out all the particulars? Marvella has been wanting to bend your ear since you arrived."

"That would be lovely, sir. Give me just a moment to look around." A quick glance out the window showed the snow coming down in larger flakes. Better make it fast. He walked from room to room. The small apartment was perfect. There was a nice-sized sitting room with two large windows. Just off that was a tiny kitchen with a stove and icebox. There were rows of shelves for storage with a small broom closet at the far end of the room. Back in the sitting room there was a door to a small bathroom, and another to a decent-sized bedroom with a double bed and dresser.

He met the judge back at the door. "Thank you for thinking of me, sir. This will more than meet my needs."

"Good. Good." He clapped his gloved hands together. "Let's get out of this snow then. Marvella has something sumptuous planned, I'm sure, since we are entertaining another guest."

"Oh?"

"Yes, in fact you'll be the first to meet the new court stenographer, who has just arrived."

The evening was looking even better. One of the things he'd vowed to do on his return was to get involved in church and make some solid friendships with God-fearing men. "I haven't had much of a chance to socialize since my nose has been buried in the books." He laughed at his own joke, but the judge only smirked under his mustache. "Is he around my age?"

The older man chuckled. "It's a woman. But yes, she's probably around your age."

"A woman?" He'd never heard of such a thing—a female court reporter? "How fascinating."

"She is, quite so." Ashbury picked up the pace. "You two should get along famously. The three times I've encountered her today, *her* nose has been buried in a book as well." He quirked an eyebrow in Mark's direction. "Reminds me of when you were younger."

Oh dear . . . The judge's wife hadn't been up to her matchmaking again, had she? The woman was notorious for it and Mark didn't have any desire to be obligated to any such arrangement. But no one argued with Marvella Ashbury and won. "I'm sorry, sir. But maybe I should head back to the hotel. There is a good deal I need to accomplish this evening especially if I need to move my things." He stopped and shifted his weight to head the other direction.

"Nonsense." The judge gripped his shoulder. "I know exactly what you're thinking, and no, Marvella didn't arrange this. Your invite to dinner was entirely *my* idea."

Whew. "Oh good." His heart settled into a slower rhythm. Besides, a home-cooked meal at the Ashbury mansion wasn't something he ever wanted to turn down. No matter the company.

When they entered the spacious foyer, a maid and a footman appeared and took their hats, gloves, and coats. Mark stomped his feet to get all the snow off his boots so he wouldn't trek it across the marble floor. "Thank you." He nodded at the two.

"Yes, thank you, Mimi. Clarence." The judge straightened his waistcoat. "My dear!" His voice boomed through the cavernous entryway. "I've brought another guest for dinner."

The familiar alto timbre of Marvella Ashbury's voice answered. "How lovely." Her steps clicked toward them.

As wealthy and high society as the Ashburys had always been, one of the things Mark loved about them was their casual nature about some of society's conventions. Which was why they never seemed to have a problem speaking from room to room with raised voices. That was often entertainment in and of itself.

And there was always laughter.

Lots of laughter.

The judge put a finger over his lips.

Mark dipped his chin and grinned at the man. He would go along with the conspiracy.

"And who is it you've brought to our humble abode, Judge Ashbury?" The words jumped around from pitch to pitch as she almost sang them.

Mark envisioned the plump and vivacious judge's wife as a prima donna with the opera. He grinned at the vision in his mind. She could pull it off too.

As soon as Marvella Ashbury rounded the corner and she spotted Mark, she threw out her arms and rushed him. "Why, this isn't a guest, Judge." Wrapping Mark in a warm hug, she pulled him toward her ample bosom and squeezed. "This is family." She pushed him back to arm's length but didn't release him. "Let me look at you."

In that moment, he felt like he was the gangly boy who'd shown up in Kalispell with his father and sister all those years ago. "It's wonderful to see you, Mrs. Ashbury."

She narrowed her eyes. "We'll have none of that, now. It's Marvella and you know it."

"Yes, ma'am."

She *tsked* at him but grabbed his hand. "I hated missing the dedication for the library. After all, I'd helped to plan it, but I've been recovering from a dreadful cold. Or it might have been influenza. The doctor was uncertain."

"I hope you're much better now." Mark put his hand atop hers.

"I am, and I heard from the judge that the ceremony was quite grand and that you were well received. But how could you not be? Look at what a handsome man you've grown into. Besides, everyone here knows your family. Speaking of which, how are they?"

Mark forced the smile to remain on his face. "They're doing fine."

She stared at him for a moment, then pulled her hand away and turned. "I haven't seen Kate in a bit. Is she still enamored with that new husband of hers?"

"Yes, ma'am. They seem very happy."

"Good, good. Now follow me. Cook has fixed us a lovely supper and you need to meet Miss Whitman."

With a deep breath, he allowed himself to be led toward the parlor. Hopefully the dinner wouldn't be too long. He had a lot of reading to get to this evening. Oh, and he needed to pack his things. Perhaps he should tackle that tomorrow if things ran late.

Marvella stopped in front of him and held out an arm. "Mr. Mark Andrews, allow me to introduce you to the first woman stenographer in the *entire* state of Montana, Miss Rebecca Whitman."

A lovely woman stood from the settee and held out a hand. "It's nice to meet you, Mr. Andrews." Her dark blue eyes held the hint of a smile.

"And you as well, Miss Whitman." He gave a slight bow.

Taller than most women he knew, she had a slender build, but a hearty handshake. He wasn't used to shaking hands with women, but perhaps this was how it was done nowadays.

A good half-foot shorter than his own six-foot-two-inch frame, she didn't have to tip her head back to look up at him like Marvella did.

"What is it that you do, Mr. Andrews?" She tilted her head to the side and studied him.

"I am the director of the new Carnegie Library."

Her dark brown eyebrows shot up toward her hairline. "Oh, I do love to read."

"Wonderful." He was about to ask after her favorite books, but she turned to their hostess and started chatting about the local women's club.

Mark shrugged and turned to the judge. "Any interesting cases lately? I've been remiss in keeping up with the local news."

"Nothing of note, thank goodness. I always appreciate it when things are calmer in the winter. For the most part, the cold seems to keep people from misbehaving."

"Good thing it's not the opposite. With people cooped up during the harsh winter months, I can imagine that arguments abound."

"Let's not strike my good luck in this area, shall we?" The judge chuckled. "I don't need any more hullabaloo this winter."

"Yes, sir." Mark did his best to keep his own laughter in check.

"Dinner is served." One of the maids curtsied at the door.

He followed behind their other guest as they headed into the dining room. The crystal chandelier above was one of his favorite things about the room. Until he'd moved here with his family, he'd never seen anything so fancy.

Miss Whitman's shiny brown hair caught the light. He liked the way it was wavy, and a few curls escaped her chignon. He pulled out a chair for her and as she turned to take her seat, she sent him a smile.

"Thank you, Mr. Andrews."

"You are most welcome." Taking his seat across from her, he savored the aromas wafting toward him. Nothing quite like the food prepared at the Ashburys'.

Marvella lifted her chin from her end of the table. "Miss Whitman, how serendipitous that my husband invited our new librarian. Mr. Andrews is one of our most eligible young bachelors in town."

The judge—who had just lifted his water glass to his lips—sputtered and choked.

Rebecca laid her napkin in her lap and commanded the heat creeping up her neck to not enter her cheeks.

It didn't work.

So she reached for her own water glass and drank several long sips. While Mr. Andrews was an interesting man, he was—after all—the first man she'd met. And after her parents' warnings, she would remain stalwart in guarding her heart. Allowing the judge's wife to matchmake wouldn't do at all.

"My dear, you haven't asked the reason I was late this evening." Judge Ashbury had calmed his cough and tapped his napkin to his lips. "I was showing one of the apartments to Mark. He's going to move in right away."

Mrs. Ashbury—Marvella—didn't seem the least bit fazed. "Then you will both be living in our apartment building. How fortuitous."

The plump woman spooned potatoes from the dish the maid held to her own plate. "You know, when I saw Miss Whitman's application for the job here, I told the judge that he simply must hire her."

"That you did, my dear." He turned to Rebecca, his eyes smiling. "We are honored to have you, Miss Whitman."

"Thank you. And I greatly appreciate the invitation for this lovely dinner. You've been a tremendous assistance already, what with helping me to get moved into my apartment, arranging for the furnishings, showing me about town. It is lovely to be here."

"We are thrilled. I must say, I can't wait to see what you've done with your little apartment." The judge's wife beamed at her.

"You are welcome anytime." Perhaps a change of subject was in order. "How might I volunteer with the Woman's Suffrage movement, Mrs. Ashbury?"

Silverware clanked against the dinnerware as they filled their plates.

"Again, please call me Marvella, at least while we are in my home. And another excellent question, my dear. It's about time women around our state were taken seriously. Grief, but Wyoming has had the women's vote for years and that state is still moving along in good order. We can't allow for Montana to get behind the times, now can we?"

"No, ma'am." Rebecca tasted one of the potatoes. *Oh my!* She'd never tasted such buttery goodness back in Chicago.

Mr. Andrews set his fork down. "If anyone can help women get the vote in Montana, it's you, Marvella."

"Thank you, my boy." She winked across the table.

Rebecca wanted to giggle. The relationship these people shared was rich indeed. What would it be like to have that? She had her family back home, but nothing like this.

"Rebecca, did you know that our local women's club started the library years ago? Of course, Alicia Conrad and I were the ones to light a fire under the community. Our dream was to see the library expanded, and *now* look. What with the grant from Mr. Carnegie, we have ourselves a library of which to be proud."

Apparently, nothing happened in this town without Marvella Ashbury's nudge and approval. Rebecca better take note of that. For some reason though, it didn't upset her at all. In fact, she found the woman to be positively lovely. It would be good to have Marvella in her corner.

"I shall run it to the very best of my ability." Mr. Andrews lifted his glass to the older woman.

"It's simply good to see you understand the value of our library and your position. The entire Flathead region comes to it, you know." Marvella's voice was almost musical.

"Yes, ma'am. I am well aware." Mr. Andrews nodded and cut his meat with his fork and knife. "This job is an honor for me and rest assured, I take it very seriously. Your trust in me is invaluable."

One thing was for certain, the man knew how to handle Marvella because she cooed and tittered and smiled for the next few moments.

Dinner progressed with lively conversation. And not just from Marvella. The judge had quite a sense of humor and—when his wife let him get in a word edgewise—it was fun to watch his mustache and eyebrows move. He could be fierce, she'd sensed that from the moment she looked into his eyes. But there was also a light there—almost a twinkle—that set her at ease and made her wish she'd known one of her grandfathers.

Then there was Mr. Andrews. The more they talked, the more she liked the man. And the more she held his gaze, the more she couldn't look away. His brown hair had reddish highlights in it and his eyes were much bluer than hers. Lighter too. She especially liked the way they crinkled around the corners when he laughed or smiled.

He knew books—one of her favorite things in all the world. Another positive in his favor.

Sipping her water, she schooled her thoughts and features. Too bad he was the first man she'd met. But they could at least be good friends, right?

Marvella picked up a bell and rang it.

A maid appeared in a matter of seconds. "Yes, ma'am?"

"We're going to move to the small parlor to have our dessert and coffee. Please bring it there."

"Of course, ma'am." The maid disappeared just as quickly as she'd come.

"I'm not sure I could eat another bite"—Mr. Andrews pushed back from the table—"but I would never pass up the chance to have a dessert that Marvella has planned out."

"Oh, you do not want to miss this. It's one of our favorites." She stood as the judge came to her side.

Knocking sounded at the front door, and moments later the butler appeared at the arched entry to the room.

"Mr. Samuel Tuttle is here to see the judge."

"Oh, tell him to come right in," Marvella declared. "He'll have dessert and coffee with us. Tell Mimi."

"Yes, ma'am."

The graying butler left, and a younger man appeared in his place. The judge ushered the man in. "Sam, welcome. I trust you brought me those papers."

He held out a file. "I did. I'm sorry to intrude, especially since you have company."

"It's not a problem." The judge took the file. "We were just about to have dessert and coffee. Would you care to join us?"

"Well, if it's not inconvenient." Mr. Tuttle appeared quite pleased at the prospect.

"You haven't yet met our new stenographer, Rebecca Whitman." The judge motioned Sam to where Rebecca sat.

"Miss Whitman, this is my secretary and clerk, Samuel Tuttle."

"Mr. Tuttle." She studied him and smiled. This was the man that had sent her the letter with her job offer. Would they be working together?

"And I don't know if you remember Mark Andrews or not since he's about seven years your junior."

Mark stood. "Good to see you again, Mr. Tuttle."

Rebecca watched as the two men exchanged a handshake. The judge's clerk had to look up quite a ways at Mark. He lifted his chin and shoulders and then gripped the edge of his suit coat as if he were about to make an important speech. "I remember Mark's sister better than I remember him. He was just a child when I left for my education back east." He spoke with an air of superiority. "Wells College."

What was it about men trying to outdo another? Did it make them feel stronger? More intelligent? The brief amount of time Mr. Tuttle had been in their presence, he'd tried to appear taller. Mr. Andrews dwarfed the man. Goodness, *she* probably would. So he'd lost at height. Was that why he had to throw out that Mr. Andrews was a child when he left for school? Point for Tuttle! Went to school back east? Another point!

Ridiculous notion. Rebecca schooled her features so the men wouldn't see her censure.

"Mr. Andrews was also educated back east." Mrs. Ashbury slid in the comment. "Harvard, was it?"

Now why would the woman challenge these men like that? It made Rebecca want to snicker. But she held herself in check and watched the judge's clerk fidget.

"Yes, ma'am. History and biblical studies were my preference. I'm sure Mr. Tuttle here has much more interesting and demanding education credentials." Mr. Andrews took a seat.

Interesting. A man who didn't rise to the bait.

Mimi entered the room with a cart of dessert and coffee. Marvella grinned like a cat who'd found the cream. "Ah, here we are. Just look at what we have for tonight's dessert. Charlotte Russe with fresh strawberries from our neighbor's greenhouse."

Rebecca's study of the men would have to wait. She leaned forward. "I don't believe I've ever even heard of such a dessert."

"It's quite delicious and was the favorite dessert of President Martin Van Buren. The recipe was passed down to me from my mother. She and my father were personal friends of the president."

Mrs. Ashbury's parents had known the former president? It took every bit of control Rebecca had to keep her eyebrows from jumping toward the ceiling. Wait until she wrote home about that. When Mimi handed her a plate, she had to pause to refrain from licking her lips. Custard topped with strawberries was encased with little sponge cakes. It looked almost too beautiful to eat.

"I still remember the first time you served me this." Mark took a plate. "Thank you, Mimi." He glanced back at Mrs. Ashbury. "I was sixteen."

"Yes, and you ate half of the entire dessert." The judge chuckled. "Keep in mind he'd already had a healthy serving of supper."

Mark laughed too and picked up his fork. "I couldn't help myself. It was so light and delicious. I believe you served it with cherries however, rather than strawberries."

"Oh, goodness yes." Marvella lifted her fork. "They were freshly picked from the lake area. We do grow the best cherries around Flathead. Quite the treat." She motioned to the plate. "Now everyone dig in."

Mimi served the coffee, something Rebecca waved off. Coffee had a way of keeping her awake . . . even if she drank only the smallest amount. Though from the rich aroma, it was probably better than any coffee she'd ever had.

"Miss Whitman, I have to tell you that I'm not in support of women stenographers." Mr. Tuttle dipped his fork into another bite.

Rebecca tried to swallow, but it caught in her throat. She blinked several times, feeling the heat fill her face. Why on earth would the man bring that up here and now? Mimi was at her side with a glass of water in mere seconds. She sipped it, trying to form a response.

He went on, seeming not the least concerned about *her* thoughts on the matter. "I believe the information shared in the courts to be much too graphic and violent for the fairer sex."

The man clearly enjoyed listening to his own voice. She, however, did not. She swallowed the delicious dessert and looked the man in the eye. "The world is full of unpleasantries, Mr. Tuttle." She wanted to add *such as yourself,* but refrained. "And whether you support it or not, I've been a part of the National Shorthand Reporters Association, established in 1899, for the past two years. I'm qualified and certified."

He finished his last bite, set the plate down, and crossed his legs. With a hand, he waved off her remark. "Yes, that may be true, but ladies are far too delicate. They would be better off remaining under their father's protection until a suitable husband can be found."

"I respectfully disagree." Rebecca prepared herself to give an aggressive defense, but Marvella held up a hand before she could.

"Mr. Tuttle, this is 1904. Women are making exceptional strides in employment and are soon to have the right to vote." She snuck a glance at Rebecca and smiled. "I personally was involved in seeing Miss Whitman hired on, and I mean to offer her every support. She's a very intelligent and gracious young woman."

The smile he sent her made her want to throttle him. "I quite agree about her value. I find her quite beautiful and socially adept."

Did this man think that he could throw out a compliment and a smile and win her approval? Rebecca fought to keep from giggling. She glanced at Mr. Andrews, who gave her a lopsided grin, then ducked his head to focus on his plate.

He hadn't helped matters at all. In fact, Rebecca burst out laughing.

Everyone, even Mr. Andrews, fixed her with their gazes. She wanted to apologize, but she couldn't quite get her laughter under control. Thank heaven Marvella appeared amused rather than offended.

She smiled as she filled her fork with another bite. "I fear we have embarrassed poor Miss Whitman by making her the focus of our conversation."

Mr. Tuttle shook his head. "There's no need to be embarrassed by my comment. I find Miss Whitman quite charming, and as a man who is in search of a wife, I would be very proud to further explore the possibilities of courtship. Of course, if we were to progress to marriage, she would have to give up her job."

Could the man hear the antiquated words spewing from his own mouth? And he thought it would help him appeal to her? She put her napkin to her lips then set her plate aside and folded her hands. "Well, that isn't going to happen, and neither is our courtship. I came west to work, not to marry. I have no interest in *exploration*, except in the court's system."

Marvella's eyebrows had a turn at lifting toward the ceiling. But the woman didn't say a word.

Even if she'd surprised her hostess, Rebecca didn't care. She'd probably broken every societal rule, but at least she'd made herself clear.

They ate for several minutes in absolute silence, which didn't help Rebecca's mood at all. What a wonderful way to ruin the evening—why, the judge's clerk had probably worked for the older man for years. Marvella obviously didn't agree with the man, but Rebecca was still a guest in their home. And to think she hadn't even started her job yet. Gracious, why did she have to cause a scene?

The quiet stretched and then Mr. Andrews set his plate down on Mimi's tray and looked toward Rebecca. "I must admit that I admire your gumption, Miss Whitman. You've traveled across the country to become the first woman in your field in our grand state. I, for one, applaud you."

"Amen to that." Marvella gave an emphatic nod.

The judge got to his feet. "Sam, I wonder if you would come to my office. I'd like to discuss a couple of things, and I know Miss Whitman and Mr. Andrews need to get home. Bring your coffee, if you like."

"Of course, sir."

"You are quite right, Judge." Marvella stood as well. She pointed her stare at Mr. Andrews. "Mark, please do me a favor and walk Miss Whitman home?"

"Yes, ma'am. It would be my privilege." He straightened his tie and stood.

"It was good to see you again, Mark. I'll be in touch." The judge motioned to Sam to follow him.

Mrs. Ashbury waited until they were gone before speaking. "I'm sure you two would love some time to get to know one another better without us older folks getting in the way. Besides, I'm quite tired." She patted her hand over her mouth as if she was yawning.

What a show. Rebecca wanted to laugh out loud again, but that would be quite rude. Besides, she couldn't blame the woman. It was obvious she was used to telling everyone what to do and orchestrating all that went on around her.

Mr. Andrews waited for Rebecca to stand, then escorted her to the door, where one of the many servants held out their coats.

"Thank you, Clarence." Mr. Andrews took his things.

Clarence helped her into her coat and she buttoned it up, steeling herself to brave the cold winter evening.

Once they were outside, Mr. Andrews held out his arm for her. "Be careful, it's gotten quite slick."

She took it. At least *he* was a gentleman—unlike Mr. Tuttle. Just the thought of the man made her cringe. They walked several minutes and neither one of them spoke. The awkward silence stretched. Maybe Mrs. Ashbury's hinting had gone over Mr. Andrews's head. Or perhaps he simply wasn't interested.

That thought brought a little twinge of disappointment. But no matter.

He kept his gaze on the ground. Probably watching for ice. Very gallant of him. "I hope you will visit the library soon."

For what purpose? To see him? "Why would I do that?" Oh dear. She hadn't meant to sound quite so harsh.

One of his eyebrows shot up. "Since you love books?"

Had her expression been that telltale? "Oh, yes."

"It's outstanding that you have studied and acquired this job. The judge isn't easily impressed. Your skill and intelligence must be noteworthy. My sister is quite knowledgeable too, although with her it's not so much a book learning situation. She's more hands-on."

Rebecca didn't know why, but his comment irked her. "Hands on what?"

He laughed. "Ranch work. She loves ranching. She's not afraid to get dirty."

"Do you suppose that I am?" She bit her lip. *Why* was she taking such offense?

"I don't know you well enough to suppose anything." His eyebrows dipped, but it was his tone that gave her a hint Mr. Andrews was beginning to get irritated.

Rebecca fought to control her mouth and mind. She had no reason to be angry with him. It wasn't like he'd said what Mr. Tuttle had. "I'm sorry. I don't know what's come over me, except that I'm tired and didn't care at all for Mr. Tuttle's attitude."

"I can understand that. My father is of a mind that I need to be involved in the ranch—that my sister can't handle it alone. But she does a wonderful job and has no need of me. I would only get in the way."

Her nerves calmed a touch. At least he didn't seem to be against women using their minds and their skills, unlike the other man she'd met that evening. "I doubt that. You seem to be the kind of man who accomplishes what he sets out to do."

"Now, you don't really know me well enough to suppose that." He smiled. "But somehow you've managed to figure me out. I'm exactly that way."

She smiled. "I hope you'll forgive me for my earlier rudeness."

"Already forgotten. There is one thing, however, that I must make clear."

They reached the apartment building and as she released his arm, he touched her elbow. "Look, I hope Marvella didn't give you the wrong impression. They've known me for many years, and she means well, but I'm not looking for a relationship. And I'm definitely not one of the most eligible bachelors, if that's what *you're* looking for."

Gracious, he didn't believe that she had expressed interest in finding a husband to Mrs. Ashbury so the older woman would say something . . . did he? Granted, some women operated that way, but not Rebecca Whitman.

"Well, *I'm* not looking for a relationship either. In fact, I promised my folks that I wouldn't go to the wild west and fall in love with the first man I met. And you, Mr. Andrews, bear that unlucky title."

Something flickered in his eyes, but she couldn't decipher it, as much as she wanted to know what the man was thinking. "Didn't you report to Judge Ashbury earlier today?"

He was a smart one, she'd give him that. "Yes, but that doesn't count. He's my boss." She squared her shoulders and raised her chin, hoping it made her look strong and capable. So he would take her seriously. "Mr. Andrews, I'm here to make a career for myself. And, I might add, I'm very good at what I do, but to remain so I must be singularly focused."

He tipped his hat at her. "Good. Then we have that settled."

"Good." But why didn't it *feel* good? Did he not like her? And why did she care?

"Have a good evening." He turned on his heel and walked away.

For several moments Rebecca watched him, remembering his laughter at dinner. His easy camaraderie with the Ashburys. His delight as he talked about the library, his plans, and his passion for books and education.

He would have made a good friend.

Oh well, it was too late for that after her behavior this evening.

4

Marvella walked out to her gardens in the back of their large home and hunted for their gardener, Jacob. At least the little pathways had been shoveled of snow. She'd have to commend him for that. A lady hated getting her garden boots covered in snow. It had taken her a good bit of time to train the young gardener in her ways—which were best, of course—but he was coming along nicely.

Today was manure day. A very important day, especially for her roses.

Where *was* that man? "Jacob?" She lifted her voice and let it resonate across the lawn. "Ja-cob!" She stretched out the two syllables and raised the pitch on the last. That usually worked.

"Yes, ma'am. I'm here, ma'am." The spindly fellow skidded around the gardening shed, slipping as he went.

"Oh good." She tucked her hands over her waist. "It is manure day, is it not?"

"Yes, ma'am. I was just fetching it, ma'am." He rushed back to the shed. Clanking, scraping, a couple of loud thuds, and a groan followed.

Marvella blinked and shook her head. What it took to train a good gardener these days . . . oh, but she would stick with it. Someone had to teach them how to tend her prized roses. And she wasn't about to let the judge do it. Her husband might be the smartest and most handsome around—and he knew the law like no other—but he didn't know a thing about roses.

Jacob emerged with a wheelbarrow filled to overflowing with the dark manure.

Pulling out a clothespin she always carried tucked into her waist on gardening days, Marvella pinched it over her nose.

The way her new gardener gaped at her made her roll her eyes.

"It is for the stench, young man. It is indecent for a lady to endure the aroma for too long." Her voice was nasally— even to her own ears—but surely he understood.

His eyebrows shot up as his jaw dropped. "Oh. Of course. I see."

"Come along." She stepped toward the first row of roses.

Last week she'd given him an hour tour of just her roses. Explained how everything was done. Showed him the pruning that had been done in the fall. Today was most important. "Once a month, I want fresh manure mounded around the bases."

He took the shovel, scooped up some of the manure, and sprinkled it around the base of a bush.

"No, Jacob. Mound it. Mooooooooound it." She made an example with her hands.

"Oh, of course." He shoveled it and eyed her. Shoveled some more. Glanced. Shoveled some more.

When it reached the appropriate height, she gave a deep nod and pointed at him. "Good job. Now that is a mound to be proud of."

"Yes, ma'am." He started working on the next one.

By the time they finished the row, he'd had to refill the wheelbarrow three times. Sweat poured from the young man's brow even though it was quite chilly outside.

"Now, the next important task is to check the moisture level at least once a week. Then, when a warmer day comes around, poke a hole in the mound and pour some warm water in. Not hot. Warm. Just enough to make sure the roses are getting their nourishment."

"Yes, ma'am." His gloves were covered in manure.

"Make sure you go back to your quarters and make notes of this."

"Yes, ma'am."

She glanced down at the watch pinned to her coat. "It is time for me to get ready for my women's club. Rest assured, I will come check the progress later today." She turned but then thought better of it. "Why don't you tell me what needs to be done. I might have gone too fast." With a smile, she raised her eyebrows.

He licked his lips and then ran down the list of all she'd said. It wasn't word for word, but good heavens, it was close enough.

"Well done, Jacob." With a hand to her skirts, she turned to the house but threw over her shoulder: "I shall ask Mr. Jefferies to leave you a special treat in your room."

The young lad needed some fattening up as it was, and a well-placed treat was powerful incentive.

She pulled the clothespin from her face and wiggled her nose. The pinch was always a bit painful, but it was better than the alternative. Ah, fresh air. What a lovely, crisp day.

When she entered the house, Mimi waited for her and took her things. "I have your gown laid out for the Women's Club meeting, ma'am."

"Wonderful. And you made sure that Miss Whitman received an invitation?"

"Yes, ma'am. She sent a reply that she would attend."

"Perfect."

The judge walked into the room and kissed her cheek. "What is perfect, my dear? Manure day, is it?"

"Yes, it is, but we were speaking of Miss Whitman coming to the Women's Club meeting."

"Ah." He tucked his hands into the pockets of his smoking jacket. "Is that today as well? Busy, busy, aren't we?"

"Yes, Judge. Which means you either need to hide in your study or venture out to the courthouse." The courthouse would be best. It was good for him to get out.

"Of course, dear." He winked at her and leaned down to kiss her again. "I look forward to hearing all about the meeting over dinner." His eyebrows waggled at her and then he walked away.

Oh, that man. It was a good thing she had him as trained as she did. What kind of mess would he be without her? But after forty years of marriage, he not only was a fine specimen of a man, but he was a prominent judge. Who took her advice on everything.

Proof of his brilliance.

She couldn't help but grin as she headed up the stairs to change. It thrilled her to no end that she had been the one to suggest Rebecca Whitman. It was about time their state moved out of the dark ages. Bringing on a female court reporter was brilliant and had already made waves in the papers. Exactly as she had planned.

The women's suffrage movement would benefit greatly from this huge step forward.

And the court would probably run smoother too.

Even though Marvella might run the judge like a well-oiled machine, she didn't have control over everyone.

Which was a pity. But with Rebecca there now? Things would be shipshape in no time.

Mimi waited for her once again at the top of the stairs. "What's put that grin on your face, ma'am?"

She tapped Mimi on the shoulder. "I think Miss Whitman will be my new personal project. I'm quite impressed with her, and I have a feeling there's a lot of potential there."

Mimi followed her into her dressing room. "I agree, ma'am. You do always choose the best recipients of your goodwill. Miss Whitman is an excellent choice."

"She is, isn't she?" She lifted her chin. "Once she arrives, please invite her to dinner after church tomorrow. That way we can have a nice, long chat."

Mimi smiled at her in the dressing mirror. "Of course. I'll take care of everything." She pulled the pins out of Marvella's hair and began to brush it. "Now . . . how would you like to wear your hair for the meeting, ma'am?"

The walk to the Ashbury mansion put a skip in Rebecca's step. The sun was shining. The air was crisp. The snow sparkled.

And she was on her way to her very first Kalispell Women's Club meeting. To say she was excited was the understatement of the week. The Ashbury home, like the Conrad mansion, was on the outskirts of town and she relished the time to revel in her thoughts on the way there.

For years, she'd longed to get involved in active women's groups, but her mother and father hadn't been too keen on it. Of course, after the incident at the parade all those years ago, they had done their level best to protect her from much of the goings-on of the world.

A shiver raced up her spine, and she shook it away. She would not think of that now.

The lovely apartment the Ashburys rented to her was perfect. Located in the center of Kalispell, it was only a block to the current courthouse. Everything else was within walking distance. The new courthouse being constructed would be a good deal farther, but she could handle the eight- or nine-block walk. Her first day, she'd walked the length of town, which was only thirteen blocks. Going north and south it was only about eight blocks. But it was expanding. Even so, it was the perfect-sized town for her.

And the apartment! Oh, the apartment. It was much more space than she'd been accustomed to. She'd never had a bedroom to herself, much less an entire home with bedroom, sitting room, kitchen, and bathroom. The furnishings were new and stylish—Marvella wouldn't abide by anything else. Rebecca had already added to it by making her first purchase of her very own: a teakettle and a set of towels.

Over time, it would be wonderful to add a bookshelf and books to her belongings. But until she could afford it, she'd just have to visit the library often.

Which was less than three blocks away.

Since that awkward conversation Tuesday evening with Mr. Andrews, she'd seen him several times in the foyer of their apartment building, and they shared pleasantries. He was a nice enough man. Perhaps if she visited the library, they could become friends. And he'd come to realize that, contrary to Mrs. Ashbury's comments, she was *not* in the market for the most eligible bachelor in Kalispell.

"Miss Whitman! Please wait."

She turned and found Sam Tuttle following her at a brisk pace. He waved and Rebecca nodded. Good grief, she didn't wish to deal with him right now. It was bad enough she was going to have to work with him, but now he was following her.

"Good afternoon, Miss Whitman." His rather breathless voice had a pinched, high-pitched tone. "I hope you don't mind my stopping you."

"What seems to be the problem?" She closed her mouth against telling him how annoying she found him.

"There's no problem, I just thought you might like to have dinner with me tonight. I didn't have a chance to ask you after dessert the other night because, well, as you know, the judge needed my expertise on a matter."

She stopped herself from audibly sighing. "Yes, I'm sure he did. I'm headed to the Ashbury house right now to attend the Kalispell Women's Club meeting."

He frowned. "Do you think that wise, Miss Whitman? Most of the attendees are older women—those who have raised their families and now do pretty much as they desire. Their husbands are hard-pressed to keep them under control, and their sole purpose in gathering is to complain about the very hand that feeds them."

"I beg your pardon." Did he actually believe these were the words to woo a woman?

"Well, it's true. I've heard the judge himself complain about those women taking over his house, and the fact that they have done their best to take over this town. They complain about their husbands and families and bemoan their lack of power." He gave a *tsking* sound. "Miss Whitman, that would be putting a bad foot forward."

Enough. "I hardly think so. Women have wonderful ideas and are responsible for civilizing the west. We are beholden to these ladies here in Kalispell for getting the library started, as well as various charities. Really, Mr. Tuttle, you shouldn't judge so harshly when you know so little about them." She stopped herself before she *really* got riled up.

With a glance down his nose at her—even though they were the same height—he cajoled. "I know plenty. I've been in the company of their husbands." He softened his tone. "Miss Whitman, you are a lovely young woman, and I would hate to see your reputation damaged by the company you keep."

"I see. Then perhaps it's best I not associate with too many people." Him, for starters.

He nodded and dipped his brow as though he was very serious about her well-being. "I think you would benefit from that. After all, you wouldn't want to be led further astray. The judge and Mrs. Ashbury are fine people, but everyone knows that Marvella does her best to wear the pants in the family. I would probably avoid her as well."

"I thought rather to avoid *you*, Mr. Tuttle. I know we must work together, but that doesn't mean I need associate with you for any other reason." Her temper was getting shorter by the minute.

"You are clearly offended, but that wasn't my intent. I would like to know you better. As I mentioned during dessert, I believe it would be nice to get to know one another, perhaps for the sake of something more serious." His hand touched her elbow.

She yanked out of his grip. "I *am* offended. And frankly, it *was* your intent because you believe you are correct and want to spout off your belittling words. I'm sorry, Mr. Tuttle. I have no interest in knowing you outside of work. Even there, I hope we shall limit our association." She turned on her heel and took swift steps away from the opinionated, short, obnoxious man.

But somehow, he kept pace with her. "Miss Whitman, I do apologize if I have upset your delicate constitution. I should have considered that speaking out so boldly might cause you distress."

She stopped and squared her shoulders as she faced him. "Mr. Tuttle, I am not in distress, nor is my constitution delicate. Please understand that I have no interest in knowing you any better than I do. You have no respect for what I do, nor are you respectful of women in general."

"I beg your pardon! I have the utmost respect for women. Why, you can ask my sainted mother. I am constantly attending to her needs now that my father is gone. She will tell you that I have been nothing but attentive and considerate of her and have learned a great deal about the lesser sex."

So now they'd gone from the fairer sex to the lesser sex? The man was abominable. "Then I suggest you go keep the company of your sainted mother and leave me alone." This time, she practically ran to get away from him.

He didn't follow.

After a minute of convincing herself to calm down, she dared a glance over her shoulder. Tuttle was gone, thank goodness.

She forced aside thoughts of Mr. Tuttle and his unpleasant nature. To think, he wanted to have a serious relationship with her! It soured her stomach.

She slowed her steps and forced her mind back to more pleasant things.

The beautiful day. The Women's Club meeting ahead of her. The opportunity to meet other ladies in town.

The Ashbury home was before her, so Rebecca took a deep, calming breath and hurried up the steps to the stately three-story mansion. It was red brick, like the apartment building she lived in. Marvella told her that she wanted the red brick to stand out against the white columns and trim and so that their home wasn't too similar to the Conrad mansion, which was dark shingles and brick.

A little thrill rushed through Rebecca at the thought of meeting Mrs. Conrad. Alicia—known as Lettie, according to Marvella—was the widow of the man who founded Kalispell. It was going to be like being in the presence of the President's wife!

Mimi opened the door for her before she could even ring the bell. "Good afternoon, Miss Whitman."

"Mimi. How lovely to see you again."

"And you, miss. May I take your things?" The woman was tall and thin, with broad shoulders and black hair that shone in the light from the foyer's chandelier.

Oh, to have straight, shiny, smooth hair. But alas, hers was a constant wave and what her mother called *frizzy*. "Yes, thank you very much." The maid helped her out of her outer coat, hat, and gloves.

Feminine voices lifted in conversation reached her ears and she put a hand to her stomach. She shouldn't be nervous. Marvella had told her that she would talk her up to the ladies and that Rebecca should enter with her head held high.

Hearing that and doing it were two completely different things.

Mimi nudged her in the back. "Go ahead and join them in the parlor, Miss Whitman. They are all quite excited to meet you."

The prodding was exactly what she needed. With a deep breath, she gave a nod to the maid. "Thank you." And then headed toward the parlor.

As soon as she reached the large, double-door entry, her heart had tripled its beat. At least that's how it struck her.

Marvella spotted her and held out a hand. "Ladies . . . la-dies!" She glided over to Rebecca, whose feet seemed to be lodged in cement. "Allow me to introduce you to the first female court stenographer in all of Montana. Miss Rebecca Whitman."

Applause filled the room as Rebecca took in all the faces. All the ladies dressed in their finery. Jewels glistening. Oh, she didn't fit in at all! She pasted on a smile. "Thank you for having me."

Marvella tugged at her elbow and her feet begrudgingly moved. From one woman to the next, she was paraded and introduced. Then at last they reached the end of the circle.

"Mrs. Conrad." Marvella's tone held pride and adoration.

"Please . . . call me Lettie." The woman was gracious. Composed. Lovely. "We are thrilled that you are here, Miss Whitman. And excited to see what changes you help us to bring about."

"Changes?" Rebecca swallowed. Her? She wasn't capable of doing anything like that . . . was she?

"Don't you worry." Lettie patted her arm. "We've been working toward this for many years and we are proud to have you among our numbers. Here"—she pointed to a chair—"why don't you sit next to me while Marvella gets things started."

Another big swallow followed by a short intake of breath. "Thank you." She took her seat and folded her hands in her lap. Whew. At least she'd made it this far. The introductions were done. Over time, she'd come to know each of these ladies and hopefully be able to call them friends.

Friends.

Something she'd hoped and longed for—for longer than she cared to admit.

Mrs. O'Neil—the Ashburys' housekeeper—wheeled a tray around offering each lady a dainty plate, cup, and saucer. Tea and coffee were served from her rolling contraption, while little platters of sandwiches, pastries, and other items—the ladies called them *finger foods*—were passed around the circle of women. All in all, there were fifteen women present. Quite an impressive number for a small town.

At first, Rebecca didn't think she would take anything

because she was sure she would spill something until Lettie showed her the small table beside her. Covered in a tiny doily, it was just big enough for her tea and plate.

Glancing around the room, she noticed a multitude of the tiny wood tables, each with a pedestal and Queen–Anne–style legs.

Lettie leaned close to her. "Aren't they divine? Marvella commissioned a local carpenter, a Mr. Joseph Cameron, to make these for the singular purpose of our meetings."

"They're lovely. A perfect design to be sure." Rebecca smiled and took a sip of her tea. What would it be like to have the money to order fifteen identical tables? Their only use that of a ladies' club meeting. It made her mind swim. Especially since she had regarded a similar small table while they'd been shopping for her apartment. The cost was a whole dollar and fifty cents!

But Lettie Conrad sure wouldn't understand the shock this was to Rebecca's senses. Rebecca had seen the Conrad mansion and it was breathtaking. Even larger than the Ashburys' home.

Conversation traveled around the room. Business must come later as the ladies enjoyed their refreshments and tea. The more she listened, the more she concluded that women didn't have any shame sharing their marriage woes and troubles.

One woman was married to the manager of the First National Bank and her husband never seemed to have enough money to help her beautify their yard. The other ladies groaned and encouraged her to keep her chin up.

Another woman—a bit closer to Rebecca's own age as most of the women were more mature—complained about her children and her husband's lack of interest in their futures.

An equal amount of bolstering and understanding was given for the second woman.

Then, one of the eldest ladies in the group shared about how she hadn't spoken to her husband in a week because he worked so late and she was already asleep by the time he returned.

More comfort and empathy were given.

Goodness, was Mr. Tuttle right? Were these women so miserable in their married lives that they gathered just to complain about their husbands?

During the next lull in the conversation, Marvella glanced at her. "Why, whatever is the matter, my dear?"

Rebecca set her teacup down. If these women could be so honest with one another, then so could she. "Ladies, I understand that I am new here and I greatly appreciate you welcoming me into your midst. But I must say . . . I'm a bit confused. Are any of you happy in your marriages?"

Silence greeted her, along with several shocked expressions. Oh gracious, had she offended them? Perhaps she should have read up on what went on at these types of meetings so she would have been prepared.

Lettie started to laugh. Then Marvella. Then the rest of the group.

Rebecca glanced from one woman to the next, awaiting an explanation from someone. Anyone.

Marvella put her napkin to her mouth and the laughter subsided. "Oh, my dear. Of course we are happy. What would make you think that we aren't?"

"Well . . . that is . . . there was . . . I guess . . ."

Lettie saved her. "A lot of complaining going on?"

Rebecca grimaced and nodded.

Marvella waved her hand. "Oh my dear, this is simply what married women do."

She stiffened her shoulders. "I never once heard my mother complain. In fact, it wasn't until I was leaving Chicago that my mother even expressed any hardship whatsoever. She simply warned me not to marry for the wrong reasons, or to fall for the first man who showed me attention or spoke flowery words. She wanted me to know that life could be very hard." At this point she couldn't take the confession back. "I'm beginning to wonder if marriage is worth it at all if this is what is to be expected." Perhaps she hadn't calmed herself enough after her conversation with the despicable Mr. Tuttle. It would have been better for her to keep her mouth shut. What did she know of marriage?

Several women spoke at once.

A small woman next to Marvella spoke up. "Dear, what a horrible example we have been to you." She glanced around the circle of women. "Perhaps we should remember that our lips should be speaking only that which is edifying."

Words of affirmation and nods rounded the room.

Marvella pinned Rebecca with a stare. "I am sorry, my dear. Women often bear a difficult life. That burden is especially hard when they're poor, but that doesn't mean marriage is horrible or that we are all miserable. Women are the glue that holds the country together. God made us that way. We are the nurturers, the encouragers. Without us, men would wander around punching things and never get anything accomplished."

Every woman nodded. "Yes" and "that's true" came out of almost every mouth.

"That's why a relationship with God is so very important. He has given us an incredible job. A mission," Marvella continued, her chin high.

A relationship with God?

Rebecca believed in God. Her parents often talked of God providing. And when they had time, they'd gone to a church up the street. But only if all of them had decent clothes to wear and had been bathed. Because lots of rich people went to that church. She didn't remember the reverend ever saying much about a relationship with God though.

"I see we have puzzled you." Lettie placed a hand on Rebecca's knee.

Rebecca blinked and gazed around the room. Every woman watched her. Oh what she wouldn't give to learn how to school her features. Papa warned her many times that she wore her feelings on her sleeve. "I'm sorry. I am simply trying to understand what you mean by a relationship with God."

Several gasps were heard, and Marvella came out of her seat at the same time Mrs. O'Neil entered with her wheeled tray and a beautifully decorated cake.

Marvella sent Rebecca a smile and smoothed the front of her skirt as she sat down again. "That's quite all right, my dear Miss Whitman. No need to worry, ladies, I've determined to take our sweet Rebecca here under my wing and you know I cannot and will not abide having a protégé who is a heathen. But the hour is late and it's time for cake, so rest assured I will get her saved in the morning."

5

SATURDAY, JANUARY 30, 1904

The library had been busier today than any day so far. Mark shelved several books and then tidied up the space around his desk. It was almost closing time, and his feet were telling him they needed a rest.

Once home, he would put his feet up and read a good book. Something he hadn't had the luxury of doing all week since he'd been settling into his new apartment. Every time he thought he was finished, he realized how unprepared he was to cook and fend for himself.

The front door opened, and Mark looked up. A smile stretched across his face. "Why, hello, Judge. What brings you to the library today?" He pointed to the clock on the wall. "It's almost time for me to lock up, but I'm sure I can help you find whatever you're looking for right quick."

Judge Ashbury grinned underneath his mustache. "Don't worry about me, son. I'm here to see you. Marvella had the ladies over for one of her meetings and I chose to make myself scarce. Go ahead and do whatever you need to do, then perhaps we can chat for a bit?"

"Sounds wonderful." He straightened the stack on his desk. "Just give me a couple minutes." Mark left his desk area and wandered through the bookshelves. As far as he knew there were only two people left in the library. He found them, directed them to what they needed, then helped them check out the books. He locked up behind them, then walked across the hardwood floors of the entryway and found the judge studying a tome on ancient Greece. "All right, Judge. All locked up for the night."

"Splendid."

"Why don't we sit in my office." Mark led the way. Something must be on the man's mind for him to wander into the library on a Saturday.

"Tell me about things here. Is everything proceeding as you'd hoped?"

Mark nodded, a strong sense of contentment washing over him as he leaned back in his chair. "Yes, sir. I have big dreams and plans for this place, mind you. But it will take time."

"And your family? I bet Angus and Kate are thrilled to have you back."

Kate might be thrilled. Dad? Not so much. But Mark filled the judge in on his dad's condition and that he hoped to get out to the ranch tomorrow. When he got to the part of his father disowning him, the judge laughed.

"Oh, Angus. Your father's always been a bit of a hothead. Must be his Scottish heritage. But he didn't mean it, I'm sure of it."

Mark released a breath. "I know. I just wish I could get him to understand that what I do is important."

Judge Ashbury leaned forward. "Nothing is important except that ranch—at least in your dad's mind. I don't think you're going to be able to change that."

Mark mulled that over for several moments. "You're probably right." Tapping his fingers on the desk, he eyed the man he most trusted. "So tell me what you know about Harvey Monroe."

The older man leaned back and fiddled with his mustache and then his beard. "Well . . . let's see. He showed up in town one day last October, if I recall. The ladies were all dancing jigs to meet him at church and social events because he *is* a handsome man. Your sister happened to be the one to get his attention and funny . . . now that I think about it, I don't think she was one of the ones clamoring over him." He shrugged. "But anyway, Monroe wooed Kate and they married in December. Your dad sings his praises and says he's very attentive about the ranch and Kate, so when Harvey asked for Kate's hand in marriage—even though they'd only known each other a few weeks—Angus didn't object. With you gone, he knew they would need help."

A twinge of guilt hit Mark in the gut.

The judge raised a bushy brow. "Why? What do you think of him?"

"I've only met him the once." He didn't want to like the man. Was that only because Kate had married so fast? *If I'd been here, would I have stopped her?* He doubted it. Kate was much older, stubborn, and once she set her mind to something, that was it. "Do you know anything about his past?"

"Far as I recall, he didn't speak about it."

Hm. That didn't necessarily mean that the man had anything to hide. . . .

"Could you, perhaps, be a bit overprotective of your sister?"

Mark shrugged. "Quite possibly."

"My advice then is to take some time and get to know Harvey. Kate is a smart woman."

"Once again, sir, you are correct."

"Have you ever thought of getting involved in politics?"

Mark's eyebrows shot up. "That was quite the change of subject, sir."

The judge laughed. "Have to admit, it's why I came by today. Been thinking on it ever since you came back to town. You've grown into a solid and respectable man, and we need more of those around here for the future of our town."

"While I'm honored, don't you think I need a bit more experience under my belt?"

"Remind me of your age, Mark?"

"Twenty-eight, sir."

The older man waved a hand at him. "You've got plenty of years behind you to run for office. Although you'll need a wife to gain more respectability." He winked.

Mark laughed and shook his head. "*Now* who's playing matchmaker?" He crossed his arms over his chest.

"Simply stating the obvious." He tapped his fingers on the arm of the chair. "I don't know where I'd be without Marvella. That woman has kept my toes to the fire for more than forty years now."

"She is definitely a powerful force, sir."

"That she is." Judge Ashbury was silent for several moments. "You're like a son to us, Mark. I hope you know that." He cleared his throat. "When the good Lord above didn't bless us with children, we were sorrowful for many years.

Then you came to town. A skinny, gangly kid who loved books." He chuckled. "But you were a gift to us."

"Thank you, sir." Mark swallowed the emotion clogging his throat. "I know I've been gone a long time—too long. But you and Marvella will always have my undying love and affection." He'd written to them regularly—more often than to his own family—because the Ashburys understood him and loved him like no one else. But he hadn't seen them in so long, he had been worried that things would be awkward when he moved back. That their relationship would have suffered from the time and distance. From the look on the judge's face as he stared out the window, Mark need not worry anymore.

He should make more time for these precious people. "I hope we will be able to spend lots of time together now that I'm back and settled."

The judge stood and swiped at his cheek. "Sounds wonderful."

"I appreciate you thinking of me for the town. I'm not sure I'm ready for politics, but I will consider it. Even though my dad believes I'm a failure of a son for not following in his footsteps, it's nice to know that you imagine me worthy of a public servant position."

"You are more than worthy, son. Your reputation is spotless. Stellar. You are a good citizen and son. You father will come around in time. He always does. It simply hurt his pride that you didn't want what he worked so hard to build. Your rejection of it felt to him like a rejection of his life's work."

Leave it to the judge to hit the nail on the head. Why hadn't Mark realized where his father's anger came from? "I needed to hear that, sir. I need to make it right even if I don't want to be a rancher." He stood and picked up his things.

The judge gripped his arm. "Might I suggest you get on your knees about it?"

"Another good point. Perhaps it's time I do that."

"The good Lord will surely guide your words if you seek Him first. Start there and work your way up to standing."

"Yes, sir."

Judge Ashbury stepped closer and wrapped Mark in a hug. He patted Mark's back several times and then released him. "I'm proud of you. Now I best get home and see how Marvella's meeting went. Who knows what wonderful things she's cooked up for the great town of Kalispell." He turned toward the door, then paused. "And don't forget what I said about public office. Pray about that too."

"I will. I promise."

Mark's heart swelled as he let the judge out of the library and then went back for his coat and hat. Twice since he'd arrived, the older man had told him he was proud of him.

And that held more weight than anything he'd heard his whole life.

Sunday, January 31, 1904

"Rebecca."

Huh? Everything was dark. Of course, her eyes were closed. She was asleep. Must be a dream.

"Rebecca."

Why was her name being whispered? And by whom? She rolled over in her bed and pulled the covers up over her head.

"Rebecca Whitman. It is imperative that we speak this instant."

Why on earth was she dreaming about Marvella Ashbury?

"Rebecca. Whitman."

She lowered the covers and cracked one eyelid open. "Ahhhhh!"

Inches above her face, Marvella stared down at her, gray eyes wide.

With another squeal, Rebecca scrambled across her bed, away from the older woman, sat up, and pulled the covers up to her chest. "What are you doing here?" She pushed her unruly hair out of her face.

Marvella chuckled. "Why, I knocked, but you didn't answer. What if the building had been on fire? Besides, you told me I was welcome anytime." She walked over to a chair and sat in it, back ramrod straight.

"You scared me." Rebecca put a hand to her chest. But she *had* said those words. And the woman owned the building. Taking several breaths, she blinked away the remnants of sleep and yawned. She'd always been a hard sleeper. "What time is it?"

"Almost six a.m."

Good heavens. No wonder she was so exhausted. She'd set her book down at two a.m. But it was Sunday. No need to rise early on a Sunday.

Except, of course, when your landlord and the woman who basically ran the town decided to give a wake-up call in person. She swiped a hand down her face. "Awfully early for a social visit, isn't it?"

Marvella removed her lace gloves and kept her hands on

her pocketbook in her lap. "This isn't a social visit, my dear. This is critically important. It's about your soul."

"My soul." Oh dear. She'd hoped Marvella had let go of this last night.

"Yes, dear. You simply must get right with God. This morning, if at all possible."

"Before breakfast?" She drew her knees up to her chest.

"Oh, definitely. This is the most important thing you will ever do. Everything is so much clearer when a person has their life in order with the Almighty."

"I believe in God. I've always believed in God."

"Good." Marvella nodded. "That is a lovely start. But even the devil himself believes in God, dear."

Ouch. Nothing like being compared to the devil first thing in the morning. She wasn't awake enough for this. Perhaps she could persuade the woman to allow her to make some coffee first? No. That wouldn't do. Rebecca was in her nightdress. She wasn't about to go parading about in front of this prestigious woman without proper clothes on. She'd just have to face the onslaught without coffee. Rubbing at her eyes, she grasped for clarity of thought. It had to be somewhere within reach.

"It's not enough to simply believe in God, Rebecca."

"Okay. What do I need to do?"

"You must recognize that you are a sinner."

She was a relatively good and decent person. But okay, she wasn't perfect. "I can admit that."

"Good. You are in need of a savior because of your sins. Jesus is *the* Savior. He died for you because He loves you."

Why would anyone die for her? That was ludicrous. But she couldn't say that. Marvella obviously thought this was important enough to come into her apartment before six in the morning and tell her. Every woman at the meeting yesterday seemed adamant on the saving of Rebecca's soul as soon as possible. But why?

She needed a good deal more information to understand all this. "Isn't it enough that I know God exists and I strive to live a good and honorable life?"

"No." The sorrow that crossed the woman's face made Rebecca feel bad for asking the question. Marvella might be a bit nosey and eccentric, but the woman cared a great deal about people. That much was obvious. "Good works are just filthy rags without a true heart."

"Isn't my heart true?" She yawned again and covered her mouth with her hand.

"My dear, you have a beautiful heart from what I have seen thus far, but God wants your heart devoted to Him." Marvella stood and pulled a book out of her pocketbook. "Here. I had a feeling you might not have one." She held out a leather volume.

Heart pounding, she had a little thrill. Oh, how she loved books. Then she saw the cover. *Holy Bible*. Well, she'd never read it, but she'd seen one at the reverend's back in Chicago. Wasn't it just a boring old book of stories? She took the book and ran her hand over the cover. "Thank you." She pasted on a smile, but another yawn interrupted it.

"I can see that you are exhausted so I will take my leave for now." Marvella walked back to the bedroom door. "I will see myself out, but I expect to see you in church at eleven o'clock sharp. The judge and I will save you a seat. Then perhaps this afternoon after dinner at our home you can read in your Bible. I took the liberty of marking some of my favorite passages. The judge and I will be glad to discuss any questions that you have."

"Thank you." Anything for the woman to leave. Her eyes drooped and she wanted nothing more than to burrow under the covers once again and forget this meeting ever happened.

"Eleven o'clock," Marvella called over her shoulder.

"Yes, ma'am," Rebecca hollered back.

She heard the clicking of the front door, pulled the covers over her head, and closed her eyes.

But then her eyelids popped open. If she didn't set an alarm, she would surely miss the church service. And if she did that, Marvella Ashbury would call in the cavalry and next time, instead of being awakened by just the judge's wife, Rebecca was quite certain the constable would be there.

Accompanied by every woman of the Kalispell Women's Club.

Rebecca suppressed a yawn as she listened to the preacher talk about the importance of loving God with one's whole heart. She'd never considered such a thing before now. Love had always been reserved for her family. Fear was what she exhibited toward God. After all, God was . . . well . . . He was God. He had all power and all knowledge. He knew everything about everything. He was the one who had the ability to punish you for wrong-doing and reward you for good. How did a mere human being love God?

The pastor suggested it was done in obedience, praise, and good works. But Marvella had said that good works were the same as filthy rags without a true heart. Goodness, but it was all so confusing.

It wasn't long before the services concluded, and Marvella introduced Rebecca to the pastor and his wife.

"These are the Watkinses," Marvella declared. "Woodrow and Henrietta Watkins."

The pastor smiled. "You can just call me Pastor Woody. Everybody does."

His wife reached out and took hold of Rebecca's hand. "And please, call me Henrietta. I was certainly sorry to miss the ladies meeting yesterday. I so wanted to meet you and get a chance to know you better."

"How is poor Grandma Olson?" Marvella asked the pastor's wife then whispered to Rebecca. "Henrietta went to sit with Grandma Olson. She's in her nineties and soon to go home to the Lord."

"She slept the entire time. The doctor says it won't be long now."

"A good woman, and I know all of heaven will rejoice to welcome her home."

Rebecca tried to hide any sign of curiosity about Grandma Olson's homecoming. Although she had plenty of questions. Uncertain about the matters of heaven and hell, she wasn't about to show her ignorance right now. That would be all the fuel Marvella needed. And Rebecca was in desperate need of another cup of coffee before she could tackle the continuation of that conversation.

Hadn't she always been told that God had the power to send a person one place or another and that was the reason one was to respect Him? However, Pastor Watkins seemed to believe that loving God was important to each person, and Marvella declared that God wanted to have a relationship with her. Was that how it worked? Hard to even fathom.

Henrietta Watkins touched Rebecca's shoulder. "You look like you want to say something. What is it, dear?"

Rebecca startled and could see that all eyes had turned to her. "I . . . uh . . . nothing really." She forced a smile. "I'm just trying to remember all the different names of the people I've met."

Marvella laughed and shook her head. "It'll come to you in time, my dear. And we hope you'll be with us a long time."

Even though the woman's words were meant in a different context, Rebecca hoped that wrapping her mind around a relationship with God would indeed come to her in time.

If not, she just might wake up to Marvella in her apartment every morning and that was *not* acceptable. The salvation of her soul might be on the top of Marvella's to-do list, but Rebecca needed a trip to the grocers for more coffee. Oh, and a stop at the hardware store.

To purchase a door chain.

6

Rebecca gripped her handbag as she headed to the library. The first day of work at the courthouse had been easy. On days when the court wasn't in session for a trial, Judge Ashbury only needed her until two in the afternoon. Which left her plenty of time to explore the volumes at the new Carnegie Library. She'd been looking forward to this all day.

Especially since she'd had to deal with the obnoxious Samuel Tuttle, the judge's secretary. Rebecca had sensed him watching her time and again. The judge must have noticed too because he finally sent Sam to his house to retrieve a couple of law books.

"You'll have to excuse Sam's enthusiasm toward you," the judge had told her. "He's thirty-five and anxious to take a wife."

"Well, it won't be me." Her blunt statement had garnered a chuckle from her boss. His amusement helped to calm her frustration.

Now she could head to a sanctuary full of books. Perhaps Mr. Andrews would be able to help her find something worthy to read. That is, if they could get past their last awkward conversation. Just because they weren't interested in a relationship didn't mean they couldn't be friends.

As the librarian, hopefully he'd help her find something other than the Bible. She'd read it for seven hours yesterday after dinner. Seven.

And every hour had been interspersed with plenty of questions to the Ashburys.

The judge had been eager to help her, and they laughed a good deal together. In contrast, Marvella had been most serious. But the woman had a soft heart. Rebecca was certain she would do anything for her.

"Good afternoon, Miss Whitman." The pastor's wife smiled at her as they crossed First Avenue East headed in opposite directions.

"Good afternoon."

"It was lovely to meet you yesterday. I do hope you will come back."

"I plan to. I doubt Marvella would have it any other way." Rebecca bit her lip. Sometimes her bluntness got her in trouble. Hopefully the pastor's wife didn't take that the wrong way.

The woman laughed. "I know exactly what you mean, my dear. I'm in a hurry or I'd suggest we stop for tea. Maybe next time."

"I'd like that."

Rebecca was grateful the woman didn't pursue a longer conversation and keep her from the library. Reading had been a great love of hers since she could first form letters into words. She'd only read three books since her arrival in Kalispell. Three!

Still, she wouldn't mind taking tea with Henrietta Watkins. The woman was kind. She and her husband had been most welcoming, and the church service had been nice. In fact, she'd enjoyed it much more than church growing up. Pastor Watkins taught in a conversational style. No pounding of the pulpit. No wide eyes. No yelling. He was quite soft-spoken, which was a surprise. And Rebecca was still thinking about his urging to love God.

Even though it had been awkward at first, she'd settled into the pew and liked the service. The songs were lovely. The pianist played with great flourish. And the pastor's sermon was quite enlightening.

But Marvella's quest to have her saved by the end of the day hadn't come to fruition.

The judge told her that was just fine. She needed time to investigate. Needed time to read and understand. He even convinced his wife that it would be just fine if Rebecca wanted to read the Bible from cover to cover before she made any decisions.

Mrs. Ashbury's usual bluster disappeared as she'd considered her husband's words. She'd even hugged Rebecca goodbye.

Would wonders never cease?

Perhaps God did miracles such as that to prove Himself to people like her.

With a shrug and a smile, she walked the last block to the library.

The beautiful building greeted her from afar, its dome beckoning her like an old friend. Libraries were the very best places in all the world and Rebecca could think of nowhere she'd rather be.

When she entered the large double doors, she had the distinct feeling that she was at home. Smiling, she strode up to the front desk. No one was there. Mr. Andrews probably was helping other guests.

"Good afternoon, Miss Whitman." The masculine voice surprised her from a room on the left full of bookcases.

She put a hand to her throat and chuckled. "I didn't see you there, Mr. Andrews. Good afternoon."

"I didn't mean to startle you. That was not my intention. How may I help you?" His smile made creases appear on the sides of his mouth. It was quite attractive.

She pushed the thought aside. "I was hoping you could help me find some good books to read."

"Exactly my favorite job." He laughed. "Tell me a bit about what you've read. Do you have a favorite genre?"

"Hm. Well, I love adventure. I read *The Call of the Wild* in Chicago just before I left. *The Count of Monte Cristo* is another favorite." She bit her lip. Should she tell him the truth about what she enjoyed the most? The librarian back in Chicago told her it was unladylike to read murder mysteries and the like but that hadn't stopped her from reading every one she could get her hands on. Especially the serial publications. Spying a book on his desk, she pointed. "Is that a good one? What's the title?"

"*Poems* by Tennyson." He stepped over and picked it up. "Have you ever read any of his work?"

She shook her head, her lip still between her teeth. Poetry had never been on her reading list. Of course, ladies were supposed to love that sort of thing, weren't they?

What would he think of her? Maybe she could give it a try. Show him that she loved to read all genres. Then perhaps it wouldn't be shocking when she asked for her favorites.

"Oh, then I must insist you start with this. 'The Lady of Shalott' and 'The Charge of the Light Brigade' are my favorites. I had a professor in college who was a loyal Tennyson fan and I find myself returning to it every year or so."

She took the offered book. "Is this your personal copy or the library's?"

"The library's. I'll help you sign it out." He wrote on a small card. "Next time you come in, I'll be sure to pull some adventurous stories for you."

"That would be much appreciated. Thank you." She studied him. The man actually listened. Interesting.

"How are you liking Kalispell?" He bent over a large ledger and wrote down her name and the title of the book.

"It's so different than Chicago. I love it. The mountains, the fresh air. And the Ashburys have been wonderful to me."

"They are an incredible couple." He handed her a small slip. "Just tuck that inside the front of the book and it will remind you to bring it back. It was nice to see you at church yesterday."

"I enjoyed it." Was that the best she could do? "Much different than my church at home."

"Oh?"

She placed her hand on the counter. "Not in a bad way, I promise. I rarely learned from the reverend back in Chicago. He was always yelling and pounding the pulpit."

He crossed his arms over his chest and nodded. "I've seen quite a few of those types of preachers myself."

Studying him for a moment, she decided to be brave and

ask him a question or two. "Let me ask you this, Mr. Andrews. If God is good and fair, why doesn't He judge a person by their works—if *they* are good and fair?"

The shift in his expression couldn't be deciphered. Did he think less of her? Or was he marveling at her intellect?

She chose to believe the latter.

Mark cleared his throat and rubbed his chin with his hand. "Good and fair isn't enough."

"Enough for what?"

"To cover the debt we have to pay for our sins."

She stiffened at those words. "While I'm no saint, Mr. Andrews, I assure you I haven't done anything *that* atrocious." Especially not like the crime she'd witnessed as a child. She'd done her best to tell everyone the truth and yet no one believed her. She'd tried to right the wrong! Didn't that count for something?

His posture relaxed and he leaned over the counter. "Sin simply means missing the mark. God is perfect. Holy. Righteous in all things . . ." His stare changed and he narrowed his eyes. "I have an idea. I'll be right back."

"All right." This was puzzling. Good and fair seemed . . . *good*, right? She'd always been taught to be a *good* and decent person. To help other people. To show them love. Not hate. That if she did enough *good* things, it would give her basically what amounted to a better grade. Like in school. Was that not how all of it worked? How God worked?

Mark returned with two pieces of white paper. "All right, I'm going to turn these around and you tell me what you see."

When he flipped the sheets of paper, she compared them. "There's a small black dot in the center of that one."

"Good eye." He laid the sheets down. Pulled out a handkerchief from his jacket pocket. "That small black dot represents sin. It doesn't look like much. Just one little lie. The paper is still good enough, right?"

She shrugged. "Well, it's not perfectly clean anymore. . . ."

But then he took that handkerchief and swiped at the dot. Suddenly the paper was covered in black and gray smudges. He held up the handkerchief. It was smudged and marked up as well. "Would you like to wipe your face with this handkerchief now?"

"No, thank you."

"What if I were to wipe this sheet of paper on your skirt?"

Shaking her head, she turned up her nose. "I see what you're doing, Mr. Andrews. You're showing that once marred by sin, we can't clean it up. Just like that paper will never be white again and your handkerchief—sadly—will be permanently stained." It made sense from what she heard Pastor Watkins speak about on Sunday. "What I don't understand is why we are taught to be good people, to do good things, when none of that actually helps us?"

"Very astute question." He leaned back against his desk with his arms over his chest again. "God loves it when we do good things, love people, help one another. But the whole point is that we must understand that without Him, we are nothing. We can't *do* anything to work our way into heaven. God was the only One who could do something. Jesus paid the price that we were supposed to pay."

She bit her lip again and thought through the words. All her life, she'd been taught about God. That He was the Almighty. Creator. Ruler of the universe. But other than that, she didn't have much religious education. Oh, several people had talked about God the Father sending His son Jesus to be the sacrifice for the world. He died on the cross and rose on the third day. That was what Easter Sunday was all about.

But Marvella, Judge Milton, Mr. Andrews—in fact all of the ladies at the club meeting on Saturday—they seemed to believe differently. That everyone needed saving. A relationship with God. A very personal relationship.

"I hope I haven't confused you." He sent her a teasing smile. "I'm no great theologian and I probably bungled up the whole thing—"

"No. You didn't bungle up anything. You made perfect sense. I'm just bewildered by the different teachings. It's made me . . . reflective. I want to learn, I truly do. But apparently, I have a lot more reading and studying to do before I understand it." She tucked the book of poems into her handbag. "I'll be back tomorrow, Mr. Andrews. But thank you for your time."

As she left the building, she took her time heading down the steps. Had she missed the mark so much that God saw her as that ink-smudged paper? The thought was horrifying.

She was a good person. Had worked hard. Honored her parents.

Hm. If Marvella had anything to say about it, she'd tell Rebecca to read the whole Bible and get saved.

Whatever that truly meant.

It had been too long since he'd had a decent drink and things had not gone his way today. He wasn't about to waste his chance for a card game or two up on the second floor of the Brewery Saloon. No one acquainted with him or his family would be out this late. His wife had been in bed for an hour already and as heavy as she slept, she'd never miss him.

Might as well risk it. This winter seemed to drag on forever.

What was it with all the locals talking about how winter hadn't even arrived yet? By thunder, it was already February. What were they thinking? By this time of year, most people were looking forward to spring. Maybe Montana hadn't been a great choice after all.

He kept his hat tucked low as he sauntered up the stairs. A cute little barmaid offered to bring him a beer. Of course, he wasn't about to turn that down. Especially if she was willing to occupy his lap while he played cards.

He allowed the first two hands to go to other players. The imbeciles. They probably didn't even know how to spell poker. Or read, for that matter. When he started winning and the beer kept coming, they'd have no idea what hit them.

"Washburn."

A familiar voice made him cringe. No one here knew that name.

"Whatcha doin' all the way out here in Montana?" The man was entirely too loud. Horace Bradstreet. The weasel.

Every eye in the room glanced in his direction for a second or two.

He pulled his hat lower. "Mind yer own business, gents."

Several shrugs, snarls, and grunts were sent his way. But it did the trick, they all went back to their cards.

Then that no-good Bradstreet had the gall to lay a hand on his shoulder. "I was talkin' to ya, Washburn. Kinda rude to ignore yer friends."

The man was drunk. "Lower your voice. You're embarrassing yourself."

Horace dragged a chair across the floor and set it right next to him. "You and me back at it again, huh? Ain't that a kick?" He slapped an arm around his shoulder.

"Sleep it off."

"Not a chance. Not while yer winning like that. You need me to cheer you on."

Hardly. He won the hand, and the rest of the table took off with choice words for Bradstreet. Big surprise.

"Good. Now we can get down to business." The man's breath was horrid as he whisper-shouted.

He narrowed his eyes. "If you want to keep all your fingers, I suggest you lower your voice."

Horace swallowed. "You got it." This time the whisper was much lower. "Now, who're ya married to this time? Can I get in on this little scheme of yers?"

"Shut *up*." He grabbed the man by the collar, dragging him down the stairs and outside, where he threw Horace up against the wall.

That brought him a bit more to his senses. "Don't do that again, Washburn." Fire lit the man's eyes. "I know what game yer playin.' I know where yer *real* wife is and I wouldn't have no problem whatsoever tellin' her where yer at."

The threat made him seethe. "If you know what's good for you, you'll get out of Kalispell and keep your mouth shut."

Horace Bradstreet sauntered closer. Smacked his lips. Rubbed his unshaven jaw. "I'm on my way home to California, but I ran out of money. Maybe we can work somethin' out."

He hated swindlers. Especially the stupid ones. "How much do you need?"

"Depends on how soon you want me to leave."

"Tomorrow."

"Hundred dollars should do it."

"*What?*" The idiot had lost his mind.

But all he did was raise his eyebrows.

"You're greedy."

"Nope. It ain't cheap no more. Do you want me to go find yer wife or not?" He stepped even closer.

"Fine." He held up a hand. "Meet me here at ten p.m. tomorrow evening. I'll have some money for you."

"A hundred dollars."

So Bradstreet wasn't as stupid as he looked. "One hundred dollars." He stuck out a hand. "A deal's a deal."

"Yup." Horace sniffed and shook. "See you tomorrow night."

As Horace walked away, he studied him. Now he had to figure out a way to get his hands on a hundred dollars by tomorrow night. Because Horace Bradstreet had to go.

One way or another.

7

THURSDAY, FEBRUARY 4, 1904

Perusing the shelves at the library, Rebecca watched for Mark to return to the main desk of the library. So far, he'd helped three women and an older gentleman. But she wanted to catch him when things weren't so busy.

That way they would have more time to talk.

After coming to the library every day after work, she was finally ready to admit to him her love for mysteries and hope that he didn't scold her or laugh her out of the library. She'd been correct in her assessment. He was a good friend.

Twenty minutes later, he walked back to his desk. Alone. Finally.

Rebecca stepped over to the desk and laid down the latest book of poems he'd suggested.

Looking up, he raised his eyebrows. "Let me guess. You've finished that one too?"

"Yes." She gave him a coy smile. "It was a beautiful book. Thank you for suggesting it."

"I'm glad you liked it. You are quite obviously a voracious reader. What else has kept that mind of yours occupied?"

"Well . . ."

"By the look on your face, the poetry wasn't your favorite?"

Goodness, she needed to learn how to school her features. Perhaps there was a book on that? She released a tiny huff. "I mean no offense, Mr. Andrews, but I've been reading the Old Testament. I must say that it confuses me. All the sacrifices God demanded of His people. Their penchant to go wherever the wind blows rather than stick with what they knew was right. And the wrath of God. Goodness gracious, I'm thankful to live in the modern world."

He chuckled and nodded. "I hear what you're saying. The Old Testament can be quite a tough read."

Instead of making her feel uncomfortable with her opinions, he'd agreed with her. That puzzled her even more. Maybe it was perfectly safe to tell him what she thought. It would be nice to have someone to speak to about what she'd read in the Bible. Marvella and Milton were wonderful, but Marvella still didn't understand why Rebecca didn't just dive into faith immediately.

Mark's head was bent over some paperwork.

She opened her mouth.

"Now, what is it that you would like to read next?" He finished writing something and cast a glance up at her.

With a smack, she clapped her lips shut. Perhaps another time. No. She should just tell him the reason she was here. "You know, I haven't wanted to admit it to you because my librarian back in Chicago told me it wasn't what a lady should be reading."

"Oh?" He didn't seem fazed.

"Mysteries. I love mysteries. You know the ones, where you try to figure out who did it while you're reading? Those are my favorite."

He broke into one of those wide grins that made the creases in his cheeks show up. Every time that happened, her heart kicked up a notch. "I know just the thing. Would you like to come with me?"

"Oh, yes, please."

As he came out of the office area, she followed him around several bookshelves as they wove in and out. He touched a shelf here and there, a smile on his face. Did he do that on purpose, so they could both relish all the books on the shelves? He clearly knew where everything was placed—this was *his* library after all.

"Here they are." He pointed to the bottom shelf. "This entire shelf is nothing but serials published in London. My particular favorite. There's more than two hundred and seventy-five here. That should keep you busy for at least a week." He wiggled his eyebrows at her.

She couldn't help but laugh. She could kiss him, she was so ecstatic.

On the cheek of course.

A very chaste one.

Her thoughts made her giggle even harder. "Thank you, Mr. Andrews."

"Please. I insist that you call me Mark. We live in the same building after all, and we see each other every day."

"Thank you, Mark." She picked up the first five serials. "You may call me Rebecca. May I check out this many?"

"Of course. And I'm sure you'll be back tomorrow for more."

A throat cleared behind her. "I thought that was you heading into the library a while ago, Miss Whitman."

Oh . . . *bother!* Rebecca turned to Sam Tuttle. Wasn't it enough that she saw him every day at work? "Yes, it's me."

Mark turned his attention to the man. "Sam. Are you here to pick out a book?"

"Hardly. I spend my days going through all sorts of legal books. You understand. I am certainly not looking to spend my evening reading." He smiled to Rebecca. "No, I thought I would ask Miss Whitman to join me for an early supper."

Rebecca frowned, then fought to make her expression neutral. She snapped her eyes to Mark.

He surveyed her with a hint of a grin, raising his brow as if to seek her answer to Mr. Tuttle's invitation.

"I'm sorry, I cannot join you for supper, Mr. Tuttle." She hoped her manner of speech made it clear that there was no room for debate or question. Unfortunately, Sam Tuttle didn't take the hint.

"You have to eat. There's no reason not to say yes." He should have been a lawyer since he seemed to spend all his time arguing with her.

"I have plenty to do tonight, Mr. Tuttle. So you will have to excuse me." She cradled her books a little closer. "Besides that, I've tried to make it clear to you that I have no interest in knowing you better."

"I know it bothers you that I don't believe in women working, but in time you'll appreciate my point of view." He sent a smug smile to Mark. Was he hoping for encouragement? The man was oblivious.

"Why should she do that, Sam? Miss Whitman has an

amazing intellect and enjoys her job. To appreciate your point of view, she would have to give up both."

Rebecca pressed her lips together. Hard. Because she would love nothing more than to cheer Mr. Andrews on.

Tuttle turned to his new debater. "As men, we both know that women working has done nothing but cause problems. There are certain things that God never intended, and this is one of those things."

"I believe you are discrediting God." Mark crossed his arms over his chest. "He created woman out of man's side, because man wasn't good enough alone. Have you never read Proverbs thirty-one? The woman described clearly goes against what you say God intended."

"You are still young, Mr. Andrews. Perhaps you are the one who needs to read your Bible more thoroughly. Godly women should be quiet. And stay at home."

"Mr. Tuttle!" Rebecca interjected. "It baffles me that you would continue to pursue me when you know full well I speak my mind. I am not married. Nor do I have children to care for. But I've been given a brain and it works quite well. There is no reason for me to stay at home. If I recall, the Bible also talks about not being idle. I am quite good at my job. I would thank you to remember that and appreciate it. And please, *please* stay out of my affairs. I have no personal interest in you. However, our jobs will intersect at times, so I would like for us to remain on amicable terms."

Sam shook his head. "You are a victim of the world's fast thinking, Miss Whitman, and I intend to show you a better way."

Mark laid a hand on the shorter man's shoulder. "I think she's found her own way, Sam. It might be best to let her figure this one out for herself. And if all else fails, she has both the judge and Marvella to watch out for her interests. I doubt they need help from you."

Rebecca nodded. "Exactly."

Sam's countenance changed for a moment. However, he raised his chin and looked them both in the eye. "Then I will bid you both good day." He turned and left without another word.

Once he was gone, Rebecca let out a sigh. "Thank you, Mark, for standing up for me. Goodness, but that man is annoying. He's been following me around for days."

"Is he the only one? I would think by now you'd have an entire flock of admirers."

Rebecca laughed. "No, just Sam. He's always telling me what he thinks I need to be doing and why. Thanks for trying to help. I'm sure he didn't hear a word either of us said."

"I'm sure you're right. He doesn't understand the benefit or meaning of just having a friendship. Like we have."

She thought about that for a moment. "Exactly. A friendship. Nothing more."

Mark grinned. "And nothing less."

Friday, February 5, 1904

Oh, what joy! With a pencil tucked behind her ear, two hidden away in a pocket, and another in her hand, Rebecca headed to the courtroom. Her first case. She practically bounced all the way there. The hardest part was trying not to smile like it was Christmas morning.

She failed.

Once she took her seat at the stenographer's table—*her* table, the place that only *she* was allowed to sit—she set out her things. Notebook. Pencils.

And took several deep breaths.

"All rise."

Her job had begun.

Judge Ashbury entered.

She recorded every word that was spoken in the courtroom—and who said it—using shorthand.

The speed of it thrilled her. Kept her senses sharp. Helped her to notice every detail of what was happening around her.

The case was about a stolen cart. One man said he bought it fair and square. The other insisted he was never paid.

It was a simple case, but fun to listen to the testimony of all the people involved. By the time lunch rolled around, the judge was ready to give his verdict. Given all the testimony and evidence provided, she was certain she could guess what he would say.

He announced his ruling and she smiled. Yep. She was correct. The man had no bill of sale to prove he had purchased the cart, and no witness to back up his testimony. While the cart's original owner had men to confirm that he hadn't been paid at the time of the supposed transaction.

Case closed.

Rebecca closed her notebook, picked up her pencils, and cleaned off her little desk. It wasn't quite as exciting as the mysteries she'd been reading, but she couldn't wait for the next case.

When Sunday rolled around, Rebecca had more questions about the Bible and faith than ever. She'd written down over two pages of them, planning to speak to the Ashburys after dinner. After reading about all the blood sacrifices God required of His people, she had been quite upset. Why would a good and loving God require blood? Were people really all that bad? Why couldn't they be good and earn their way to heaven?

At the church, she silenced all the swirling questions and found a seat with the older couple once again. Many people greeted her, which warmed her heart. Made her feel like this was truly her new home.

Now if she could just understand all that she'd read.

After some singing and prayer, the pastor stepped up to the pulpit and grinned. "All right, folks. Today we are going to start a new study. Please open your Bibles to the book of Jonah."

Marvella leaned over and helped her to find the right place.

Since Rebecca hadn't gotten that far in her reading, she didn't recognize it. But wait, wasn't Jonah the story of being swallowed by a whale?

She'd heard that one at some point in her life.

The pastor glanced down at his Bible. "Now, we are going to do a look at the entire book today and then we will talk about it some more over the coming weeks. But the point I want to make to you today is that people can do the right things with the wrong attitudes. Jonah didn't like God telling him to go to the Ninevites because Jonah hated them. Wrong attitude. So Jonah ran away. Wrong attitude. God got his attention and Jonah went and finally did what he was supposed to do—right thing—but guess what? As we see in chapter four, he still had the wrong attitude."

Several chuckles were heard throughout the sanctuary.

"The great thing is that God can still use us when we have the wrong attitude. But what He *wants* from us is to not only do the right things but to do them with the right attitude."

One of the men of the church—deacon so-and-so—came up to the front and read all four chapters of Jonah aloud. Rebecca followed along, finding the story quite fascinating.

But what kind of ending was *that*? Jonah, a prophet of God, was angry. First that all the people of Nineveh listened—um, wasn't that the point? Then he got mad about the plant God gave him.

The end of the book of Jonah was a little bit of a letdown. It was abrupt. Why wasn't there more?

What did God do to Jonah after that? He was supposed to be a prophet after all. Talk about the wrong attitude.

Pastor Woody smiled at the congregation. "Have you ever thought about who wrote the book of Jonah?"

He gave them a moment to ponder the question. "Most scholars believe that it was written by the prophet himself. Which made me think about how difficult it must have been to write about his failings. But remember, this is the inspired Word of God. Our Heavenly Father wanted us to see Jonah's struggle, just as we see that David was a man after God's own heart and yet was guilty of heinous sin.

"The point I'm trying to make is that sin is sin. No matter how big or small. Jonah had been asked to go witness to the Ninevites. People he hated. He would have much preferred to stay among his own people. It would have been comfortable. Safe. He was well respected as a prophet. But Jonah needed to learn to obey. No matter what. And he needed to learn compassion.

"A lot of you might be thinking that you are obedient. That you have compassion." He raised his eyes as if questioning each one of them.

Rebecca squirmed in her seat.

"But none of us is righteous. Even the slightest sin condemns us to death. We don't have compassion for one another like we should. We gossip and complain. We think we're better than others. The list can go on and on."

Picking at her thumbnail, she looked down. Too many thoughts swirled in her mind. She didn't understand God. Why did He allow an innocent man to go to jail? Why didn't He convince the police to listen to her?

All her life, she'd dreamed of making her place in the world so that people would listen to her. They hadn't when she was young. And a man had died.

It wasn't fair. Or right.

Why wasn't it good enough that she was trying to do the right thing?

She would have to speak to Marvella and Milton about this.

SUNDAY, FEBRUARY 7, 1904

Mark waited at the corner across the street from the church until everyone had gone inside. Then with swift strides, he crossed the road and took the front steps two at a time. Kate had warned him with a note that their father was on a rampage and wanted to speak to him before church about calving season.

Was he being a horrible son for completely avoiding the conversation and arriving just as the first song was being played?

He winced and made his way to the family pew. At least he could sit with his family. After the service though, he'd have to figure out a way to skedaddle as quick as possible.

The pastor gave a wonderful overview of the book of Jonah, and Mark appreciated the fresh approach to the timeless story. The story itself? It convicted him.

How many times had he done the right thing, but with the wrong attitude? He could do better than that.

When the service was over, Kate came to his side and gave him a hug. "I'm sorry to leave you without chatting, but we've got to get back. Calving has started and I need to be there." She hugged him again and looked over her shoulder at her husband. "Harvey has been a huge help." The smile she sent the man shone with admiration and love.

At least she was happy.

But as Mark studied Harvey, his protective-brother mode kicked into high gear.

Harvey was a good deal older than his sister. Mark wasn't sure how much and when he'd asked Kate, she put him off. Harvey also was one of the best-looking men around. The man drew stares from almost every woman he passed. Little wonder. He was tall. Obviously strong. And seemed to have a smile for everyone.

At least all the ladies.

What did Kate see in him? Other than his handsome face?

There had to be something. His sister wasn't stupid. In fact, she was one of the smartest people he knew.

"Harvey's a good man. It's been tremendous of him to work with Kate around the ranch." Dad's words brought him out of his thoughts.

Mark turned to face his father. "And you like him?"

"Of course." He cleared his throat. "Now son, it's time we talked about calving season. We need you at home to help. Harvey's not my son, you are, and you have a responsibility to the ranch."

"We've been over this before, Dad." *Lord, guide my words. Help me to be honorable.* Because right now, he didn't want to be. His father never listened. "I have a job and responsibilities at the library." He kept his tone calm and smiled at Dad.

"You always were a dreamer, but cattle don't get fed off of dreams. I tolerated your head in the clouds, even let you go off to college to study whatever you wanted. Because you were smart. I knew eventually you'd recognize where you belonged . . . where you were needed. Now the time has come for you to show your gratitude for all that was given you."

"I am grateful, Dad. I've told you that over and over. I'm just not a rancher." It was becoming harder by the minute to keep his ire down.

"Bah! You were born with ranching in your blood. You're my son and you need to start acting like i—"

"Good afternoon, Mark . . . Angus." Marvella's voice cut off Dad's reply. "Would the two of you like to join us for lunch?"

Mark lifted an eyebrow and looked to his dad. When Marvella asked, it usually wasn't meant as a question. More of a demand. Even Dad wouldn't ignore her summons.

"That would be nice. Maybe you can help me talk some

sense into my boy here." Angus squared his shoulders and nodded at the woman.

"Or help explain to my father that I have an important full-time job with the library," Mark countered.

Her pointed look silenced them both. "Lunch first. Family brawls afterward while we're having our coffee and dessert."

Mark hadn't said a word since arriving at the palatial Ashbury home. Marvella had seen to that by filling up every moment. But when they walked in the door and he spotted Miss Whitman—Rebecca—he grinned.

The old lady was up to her shenanigans again. He couldn't blame her for trying. Thank goodness he and Rebecca had an agreement.

Marvella beamed. "Mr. Angus Andrews, I'd like to introduce you to Miss Rebecca Whitman. She's the new court stenographer and she lives in one of our apartments as well. Just like Mark."

"Pleased to make your acquaintance, miss." Dad gave a little bow and then turned an irritated glance toward him. "I didn't realize you'd moved into one of the Ashbury's apartments?"

"You're Mark's father?" Rebecca's gaze darted between the two of them. Her welcome interruption steered Dad back to safer waters.

"Indeed I am."

"And what do you do, Mr. Andrews? Other than having raised such a wonderful son." It seemed Rebecca was quite good at pouring on the charm as well. Marvella must be rubbing off on her.

"I have a ranch. I find it hard to believe that Mark hasn't mentioned it to you?"

"Now that you mention it, he did." She tapped her lip. "And I presume that you raise cattle?"

"Indeed." Dad's chest puffed out. "The best cattle in the entire Flathead Valley."

Marvella moved them all into the dining room and Mark prayed for civil conversation. Dad obviously wasn't over his anger yet. That could become a problem.

Dinner was served, and he had a lively conversation with the Ashburys about the pastor's sermon. Rebecca's brow furrowed the whole time, but Mark found it odd that she never voiced her questions. Hm. Perhaps she was listening and would speak to the Ashburys about it later.

He found her intellect refreshing. It didn't bother him one bit that she wasn't a believer yet. As her friend, he hoped to help her understand faith in a real way. But there was no need to rush her. At least she was honest about her feelings and wanted to pursue the knowledge and understanding on her own.

"Honestly, Milton, I could use your support here," Dad boomed.

Oh boy. What had he missed?

"I need Mark at the ranch. I built the River View Ranch for him and Kate. He needs to do his part." When Dad got riled, his Scottish accent came out in full force. "Grief, the boy was born on a ranch in Texas. Right next to the cows."

"Dad, I know you grew up in a different time than I did. Life in Scotland was difficult and it was an absolute joy to come here and have land. And lots of it. But my heart has never been in the land or in the cattle. You know that. I did my part growing up. Obeyed you because that's what I was supposed to do. I did my best to be a good son. But I was always honest with you and Kate about my love of books and learning and my desire to leave the ranch one day for a different career. Plain and simple, I don't feel God calling me to ranch. I thought when I left for college you finally understood that."

"Ungrateful boy, I let you go wander off to college so some sense would be knocked into you." He pounded the table with his fist. "Now I say it's time for you to come—"

"Ex*cuse* me." Marvella stood in a flourish. "Gentlemen, this is my home. Angus, let me remind you that it's Sunday and you are a guest here. We will have a pleasant visit together." She lifted her chin. "The judge and I would like to invite you to have dessert with us in the parlor."

Judge Ashbury stood and nodded at his wife. He went to the back of Rebecca's chair. "Shall I accompany you, my dears?" With one arm out to Rebecca, he offered his other to his wife.

The threesome walked toward the parlor.

Mark stood, placed his napkin on the table, and then looked back to his father. "I love you, Dad. That's not going to change. I simply want you to be proud of the man I've become." He turned and walked away as his father sputtered.

As Clarence opened the massive front doors for their little entourage to leave, Marvella lifted her fur collar a bit higher. She nodded to her footman as she stepped out. "Thank you, Clarence."

"Ma'am." He dipped his head.

The afternoon sun was bright and cheery even if it was beyond chilly. Marvella shivered but kept her chin up. Asking the young couple to accompany her and Sir Theophilus on a casual Sunday afternoon stroll had been her idea after all. Something had to be done after the disastrous conversation at dinner. Given enough time together, Mark and Rebecca would fall in love and Marvella would be proven correct once again.

Gracious, her skills were extraordinary—if she did say so herself.

It made her laugh softly as she set Sir Theophilus on the ground and kept hold of his leash. The small dog bounced around a few times and then settled into tiny steps forward.

"Shall we head toward town or the country?" Not that she planned on going *that* far, but it was best to give these young people an option.

"I spend all my time in town, so I'd love to see a bit more beyond its borders." Rebecca's sweet voice lifted on the soft breeze.

Marvella glanced at Mark and lifted an eyebrow.

With his hands shoved deep into his coat pockets, he gave a shrug. "Sounds good to me."

"Off to the country it is then." With her shoulders back and head held high, she tugged on the leash and pointed Sir Theophilus away from town. Setting a brisk pace, she led her little troupe. Now all she needed to do was get the two of them talking about a subject they both enjoyed.

But after a couple blocks, she found herself quite out of breath.

Rebecca placed a hand on her arm. "Perhaps we could

slow down a bit? I don't believe my shoes are the best for this quick pace. Especially given there's more snow out here."

"Of course, my dear."

But just as she slowed, a squirrel took off across the street, and Sir Theophilus went into a tizzy barking and bouncing. The little thing took off after the squirrel and pulled the leash right out of Marvella's hands.

"No! Come back!"

Mark and Rebecca both took off after her little white dog at the same moment. Sir Theophilus disappeared into a snow drift, then bounced back up. The snow and dog were very nearly the same shade.

Marvella blinked. It wasn't ladylike for a woman to run—especially not one of her years—but it was *her* dog after all. She couldn't allow the young people to do all the chasing.

They were outside the town anyway. No one would see.

Lifting her skirts a bit, Marvella stepped a bit livelier than usual. Whether it could be called a half-walk, half-run, or simply a bouncing stride, it didn't matter. Her little dog was chasing the squirrel from corner to corner. Across snowy empty lots. Through several rogue bushes. And when the squirrel jumped to the top of the fence and ran across the top, Sir Theophilus gave chase on the ground.

Back and forth. Back and forth.

All with Rebecca and Mark giving their own chase. Calling out to the dog.

After only a minute or two of her pursuit, Marvella stopped and placed her hands on her hips. Good heavens, it was difficult to breathe in a corset while she raced around. She took several long deep breaths and kept watch of the game of who-can-catch-the-tiny-dog in front of her.

Mark and Rebecca shouted back and forth to one another their ideas of how to trap the dog. Mark would dart one way, Rebecca the other. Sir Theophilus seemed so focused on the squirrel that the humans didn't even faze him as he bounced and ran this way and that.

Marvella put a hand to her mouth to cover her laughter. How could it be that a dog of barely five pounds could best all of them?

Then all at once Mark and Rebecca were on a collision course with the dog in the middle. Diving at the same moment, the couple missed Sir Theophilus and ended up in a snowbank practically in each other's arms.

Her little white dog raced toward her, and she scooped him up.

"I'm so sorry." Mark scrambled backward, snow powdering his face.

Rebecca struggled to sit up. She dusted snow from her hat and hair. "Where's the dog?"

They turned to find the pup in Marvella's arms. She looked down at the couple and smiled. "You must have scared him with your crash into the snow. He came right to me."

Mark got up and helped Rebecca to her feet. He was quite attentive. Good man. Marvella couldn't help but smile. They did make the cutest of couples.

"I think we should make our way back." Marvella nestled her pet against her coat. "Perhaps some hot chocolate will thaw you out."

"That's all right." Mark shook his head. "I have some things to attend to back at the apartment."

"As do I." Rebecca brushed snow from her coat. Pink tinged her cheeks.

"Well then, see us home," Marvella insisted, "and then, Mark, I trust that you will deliver Rebecca safely to her apartment. The roads are such a mess. If you're too worn out to walk, I can have the carriage made ready."

"No, I'll be fine. But thank you." Rebecca stuck close to Marvella's side. Interesting that she wouldn't even look at Mark.

Once they reached her home, Marvella said her goodbyes and took Sir Theophilus inside. As she watched from the foyer window, Mark offered Rebecca his arm. She smiled.

"Looks like someone is rather pleased with herself."

Marvella turned to find Milton watching her, that knowing look on his face. She shook her head. "I'm merely grateful to be back inside. It was quite cold out there." She placed the dog on the floor and he scurried away before she could even manage to take off his leash.

The judge came and put his arm around her. "Come sit by the fire and warm up then. I'm sure Mark and Rebecca don't need you keeping watch over them. They seem completely capable of fending for themselves."

"You, sir, know very little about the ways of the heart. Some folks need a great deal of help, and I intend to lend that assistance, if necessary."

He laughed and pulled her along to the parlor. "It's a wonder any romance thrives without your involvement, my dear."

"It is, isn't it?" She gave him a smug look, which only caused him to chuckle. He was a dear, but when it came to matching two people together . . . well . . . it took an experienced authority.

Such as herself.

He needed to apologize for all that happened between him and his father. He didn't want Rebecca feeling uneasy about the whole thing. He sure did.

"I . . . I don't know exactly where to begin." He walked beside Rebecca back to the apartment building. "I'm sorry you had to be in the middle of the arguing between Dad and me. I never intended it to be like that. My hope was that the Ashburys could help get my point across to him, but he just won't listen to anyone. I didn't mean to sound so disrespectful, but sometimes I have to push back hard to get Dad's attention."

"I thought you handled yourself quite well." Rebecca's tone was supportive.

Mark glanced over at her as they continued to walk. "I've never been the son Dad wanted me to be. I've failed him over and over."

"Somehow, I doubt that. Look at what you've accomplished. Honestly, if he can't appreciate that for himself, I wouldn't let it bother you." She smiled up at him. "There are plenty of folks who admire you and approve of the job you've done."

"Am I wrong to want his approval as well?"

She shook her head. "Not at all. Every child wants their parents' approval. I do. I was so proud of accomplishing what I have. I'm the first female stenographer for the courts in Montana. I've managed to do what I've set out to do and so have you. Take satisfaction in that. Don't live for the approval of others. Not even your dad's. You'll always be disappointed if you do. He will no doubt have his own opinions and so will you. Just as you don't feel the job he does is worthy of your interest, he doesn't feel your job is worthy of his."

"It's not that I don't see the worthiness of ranching. It's just not for me." He shrugged. "I put in plenty of years at it, so I should know."

"I doubt your father sees it that way. To reject the thing he holds most dear—the job he loves—is to reject him." Two different people had said that to him now.

"But that's not at all how I feel."

"Isn't it, but in reverse?" She stopped walking and turned to face him. "Don't you feel that his rejection of the library and the job you have there is something of a rejection of you?"

Mark never considered it that way, but she was right. She was absolutely right. "How did you manage to figure out something that has bothered me for years in such a short time of knowing me?" He sent her a sideways smile, trying to cover up his own discomfort.

She shrugged. "I pay attention to details—to people." She took hold of his arm again. "We should probably keep walking. It's nearly dark."

Mark moved on again. They walked in silence for several long moments. There was much to think about in what she'd said, but he didn't like the silence hanging between them.

"It's good to have a friend to talk things out with and reason out problems. Thank you. I don't think I've ever had a friend quite like you."

Rebecca kept her gaze forward. "I know I've never had a friend like you. I have to say, it agrees with me. You don't look down on what I like to read, or the questions I have about God. I'd say you're just about the most perfect friend a girl could have."

Mark's stomach did a sort of flip. Why did Rebecca's comment make him feel uncomfortable? They were friends after all. He had no problem with that. None whatsoever.

8

Sitting on a bench outside the library, Rebecca ate an orange from a gift basket Marvella had delivered to her apartment.

Oh, how she loved fresh fruit, especially in the dead of winter. Her landlady had friends everywhere. One in Florida sent an entire crate of the juicy fruit for Marvella to share.

What a blessing she was one of the lucky recipients.

A bit of juice dribbled down her chin and she swiped it away with her hankie. In Chicago, they never had local fresh fruit in the winter, and imported fruit was much too expensive. A few of her friends who lived on the farms had saved fruit in their cellars from previous orchard harvests. But her parents rarely had the funds to purchase enough of it for the whole family to enjoy in the winter.

And of course, oranges didn't grow near Chicago. So this was a special blessing.

The sweet, citrusy scent made her mouth water before

each bite. Such a wonderful thing. If only she could share it with her family.

She'd written home twice and received one response so far, which was quite fast considering the distance between Montana and Illinois. She was grateful for the word from home. Everyone was well. And she missed them, she did.

But now that she was on her own for the first time in her life, she found herself contemplating much deeper things than ever before.

Her thoughts had been focused for so long on getting a job, spreading her wings, and what next great book she would borrow from the library. Now, she thought about the meaning of life, paying her bills, and . . . faith in God.

She'd finished reading the Old and New Testaments. It had been almost two weeks since Marvella gave her the Bible. As much as she loved reading the other books from the library, the Good Book was the one she kept picking up. She'd spent hours reading it each day. After dinner with the Ashburys on Sundays, she went home and read for hours. She'd done the same as soon as she was done with work. It hadn't been clear to her why—other than wanting to finish and to find out the end of the story.

Only thing was, she found out the story wasn't over yet. And now . . .

She wanted to be part of that story.

Last night she'd read a verse in First Corinthians that she wrote down in her notebook: "When I was a child, I spake as a child, I understood as a child, I thought as a child: but when I became a man, I put away childish things."

The impact on her was profound. She didn't care to be a child any more than she wanted to court Mr. Tuttle. She longed to learn and grow. So she'd memorized that verse. Then, as she'd finished out the book with Revelation, her heart pounded. John's vision was so vivid, she'd been able to see it in her mind. Deep within a longing grew to be at the throne and cry, "Worthy is the Lamb!"

Did this mean she now believed?

As soon as she'd started reading the Gospel of John, things began to fall into place. According to John, Jesus was the replacement for all the sacrifices. In fact, He'd paid any and all debt anyone owed to God. He fulfilled the prophecies. He was the answer. Not just to one question, but to all of them.

When the Old Testament had talked about all the feasts and sacrifices that went along with them, she'd been confused. But once she read the New Testament, it finally made sense.

All along, everything had pointed to the need for the ultimate sacrifice. The Savior.

The thing she still couldn't quite put her finger on was the why.

Why would Almighty God love them all so much?

Why would He sacrifice His much-loved Son to save them?

It didn't make any sense. Seemed like it would be easier to simply start over with a fresh batch of human beings who wouldn't get caught up in sin . . . wouldn't it?

If she were the writer of the story, that's what she would do.

She savored the last bit of orange, then crossed her arms over her chest and watched some children run and play. Their simple joy in tossing snow in the air, the roses in their cheeks, their laughter . . . all of it made her smile. What if those kids were hers? How much more joy would she find in watching them?

Was that how God felt about her? About each person on the earth?

It boggled the mind. But from what she'd read, that seemed to be the case. It was such a shame that she hadn't grown up reading the Bible. God's love for His creation was clear throughout the book. That would have been a wonderful thing to understand as a child. It would have helped her through the horrible time after she'd witnessed the beating of that poor man. And when no one but her family believed her.

Was that why she pushed so hard? Her love of the law and justice stemmed from the incident in her childhood. She'd never said it out loud, but deep down, she knew.

Rebecca shivered and stood up from the bench and headed toward the steps of the library. Her home away from home. She hadn't finished all the serials she'd taken home since she had been reading the Bible instead, but she'd promised herself last night that she would be brave and ask Mark a question or two.

Even though she'd met lots of other people, she didn't really know anyone yet. Other than Marvella and the judge.

Mark, on the other hand, had become a friend. Seeing him every day brought a smile to her face.

The warmth of the library greeted her as she opened the door and the smell of books made her happy inside.

"Good afternoon, Miss Whitman." Mark's voice was chipper. "Ah, I am well acquainted with that look. It's the tantalizing aroma of books, isn't it?"

"Goodness, yes, Mr. Andrews." Her shoulders lifted and she let out a large sigh. "I think it is one of my favorite smells in all the world."

She drew closer and he tilted his head into the air and gave a sniff. "And if I'm not mistaken, I detect the scent of oranges."

Rebecca laughed. "Yes, you do. I just ate an orange and didn't wish to litter so the peel is in my pocket. I have to admit, I like carrying the scent with me."

"I have a bin right here if you want to give them to me. They'll mingle with the book scent and keep the place smelling wonderful."

She reached into her pocket and produced the pieces. Mark disposed of them and then pushed the hair off his forehead.

She studied him for a moment. Most men used home-made pomades or Brilliantine in their hair to keep it in place. But not Mark. While his haircut was neat, he didn't seem to use anything in it.

"Now how may I help you today?" He walked back behind the circulation desk and she stood at the counter on the outside.

A glance told her there wasn't anyone else in the close vicinity, so she leaned forward. "Do you perchance . . . have a moment or two to chat?"

He checked the clock on the wall. "Mrs. Conrad is coming in a few minutes to relieve me. I'd hoped to get out to the ranch this evening and visit my father."

"Is everything all right?" She hated to burden him when he had his own stresses to deal with at home.

"Kate told me that he hasn't been feeling too well, and

after our discussion on Sunday, I was hoping to smooth things over."

She fidgeted with her gloves. Perhaps now wasn't a good time. "Ah, I see."

"But perhaps we could chat as I walk over to the Ashburys? I'm borrowing one of their horses."

"That would be much appreciated. Thank you." She pointed to the door. "I'll just wait on the bench outside."

"There's no need. You are welcome to stay in the warmth until I'm ready."

"I need the fresh air." What she really needed was a place to pace out her nervous energy.

"All right. I shouldn't be long." He went back to his desk.

As she stepped back out into the chilly February air, she shoved her hands into the pockets of her coat and then paced in front of the library. Movement kept her warmer and helped her to focus her thoughts.

She'd only made it back and forth twice by the time Mark exited the library.

He took swift steps over to her. "All right, Miss Whitman. What shall we discuss?" He rubbed his gloved hands together and they headed in the direction of the Ashbury mansion.

"May I be frank?"

"Of course. We are friends after all, are we not?"

That smile again. So attractive. She had to turn away so she could focus. "It all amounts to this." Deep breath. "I have recently read the Bible from cover to cover for the first time."

"That's quite an accomplishment."

"Thank you." Why was she nervous? "You know about

my first meeting with the Women's Club and how Marvella was insistent that I get saved right away."

His laughter filled the air around them. "She is quite the personality, isn't she?"

The casual atmosphere helped her to be more comfortable. "That is an understatement, Mark Andrews." Allowing herself to smile, she fidgeted with her handbag and then let it hang from her wrist. Their steps weren't hurried. She could do this. "What I'm trying to ask is . . . well . . . after reading all of it in a short amount of time I'm left with the fact that God is Almighty God. He loves us. I understand that I should love Him and love all my neighbors—meaning everyone. But I don't have an explanation for all the rest of it. I don't understand how in the Old Testament there were all these rules to obey, and then in the New Testament when Jesus was asked what a man must do to be saved, he simply answered confess and believe. Am I missing something?"

Mark tucked his hands into his pockets and stopped walking.

She stopped as well.

As he turned toward her, the light in his eyes comforted her. "You're not missing anything. This is exactly why a believer can spend his whole life studying and reading Scripture and not understand all of it. It's alive and breathing. It's okay to have questions, but the most important one is what you just referenced."

"Which one?"

"What must I do to be saved? That's what was asked of Jesus. I love that you are a woman of intellect and knowledge. You love to read and ponder and ask questions. But this wasn't meant to be difficult.

"God made it easy. He did all the work. In fact, salvation—being saved—has absolutely nothing to do with anything you or I do."

She frowned. "I don't understand. . . ."

"We can't *do* anything to be saved. It's all about faith. Did you know that Christianity is the only religion in the world that doesn't require anything else?"

It seemed like everything she ever learned had been about doing good works. "Really?"

"Don't hear me wrong. Plenty of preachers will shout from their pulpits that people need to *do* things. They will say you're not a good Christian unless you're doing this or giving that. But the truth? Do you believe that God is truly God? Do you believe that you are a sinner? That God sent His son, Jesus, to die for all the sins of the world? And do you believe that God raised Him from the dead?"

"Yes." That much she knew for certain.

"Then you have your answer."

How could he be so confident and assured? But then she studied his eyes. They were filled with that light. A light she longed to have. And something else . . .

Concern. Dare she think it was for her? For her soul?

"Thank you for taking the time to answer my questions." She started walking again.

"You're welcome. Feel free to ask me questions anytime. I don't have all the answers, but I'll do my best."

They walked in silence for several moments.

Rebecca's mind spun with everything she'd learned about God and the simplicity of His free gift, but she couldn't delay Mark any longer. That would be selfish. "I know you need to get to the Ashburys." The block for their apartment building was just up ahead. "I hope things go well with your father." She placed a hand on his arm. "For what it's worth, you're the best librarian I've ever known. And I've known a good share. I'm sure your father is proud of you." He needed to hear those words, of that she was certain. But she needed to get back to her apartment and think. "I'm going to head home now."

"See you tomorrow?" He lifted an eyebrow. No pressure. No expectations. Just a friend asking a friend.

"See you tomorrow." With a nod and a smile, she turned and walked toward home.

The ride out to the ranch was cold but Mark paid it no mind. Rebecca's questions from earlier rolled through his thoughts. Had he answered her well?

God, I pray I haven't failed You. But we often try to make things so much harder than they are. I ask that You draw Rebecca to You.

Funny how he'd come to look forward to seeing her each day. It was nice to have a friend who shared so many of his interests.

When he arrived at River View, comfort and guilt warred for attention.

Comfort, because he was back home where his family lived. Guilt, because he had refused his father.

His horse brought him up to the house, where Mark dismounted. One of the hands came and took the horse to the stable.

"Mark!" Kate rushed from the front door. "It's so good to see you! What are you doing out here?"

"I got your note about Dad and thought I'd come out to check on him. Maybe have dinner with you all. Get to know my brother-in-law a bit better."

A wide grin stretched across her face. "I just sat the men down at the table. This will be the pick-me-up Dad needs. He's had some kind of sickness. Hasn't eaten for several days, so I was glad he came to the table. Why don't you join them? I've got a mama I'm watching pretty close. Think she'll probably calve tonight."

"Need my help?"

She studied him up and down. "You're not dressed for it." She winked. "Besides, Harvey already offered, but he's been working so hard I told him to get some supper. I'll be fine. You go on inside. There's plenty." Kate headed toward the barn.

"All right." He called after her. "I'll come see you after supper."

With a wave of her hand, she acknowledged him but kept up her quick pace.

Mark smacked his lips together and headed inside. Guess he'd spend some quality time with the men.

Without his sister as a buffer.

Oh boy.

He went inside and called out, "Hey Dad, Harvey. It's Mark." His boots made solid thuds on the hardwood floors.

The voice of his brother-in-law answered, "In the dining room."

Mark took a deep breath and pasted on a smile. He entered the dining room. "Dad, thought I'd drop by and see the family."

His father appeared uncharacteristically pale. His cheeks

were sallow, dark circles were under his eyes, and if Mark wasn't mistaken, the man had lost weight.

He swiped a hand down his face to cover his shock. Hadn't he just seen him on Sunday? What was going on?

"Glad you came by, son." Even Dad's voice was weak. "Sit down and have some supper with us."

Mark sat and took a plate from Kimball, the ranch's cook. The cook was tough as nails but made the best food Mark had ever eaten. Especially pastries.

Harvey was congenial. Carried on a conversation with Dad about how things were going. What was happening around the ranch. Apparently, Dad hadn't been out to see things for several weeks.

Had that ever happened before? Usually nothing could keep Dad from checking every acre himself. While Mark hated to worry, he couldn't keep it from creeping up into his mind.

"You don't look like you feel too good, Dad."

Dad waved him off. "It's nothing. I'm sure I'll be right as rain before too long. Nothing a good meal can't fix." The smile he offered didn't meet his eyes. But he bowed his head and led them all in prayer over the food before Mark could get in another word.

Topic closed for now.

The sliced beef in mushroom sauce over mashed potatoes was phenomenal. Mark did his best not to inhale the food as fast as he could. He was content to listen to Harvey talk while he ate. So far, everything the man said lined up with all he knew from Kate. He seemed like a good and decent guy.

Mark lifted his napkin to his lips after he cleaned his plate. "Where are you from, Harvey?"

"Virginia." He took another bite of his food.

"Wow, that's a long way from Montana. Did you travel all that way just to come here, or have you lived in other places?" Mark leaned forward and set his arms on the table.

Harvey chewed and swallowed, then took a sip of his water. "All the way from Virginia. I had a dream of being a rancher"—he smiled at Dad—"and read an article about Montana. So I saved up my money and headed here. Until last year, I'd never been out of the state of Virginia. Funny how the good Lord does things."

"What did you do back in Virginia since you weren't a rancher?"

"A little of this and a whole lot of that." Harvey's smile stretched to his ears. "I've done everything from working in the local mercantile to helping at the blacksmith's."

"Fascinating. I bet the work with the blacksmith was grueling."

"More than you can imagine."

Mark took a sip of water, but there was so much more he wanted—no, *needed*—to ask. "May I ask how old you are?"

Harvey leaned back a bit. "I don't mind at all. I'm forty-two."

A good deal older than Kate, but that wasn't unusual. "How long did it take you to save up for the trip to Montana?"

The man had just taken another bite. He chewed for several seconds and then swallowed. "I saved up for years. I wanted to have some money to invest in a ranch here."

"It is expensive to get started, isn't it?" He looked at Dad, who didn't seem to have interest in the conversation. Or the food. "Well, I'm glad you made it here."

Mark took a moment to drink the rest of his water. Harvey seemed upstanding enough. Dad liked him. Kate loved him. So why was he so unsettled? Maybe he'd been reading too many of those mysteries Rebecca loved. He should mention it to her and see what she said.

"God is good. That's for sure. I'm glad He brought you here. Kate loves the ranch more than anything, so I'm sure she's thrilled to have found a husband who loves it as much as she does."

"I'm the one who's thrilled. And very thankful. It's an honor to be a part of this family." He wiped his mouth and stood up. "If you'll excuse me, I'm going to check on Kate."

Mark nodded and glanced back to his father. He'd barely eaten anything. "Kate said you've been sick?"

"Nothing to worry about, son. It comes and goes. I'm sure I'll be right as rain soon enough." He pushed food around his plate with the fork. "Food just doesn't sound good anymore."

"Have you seen the doctor?"

"The old goat came out but he doesn't know what it is. Some kind of sickness that's upset my stomach." He waved it off. "How are things at the library?"

The fact that his father asked him about the library and didn't say a thing about the ranch should have made Mark happy. But all it did was convince him that Dad was *seriously* ill.

"Things are going well. Very busy."

"That's good." Dad pushed his chair back and put his hands on the table. With slow movements, he pushed up to stand. "I better hit the hay, son. Thanks for coming by."

"Get some rest, Dad. I'll be back soon. I promise."

A sad smile lifted his father's lips. "I'll hold you to it." And then he walked toward his bedroom.

Well. That was that. Looking around the table, Mark wasn't sure what to think. Things seemed to be better between him and Dad right now, but then his father wasn't well. Then there was Harvey.

He couldn't allow his sister to know what he was thinking. She'd disown him for sure. Mark had seen the way she watched Harvey, the way her eyes lit up when she talked about him.

At least, he could go talk to her for a bit out in the barn. Of course, Harvey was headed out there so they wouldn't be able to have a private conversation, but it would be good for Mark to see his sister and her husband interacting and working together.

Actually, he needed to see that. Maybe that would put his thoughts to rest.

The warm glow from the barn greeted him along with the sad sounds of a mama cow in labor. He knew that sound all too well. "Kate? Everything all right?"

"Back here," she called. "I'm having to pull the calf."

When he made it back to the stall, he frowned. "Where's Harvey? He said he was coming out to check on you?"

"Not to worry. I'm fine. I sent him out to check a couple fence lines. Rodney told me earlier that some of the more ornery bulls had made a mess of them."

Mention of one of the hands he grew up with made him laugh. "Rodney must be pushing what . . . sixty years old now?"

"Hush your mouth." Kate giggled. "He's only fifty . . .

something. I promise I won't tell him you said that if you toss me that rope?" She pointed with her head.

He did as she asked and leaned over the railing. "Sure you don't want my help?"

"Yep. I've got it. Besides, we wouldn't want to mess up your clothes. You know this stuff doesn't come out."

She wasn't wrong.

"You know, Mark. I'm happy to share the ranch with you. I don't want you to think that I want to take it from you." Her focus stayed on the mama.

"That's the furthest thing from my mind." He kicked the hay with the toe of his boot. "But I know how you love it. Your entire world is centered around the ranch."

"I'm not denying that." She pulled and out came the calf.

"Well done." He watched as she cleaned up the stall and took care of mama and baby.

Kate took off the gloves and the long sleeves she'd fashioned to cover her arms with for this very job. It at least helped to save some of her clothing. "I just don't ever want you to think that I'm trying to take your heritage away from you. It would be wonderful to have you back at the ranch, but I know your heart lies with what you're doing. You always were a different breed. You worked hard, I'll give you that. And you handled all the ranch chores like a pro. But I know you don't love it like I do."

"Yeah . . . I don't. But I appreciate Dad instilling in us the work ethic that he did. Hard work was the best thing for us growing up."

She leaned over the rail as well. "I love you and I miss you. But you need to follow your dream. I'm thankful it brought you back home. That way we can see you."

"I've missed you too. Even missed you bossing me around. At least . . . every once in a while."

She reached over and tweaked his ear. "None of that now, Mark Andrews."

"I have to admit I kinda drilled Harvey earlier."

"Of course you did. I wouldn't expect anything less from my brother." Crossing her arms over her chest, she stared him down. "And?"

"I only want the best for you . . . I hope . . . are you happy, Kate?"

"I am. I love Harvey. He loves me and cares for me. Makes me feel special. He's so tender with Dad. The perfect gentleman. He works hard, and he came into my life at a particularly difficult and lonely time. Hopefully we'll have a family one day and we can grow the ranch into the great big empire Dad always wanted."

The look on her face when she mentioned their father gave away her concern.

"You're worried about Dad, aren't you?"

"Yeah. He was strong as an ox just a few months ago, even though you could tell he was slowing down a wee bit with age." Her own Scottish brogue came out with her emotion. "But the doc is hopeful it was just some passing illness that he'll bounce back from and be his old ornery self again soon enough."

"Yeah, he didn't even harass me about coming back to the ranch. I *knew* he wasn't feeling well if he didn't have the energy." Mark let out a long breath. "I better be heading back home. Have a lot to accomplish tomorrow."

Kate came around and hugged him. "Thanks for coming out. I love you."

"Love you, too, sis."

On the way back to town, he had to pull his coat up a bit higher and his hat down lower. The wind had picked up a lot more than he'd expected.

It wasn't much past seven thirty. He shivered. He would hate to be out checking the fence lines with Harvey right now. The past few days had brought warmer temperatures, but now? The wind was downright brutal and sleet began to fall. Ugh. Prayerfully it would stop or turn to snow. Sleet was the worst.

As he came to the edge of the ranch, he spotted another rider on the road. He eased his horse into a quicker pace. It was Harvey. What was he doing out here? The fence line didn't come out this far. "Harvey?"

Mark's brother-in-law turned on his horse. An immediate smile filled his face. "Mark! Good to see you. Headed back to town?"

"Yeah, I am. You headed to town too? Everything okay?"

Harvey pulled his horse to a stop and put a hand on his hip. "Nah. I just like to ride to the edge of the ranch, get some air, and look up at the stars when I have the chance. God sure outdid Himself with the sky tonight."

Mark glanced up. Clouds were covering up most of the stars. Strange.

"Well, it's almost my bedtime, so I better head on back. Good to see ya. Glad you were able to make it out this evening."

"Thanks. Me too." Mark watched Harvey turn back toward the ranch. His explanation was decent enough. So why did the hair on the back of Mark's neck insist on standing up?

With another glance up at the brooding, dark sky, Mark shook his head. Perhaps he'd been gone so long that he just needed some time to acclimate again with the family.

And Harvey was now a part of them.

Whether Mark liked it or not.

9

Washburn stepped into the Brewery and headed up the stairs to the second floor. The week had been too cold, too long.

But at least he could get in a few hands of poker tonight. The night was young. Barely half past eight.

He sat at a table, plunked down some money, and grinned. "Deal me in."

Two hours later, he'd won over fifty dollars from all the unsuspecting fools who dared to go up against him.

"Lookie who's here."

Washburn cursed the man under his breath. Horace was supposed to be long gone by now. "Thought you left town." He kept his features neutral, but inside he seethed.

Horace tucked his thumbs into his overalls. "Oh, you know me. I had a few more things I had to accomplish."

"You two know each other?" A new player at the table spit into a spittoon. "I ain't playin." He threw down his cards and walked to another table at the back of the room.

Then the others did the same.

Bradstreet was becoming a thorn in his side. He stood and stepped close to the man, growling out his words. "What do you want?"

At least Horace had the sense to hold up his hands. "My bags are all packed. You can check my horse. I just ran out of funds. Came in here to see if I could win anything for the road."

"You spent all that money?" Stepping even closer, he was almost nose-to-nose with the filthy man. "That's your own fault, you stupid fool. We had an agreement. Now get out of town. Tonight." He glanced around to make sure no one was watching.

The degenerates that were left kept to themselves. Besides, a big cloud of smoke made everything hazy. The odds of anyone watching or listening were low. There were unwritten rules at places like this.

"I'll leave. I just need some more money."

Enough.

Washburn dragged Bradstreet out of the room by the collar. Once the door slammed behind him, he narrowed his eyes and got nose-to-nose with the two-bit blackmailer. "If you know what's good for you, you'll follow me."

He stomped down the stairs and Horace followed. Once they were outside, Washburn grabbed his horse.

Bradstreet did the same.

At least the man hadn't lied about that. It sure did appear like he was packed and ready to go.

Now how to make all of this go away?

He walked a few blocks until the streets were dark. The weather was nasty. Sleet mixed with snow had made the streets a mess of ice and mud. Good and decent folk were at home. No one out and about. No windows around him showed light or life.

Perfect.

He turned back to Horace, hand in his pocket, fingering the money he could use to bribe the man. But that hadn't worked the first time and he hated wasting money on an idiot. . . .

Too much was at stake. He forced a conceding sigh. "How much do you want?"

"Twenty dollars? I know it's a lot. But I'll leave right now. You can watch me ride outta town."

White-hot fury filled his gut. His heart pumped harder. "Sure. Sounds good." He pulled his hand from his pocket and slipped the knife out of its leather sheath on his belt.

Horace Bradstreet's eyes grew wide, but he didn't have time to make a sound. With a thrust, it was over. Bradstreet fell to the ground, Washburn's knife in his chest.

For several moments, Washburn stood and stared. After all these years, all these scams, he'd never killed a man. A few women, yeah, but not a man.

He'd threatened quite a few. But never followed through.

The question now . . . What did he do about it?

Leave him lying there?

The whole thing gave him quite a thrill. Made him feel powerful. He liked it.

A tenor voice singing "Amazing Grace" floated toward him.

More voices chattered in the distance.

What were people doing out this time of night?

Better make this look like a robbery. He searched Brad-street's pockets and found a wallet. He tucked it into his pocket. That should be good enough to cast aspersion else-where.

The singing stopped. "Hey! What's happened?"

They'd drawn closer than he expected, but he was still a block away. No one could identify him in the dark. He kept his face covered and slipped around the corner of a building, pausing to take a peek back.

A man ran toward the body. "Help, someone help! This man's been injured!"

Blast! He'd forgotten his knife. How could he be so stupid?

The man reached the body. "Help, police!" he yelled over his shoulder and knelt over Horace. "Are you okay?" He lifted his head again. "This man's been stabbed!" His voice resonated.

Whistles sounded in the distance.

The police. They'd been patrolling the streets more often thanks to Chief Crane's insane desire to clean up the streets of Kalispell. So what if the small town boasted more than forty saloons?

All right. He didn't have a lot of options. He could run away. But that wouldn't give him a scapegoat. If he stayed . . . he could blame the do-gooder over Horace right now.

The whistles came closer. He'd have to allow this to play out. Just had to play his cards right.

Washburn strode toward the scene. Wait. He looked down at his hands. Blood.

The other man pulled the knife out of Horace's chest. He flung it to the ground. "Sir, sir . . . can you hear me?" He put his hands over the wound. "Help!" The shout was aimed toward the police.

Perfect. A new plan formed in his mind.

The whistles were close, Washburn even saw shadowy figures running toward them. Now was the perfect time. He rushed up behind the Good Samaritan.

Slipping the knife sheath off his belt, he dropped it next to the knife. Then he pointed a finger at the man over Horace and shouted, "Murderer!"

More whistles. Two police officers were mere yards away.

Washburn picked up his blood-covered knife and sheath. "Look! Here's the weapon!"

Monday, February 15, 1904

The afternoon was bright and cheery. A complete contrast to Rebecca's mood.

She walked to the library while questions, ideas, thoughts . . . *everything* swirled in her mind. The day's newspaper was tucked under her arm.

Her heeled boots clicked on the library's wood floor as she made a beeline for the circulation desk.

When she got there, Mark wasn't anywhere to be seen. Of course, he had a job and that was to help the people who came into the library, so she couldn't blame him for doing his work. But still . . . she was desperate to hash out her thoughts with him.

Thrumming her fingers on the wood counter, she took several long breaths. The case she'd worked on this morning was a bit dull, especially in contrast to what she'd read in the papers. In fact, everywhere she'd gone, the town was aflutter with the murder of Horace Bradstreet. An actual murder here in Kalispell.

It happened all the time back in Chicago, but here things were different. Was it terrible that she was a bit excited to work on the case?

"Miss Whitman, how good to see you."

Mark's smile was exactly what she needed to see today. "Mr. Andrews." She couldn't help but grin in return. That helped.

"Are you back for more murder mysteries?" His conspiratorial look was almost comical.

She relaxed a bit and allowed a laugh. "I'm actually here to speak to you."

"Oh? What great theological discussion shall we have today?" He picked up a stack of books. "Care to follow me?"

"Of course." She'd gotten used to following him around the library while he shelved books and helped patrons. "And no, today won't be a theological discussion. At least, I don't think it will be."

Mark tossed her a grin over his shoulder. "Whatever it is, I look forward to it. Our discussions have become the highlight of my days."

His compliment made a shiver race up her spine. Come to think of it, she'd looked forward to talking to him every day as well. Over the past two weeks, she'd come to the library every day except Sunday. And she'd seen him at church then.

At the library, they'd chatted. Mostly about God and faith as she wrestled with all her questions. But also about books. The town. The Ashburys.

She studied his back. He was her friend. A good one at that. But she'd begun to feel a tug toward him. Wanting to see him more often. Loving his smile. "You know, they've been the highlight of mine as well." Could she be developing a slight crush on Kalispell's library director?

"So what's on your mind, Rebecca?" He slipped the last book in his hands onto a shelf and steered her back toward the circulation desk.

She blinked several times and shoved her wayward thoughts aside. Laying the paper on the counter, she pointed to the headline. "This."

"I read that this morning." Mark shook his head. "Sad to see that happen here in our town. Did you know him?"

She rested her forearms on the counter. "Not a bit. But I'm curious. The man they arrested is Joe Cameron. I *have* met him and he's a wonderful, generous fellow. Marvella introduced us. He has done a good deal of carpentry work for the Ashburys. The man who was killed—Horace Bradstreet—was a complete stranger to Kalispell. So why was he here? What had he come to do? Why would Joe kill him? If, and that's a mighty *big* if, he did."

Mark leaned over the counter on his elbows and they both hovered over the paper. His eyes narrowed. "Hm . . . those are good questions. But the real question should be, why do they think Joe did it?"

"Exactly." She stood straight again and pursed her lips. "I find the entire matter puzzling."

"Like one of your mysteries." His eyes gave away the fact that he was just as fascinated as she.

"Yes. But it's also different, because this is real." She glanced down at her handbag. "This case will be in court, I'm sure. I'll need to pay close attention to every word spoken, so I need to get my curiosity out now."

"Ah . . . I see." The clock chimed. Mark headed toward

the front door. "You know, since it's closing time and I love a good mystery myself, maybe we could get dinner together at the little café down the street." He winced and held up his hands. "Just two friends going to dinner. Nothing else."

She bit her lip. Had she made him that uncomfortable? "Well, since I forgot to go to the grocers because I got all caught up in the newspaper and came right here, I don't have anything at home to eat anyway." With a lift of her chin, she smiled. "Yes, I agree. That would be nice."

"So do you think that Joe Cameron did it?" Rebecca sipped on her cup of tea.

Mark found her curiosity amusing. They'd spent the entire dinner discussing what was in the paper, whether it was all fact or not. They'd have to wait and see. But he got caught up in her enthusiasm for the mystery. "I don't know. It doesn't seem like Mr. Cameron would be the kind of man that would commit murder." He shrugged. "But the police will have to do their investigating and then, if it goes to trial, we will have to wait and see the verdict."

She squinted and gazed out to the street. "But what if they get it wrong?" Her words came out hushed.

"I'm not sure I get what you mean." He leaned his head to the side and studied her.

Setting her cup down, she bit her lip. Then took a deep breath. "I mean . . . what if they convict the wrong person?"

He jolted back a bit. "I haven't heard of that happening. Not in our modern legal system today. Have you?"

Her eyes shimmered. She blinked away tears. "Yes."

"What?" He leaned forward again. In that moment all he wanted to do was protect her. "Where? When?"

"Will you promise to keep it a secret?"

"Of course." He glanced around the café. There weren't many people present. "Are you in some sort of trouble?"

"Me?" She frowned. "No. Of course not."

He relaxed. "Sorry. I didn't mean to imply anything. With all this talk of mysteries, my mind just went there."

"Rest assured, Mr. Andrews, I am honest and honorable. I have never been in trouble in my life." A new glimmer lit her eyes as she lifted her chin.

He wanted to laugh but didn't dare. "Not even once as a child? You're telling me you *never* got into any sort of trouble?"

She smirked and narrowed her eyes at him. A look he was beginning to appreciate more and more. "I don't think you deserve to hear my story, Mr. Andrews."

"Forgive me." He schooled his features and took another sip of his coffee. "Go ahead. I would love to hear this story." She was so much fun to banter with.

She tucked her hands into her lap. "All right. I'll tell you. It disturbs me to this day."

"What is it?"

"When I was ten years old, we were at a parade. My family and I. I don't know what it was that caught my attention, but I saw shadows struggling in an alley behind us. The noise from the parade drowned out any sound of the struggle, so I moved a little closer. One man was trying to steal another man's leather case. The victim tried to hold onto the case, but the thief started beating him until he collapsed. Eventually, the thief stole the case, kicked the man on the ground a few more times, and then ran away.

"Another man from the crowd saw the victim lying on the ground and went to help. When the police came, they found the man who tried to help leaning over the victim, and they arrested him.

"I tried to tell them he wasn't the thief, but no one would listen. Over the next few days, I convinced my parents to allow me to talk to the police. I told them everything I saw, but the police didn't believe me. The good man—the man who tried to help?—was put in jail. He *died* there months later. I've never gotten over it and have wanted to see justice served ever since."

It took him aback. Leaning up against the chair, he had a hard time imagining what that would do to a child's mind over time. "I am so sorry that you had to go through that." His heart ached for her. To see such a horrible thing as a child. But the world was full of people who did bad things. They were all sinners. He studied her for several moments.

"All these years, I've wanted to right the wrong. To show everyone what the police neglected. To shout from the rooftops that they ignored a witness. To go before the judge and argue the case. Innocent people shouldn't go to jail."

"You know . . . sounds like you would make a really good lawyer. Defending people like that. Fighting for their innocence."

Pink crept up her cheeks. "I often thought about it but going to school to become a lawyer is expensive. That's why I started with stenographer's school. I thought that would give me a chance to work in a courtroom and learn the legal process. Maybe one day I'll go back to school." She covered her mouth with her hand. "I haven't told anyone else that I've considered becoming a lawyer. Please don't say anything."

"I won't say a word. I promise." He took another sip of his coffee and pondered all she'd said. Could their justice system fail them? Sure, he imagined it could happen every once in a while, but hearing Rebecca's passion made him want to learn more about it himself.

Marvella's words last week came back to him. Hadn't Joe been the man who'd made furniture for them? She adored the carpenter.

"I wonder if you could be right about Joe Cameron."

Her face lit up. "Really?"

"Yeah. What if he didn't do it? What can we do?"

10

The newspaper that morning was full of talk of the murder. The more Mark read, the more he pondered questions about the truth. Joe was found leaning over the body with blood on his hands and the knife beside the two of them.

Apparently, there'd been a witness. At least someone who said he saw Joe approach Mr. Bradstreet with a knife. That person requested to remain anonymous until the trial for his safety, so said the press, but assured the police that he had seen it all.

But by the time of the murder, the streets would have been dark. Especially in that area of town.

The paper also reported that it was a robbery and then a stabbing. So had the police found Bradstreet's money on Joe? The paper didn't say. . . .

As he walked to the library, Mark tried to tame his thoughts. They were all over the map with the case and, mostly, with Rebecca. Her interest in the case had *him* interested. Especially after he heard what she'd gone through as a child. What a horrible burden for someone so young to have to bear.

The more he thought about her, the more things he liked about her.

He loved her inquisitive mind. She was charming.

Her interest in not only the library but the work that he did boosted his spirits. She already seemed to love this town and the people in it. Loved to read and enjoyed learning. And even though she'd never been a poetry fan, she took his suggestion and gave it a chance.

He smiled. Yes, there were many things to like about Miss Rebecca Whitman—

Stop that!

He shook the thoughts from his head and let out a huff. But as much as he'd been taken aback by Marvella's obvious attempt at matchmaking, he couldn't keep his thoughts from the lovely court stenographer. And not just about their discussions. About her.

Just her.

Even now, he could picture her wavy dark hair pulled back and those deep, dark blue eyes. Her brow was often creased in question. That was one of the things he liked about her the most.

The fact that she'd taken the time to read the entirety of Scripture just so she could know the truth astonished him. And she'd devoured it in a short amount of time. Most Christians he knew took a year or more to read the whole thing.

But when Rebecca went after something, she went after it with everything inside her.

Mark opened up the library for the day, but couldn't focus anywhere but on Rebecca.

Well, he would see her soon enough. She came into the library every day after work. Until then, perhaps he should find a project that took all of his faculties. That might make the day go by a bit faster.

Thursday, February 18, 1904

Rebecca walked to the library after work with a bounce in her step. The past few days had been so lovely. For one, she hadn't dealt with Mr. Tuttle for several days. The judge had sent him on several important errands during the day, which allowed her to work in peace. Then, every afternoon she headed to her favorite place. She and Mark had poured over the newspaper for any tidbit about the murder case. But when they'd gone over everything there was—which wasn't a whole lot at this point—they switched to discussing the mysteries in the serials.

Most of the time, Mark had certain details of each figured out before the end. She had different details figured out. It was so fascinating, the differences in how they analyzed the various scenarios. Yesterday, she'd even mentioned that if they just put their two minds together, they could figure out who killed Horace Bradstreet.

Last night, after a lot of laughter, it was time for the library to close and she'd gotten brave enough to share about her past.

She'd asked him about when he became a Christian. After all the hours she'd spent reading the Bible, all the discussions with Marvella and the judge, all the chats with Mark, she still wanted to make it personal.

He hadn't been offended at all and told her of the time when he was seven. His mom had died two years prior and his Sunday School teacher was the one who helped him understand what Jesus did for him so that he could spend eternity in heaven with God.

It wasn't a whole lot of flowery words. It wasn't do this and then that, and then a bunch of other things. Works, works, works.

Simply put, it was faith.

For so long she'd struggled with doubt. Doubting she saw what she saw. Doubting other people, especially those in authority. They hadn't believed her, so why should she believe them? And worst of all, doubting the goodness of God. Because if He was good, why was there evil? Why would He allow an innocent man to die?

But hearing Mark's simple words . . . she could finally believe it to be true.

She trusted her friend.

Armed with the knowledge of everything she'd read, the testimonies of people she knew, and the simple truth of the yearning growing inside her every day . . . she'd gotten on her knees last night beside her bed and prayed.

It had been an awkward prayer. Nothing like the beautiful and well-worded prayers she'd heard the pastor pray at church. In fact, she'd giggled several times at her own faltering. But everyone had said to simply talk to God.

So she did.

Now it was time to tell her friend. It had given her a joy all day long that she couldn't describe. If she'd had a chance to see the judge without anyone else around, she would have blurted it out to him, but his day had been filled with lots of meetings. Lawyers going in and out. Besides, when she did see him, his features told her the weight of whatever it was he was carrying. Something terribly heavy.

That might have discouraged her before last night, but today she'd prayed for him. It had eased her tension and helped her to feel useful.

Looking forward to telling Mark had rounded out her day and kept her upbeat.

Of course, Marvella would need to know. The woman had been graciously waiting for the salvation of Rebecca's soul since the Women's Club meeting.

She couldn't help but giggle as she thought of that afternoon. *"But the hour is late and it's time for cake, so rest assured I will get her saved in the morning."*

Maybe she would stop by the Ashbury home tonight. It was cruel for her to make the queen of Kalispell despair any longer over her eternal destination.

At the corner of Third Street East and Second Avenue East, Rebecca stopped and stared up at the beautiful Carnegie Library. With her hands on her hips, she tilted her head and did her best to figure out what the thingies were atop the dome and at the pinnacle of the roofs on either side. Every time she'd come by, she noticed them. What were those pointy things called? And what was their purpose?

These kinds of questions always took her mind off on little distracting trains of thought. Next time she visited Marvella, she'd ask her about them. Surely the woman knew the architect personally and could help Rebecca to put the question to rest.

"Miss Whitman, how delightful to find you here."

Startled, she spun around and shook her head. "Goodness, my apologies, Clarence. I didn't hear you approach." She put a hand to her chest.

"Yes, miss. You appeared deep in thought." The footman from the Ashbury home bowed. "Sorry for my intrusion, but I am tasked with getting an invitation to you and also Mr. Andrews."

"Oh?"

"Yes. Mrs. Ashbury would like to invite you both for dinner this evening."

The man was so formal, it made her feel like she should stand up straighter and put on her best manners. "How lovely. Please send her my acceptance. What time?"

"Seven thirty, miss. It was fortuitous that I met you here. Saves me a trip." He bowed again and headed for the steps.

"Clarence." She stopped him with her hand. "I'd be glad to pass on the invitation to Mr. Andrews. I was about to see him myself."

"Thank you, miss. How very kind of you. Do you think he will also accept?"

"While I can't speak for Mr. Andrews, I can't imagine he would decline a lovely meal with the Ashburys. If I find out different, I will deliver the message myself to the missus."

"Good enough. Thank you, miss. I shall see you at the house." And with that, he clicked his heels and headed in the other direction, back toward the Ashbury mansion.

Rebecca marched up the steps to the library. Now she had a twofold purpose for her visit. She swung open the door and went in search of Mark.

There weren't any other patrons in the library this evening. But she searched every nook and cranny, and there was no sign of Mark. What if someone had attacked him?

No. That was silly. He must be here somewhere.

After checking the entire main floor of the library again, she called out, "Mark? Are you here?"

"Sorry! I'm down in the basement. Be right up."

Thank heaven! Her heart calmed its pace and she waited by the banister.

He jogged up the steps and gave her one of his charming grins as he stopped a couple steps below the top.

It was fun to look into his eyes from above.

"Things have been slow, so I went down to check to make sure nothing down there had gotten damp."

"Oh. And?"

"Dry as a bone, as they say." He leaned on the massive corner post of the stairs.

She peeked over the banister. "What's down there?"

"It's not a finished space yet. We're hoping to expand and complete it in the coming years. But it has a great deal of old documents from the original library. Some older books and things we wouldn't want to put in circulation because they're in rough shape." With a couple strides, he ventured the rest of the way up the steps. "So what are we discussing this evening? *The Case of the Missing Priest*? *Trouble in Vienna*?"

"While both of those were intriguing stories, I wanted to share something of great import with you."

"By all means"—he held out a hand toward his office—"I'm all ears."

With a deep inhale, she walked over to the front desk and then straightened her shoulders. "I prayed last night. I finally admitted that I didn't have to know all the answers. There was nothing else holding me back, I wanted to make the decision to follow Christ. Just like the disciples."

His eyes went wide. "That's wonderful news!" He reached out and embraced her.

She froze for a moment, then wrapped her arms around him and squeezed. "Thank you for answering my questions." She spoke the words against his shoulder.

"You're welcome." He released her and stepped back. His face seemed a bit pinker than usual. He walked back behind the circulation desk.

"Thank you for not making me feel foolish at any point during our discussions. Your honesty and gentle spirit were exactly what I needed."

"I'm excited for you, Rebecca. As your friend, know that I am always here for you whenever you need a sounding board. I can't guarantee I'll have answers, but I can listen."

"Thank you." Setting her handbag down on the high wooden counter, she folded her hands. "I mean that. From the bottom of my heart . . . thank you."

"You're welcome." Then he shot her another of those smiles.

Oh, every time he showed off the creases in his cheeks like that, she melted a bit.

An older woman entered the library.

"Excuse me, Miss Whitman." Another smile.

What *was* it about that? She'd seen men with dimples before—little indentations in the cheeks—and to be honest, she thought dimples were cuter on girls. But this was different. The lines in his cheeks when he smiled were rugged. His smile was . . . handsome. Manly.

Mark was unlike any man she'd ever met. His background growing up ranching made him strong and rugged. She'd heard his nickname over town a lot: *Cowboy*. And Marvella had given her plenty of history. Young women all over the area had hoped for his attention. But he'd never shown any interest in any of them and left for college. Dashing all their hopes. Had he even known? Or had he been oblivious to the enraptured female population?

Cowboy.

The nickname fit him. It fit his smile. And she liked it very much. But now instead of cattle, he wrangled books. The thought made her chuckle.

"What has entertained you?" He was back in front of her.

She blinked and tried to think of something else. "Oh!"

"What?"

"I almost forgot. Clarence stopped by right before I came in and gave us both an invitation to the Ashburys this evening. For dinner. I told him I would be there and I assumed you would as well?" Biting her lip, she squinted at him. Hopefully she hadn't overstepped.

"I wouldn't miss it. Have you told Marvella your news yet?"

"Not yet. I plan on giving her and the judge the news this evening."

He stacked another book on top of a pile. "Perfect. What time are they expecting us? I'll walk you over."

"Seven thirty."

"All right, then. It's a date."

His evening ritual of sitting with his father-in-law the past few evenings played right into his hands.

This had been his best ruse yet. Why God decided to bless him with his good looks, he hadn't a clue, but it had helped him make a lot of money. Women loved a handsome man. Especially one with manners and genteel ways, but who could also handle the toughest of jobs.

Over the years, he'd perfected the scheme, using a number of aliases. All in some form or another related to his real name, but morphed into something new. That helped him keep them straight.

He hadn't planned on staying in Kalispell when he first came here. It was too small. Too remote. But after eight scam marriages, it seemed small and remote might work better. Especially since the last one had caused quite a stir.

Kimball had been making hot chocolate for Angus every evening after dinner for the past twenty years. So of course Harvey offered to bring it to the old man.

It thrilled Kate for her dad and husband to chat each evening.

If she only knew.

He walked back to Angus's study, careful not to spill a drop from the mug, and tapped on the doorframe, then opened the door. "I brought you some hot chocolate."

Angus sighed and leaned back in his great big leather chair. "My favorite time of day." He waved Harvey in. "How are things going with the calving?"

"Good, good." He took a seat across from the older man. "Kate has it all under control. During the day, I handle most of the births. But she likes to be there at night."

How should he go about bringing up the will again? The

old man had hemmed and hawed over it for weeks now. Telling him and Kate on a regular basis that he was just going to change it. Mark didn't want the ranch anyway. "How are you feeling? Any stronger?"

"Little bit. Guess at my age it's just going to take more time to recover from whatever that was. Today was a good day. But I'm feeling awful tuckered out tonight. This"—he raised the mug to his lips—"should do the trick."

Harvey leaned back in the chair. Yes, as a matter of fact, it would. "Good, I'm mighty glad to hear you're feeling better."

"I can't thank you enough for all you've done around here, son. You'd think threatening to disown Mark would've knocked some sense into him, but"—he huffed—"I should have known it wouldn't."

Perfect. Ol' Angus brought up the will himself. Shouldn't be too difficult to find an amicable way to talk about it now. The sooner he got things squared away, the sooner he could wrap up Kalispell and put it behind him. "He's a smart one, that son of yours. But I know it breaks your heart to have him reject everything you've worked to build."

The old man nodded. "The ranch is worth a small fortune after all these years. I wanted to leave that to my kids."

"Sir, you know that Kate will cherish it and take care of it." Almost there . . .

"I know. Kate has spent a good deal of time talking to me on the matter. About the future and all. And my will."

There it was.

"She won't allow me to change my will and disinherit Mark. And I've begun to see her point. That girl always has been the voice of reason around here."

He leaned his head back, looking weak and pitiful. Which

Harvey would have rejoiced over if it hadn't been for the words accompanying the action.

Beautiful, smart Kate. His wife. Okay, well, his ninth fake wife. Still . . . Why did she have to go and ruin it? He did his best to keep his features sympathetic, but it wasn't easy. Why couldn't things just go his way?

Angus sighed. "I often say things in anger that I don't mean. And she's correct, I didn't mean it. I still want my son to have his share. He'll probably sell it to Kate, but at least I will have given him his inheritance. He deserves that. I do love him. Can't ever break a bond between father and son." The old man was getting sentimental in his weakened state.

"No. I don't believe you can, sir." He mulled over Angus's words. Maybe he could turn this around after all. "Is there any chance that Mark would sell his share to someone else? Wouldn't that devastate Kate?" Just the right amount of concern in his features to pull at the heartstrings and gain her dad's sympathy.

"Mark would never hurt his sister like that. Never. Besides, there's a provision in the will that Kate always has first dibs. The ownership of the ranch also reverts to her if something happens to Mark."

Huh. Well . . .

Wasn't that convenient?

11

THURSDAY, FEBRUARY 18, 1904

The judge had not been playing nice of late. Marvella narrowed her eyes as she primped in front of her dressing mirror.

He knew it. She knew it. Fiddlesticks with his shutting her out. He wasn't supposed to do that. Not ever.

Well, this evening she would fix it, just wait and see.

At 7:30 sharp she walked into the dining room, where she knew their guests would be waiting. With her typical singsong flair, she cooed at the young people. "Rebecca and Mark." She held out her hands to them.

The judge stood behind his seat at the head of the table.

As she hugged the two, she stole several glances at her husband. "I'm so glad the two of you could join us this evening. I must hear all the news." The footman held out her chair and she took it. Mark assisted Rebecca. Then the men sat.

Dinner was sumptuous as usual, and they enjoyed chatter about the library and the weather.

These young people were so proper and mannerly. Not bringing up anything too interesting over the dinner table. It was ruining her plan. Oh, why didn't they bring up the news that was all over town? She simply *must* steer the discussion toward the murder. That way, her husband would have to talk about it. They had guests after all.

But when dessert was finished, Rebecca appeared to be ready to jump out of her chair.

"My dear, what is it?"

Her young protégé smiled. Beamed, really. "I have some exciting news to share with you."

"Let's hear it, Miss Whitman." The judge grinned.

Rebecca gazed back and forth between them and then shared a glance with Mark. Hm. Was something brewing there?

"I am pleased to inform you that I am no longer confused about where I stand with the Lord." She sent a cheeky grin to Marvella. "No need to worry and fret over my salvation any longer, Marvella."

"Oh!" Marvella came out of her chair, which caused the men to stand as well. "Oh my dear, praise the Lord! That is the best news I've heard all month." She went over to Rebecca and hugged her. "This calls for a celebration. Let's take our tea and coffee into the parlor where we can sing around the piano."

"Splendid idea, my dear. You do play so beautifully." The judge grinned from ear to ear. Oh, that man. He could be so handsome and melt her heart and then aggravate her all at the same time.

"Clarence, please fetch the tea tray and bring it into the parlor."

"Yes, ma'am." The footman stepped to do her bidding.

Marvella glided over to the grand piano and with a flourish, arranged her skirts over the bench and took her seat. "Let's see, I believe we should start with 'Amazing Grace.'"

As they sang, Rebecca's voice grew stronger, her eyes brighter. After they finished the last verse of the hymn, she swallowed and then laid her hand on Marvella's shoulder. "If I didn't have confirmation before that my life was truly changed, I have it now. I've known the words of this song my whole life, but they are now alive and stirring within my heart. Thank you."

"How about another, my dear." The judge turned the page for Marvella.

They made their way through several of her favorite hymns and tears kept stinging her eyes. What a marvelous thing when another soul turned their life over to Christ.

She flipped another page. "Ah, this one is perfect."

Rebecca leaned over her shoulder. "'Blessed Assurance.' Hm. I don't believe I know that one."

Marvella turned to Mark. "I think you should sing this one for us, Mark. That way Rebecca has a chance to learn it."

"I would be honored." He picked up the small hymnal and cleared his throat.

She played an introduction and sent him a nod to begin.

Mark's gorgeous baritone voice filled the entire room.

"Blessed assurance, Jesus is mine;
Oh, what a foretaste of glory divine!
Heir of salvation, purchase of God,
Born of His Spirit, washed in His blood.

This is my story, this is my song,
Praising my Savior all the day long.
This is my story, this is my song,
Praising my Savior all the day long."

Marvella risked a glance at Rebecca.

Tears were streaming down her cheeks. She swiped at them and padded across the carpet to stand next to Mark. She grabbed hold of one side of the hymnal and sang along with him on the last chorus.

"This is my story, this is my song,
Praising my Savior all the day long.
This is my story, this is my song,
Praising my Savior all the day long."

Oh! The blend of their voices was so beautiful, she thought she would cry buckets of tears then and there. Her attitude had needed an adjustment and God—in His infinite mercy—had done it without Marvella's interference or permission. *Lord, forgive me for my ways. I know I tend to stampede my way through life. Which I know You use for Your good most of the time. You need strong women here on earth . . . but I overstepped. Didn't wait for You. Please help me to do better.*

Rebecca stepped behind her and wrapped her arms around her neck. "Thank you," Rebecca whispered in her ear. "For making sure I didn't stay a heathen." The young woman's laughter filled the room and then she kissed Marvella on the cheek.

It made her giggle so hard, Marvella thought she might bust her corset.

They settled into comfortable seats in the parlor around the roaring fireplace and sipped tea and coffee.

Mark shared news from the ranch and that calving season was well under way.

Since Rebecca was from the big city of Chicago, her questions about ranching were plentiful. Funny, Marvella had never thought about people not knowing about farming or ranching.

Of course, she wasn't one to get her hands dirty unless it had something to do with her roses, but she prided herself on being knowledgeable in that area. Probably because she'd been raised on a large cattle ranch herself.

" . . . it's quite a fascinating story, don't you agree?" Rebecca was talking about something. Oh dear, what had Marvella missed?

The judge's face was stormy.

Mark's head bobbed up and down. "I know I would love your opinion, Judge. Hasn't Joe Cameron done a good deal of work for you over the years?"

The judge cleared his throat. "I will not discuss the case." He sent her a glance. "My wife knows this quite well."

"But dear"—she put on her smoothest, calmest tone—"certainly you believe that dear sweet Joe is innocent? Why that man wouldn't hurt a fly."

"I will *not* discuss the case!" He surged to his feet. "Is that *clear*? I am the district court judge and it will be my case to hear. I cannot allow myself to be influenced by *anyone's* opinions. Understood? Justice is blind. I simply *must* be able to remain unbiased as I hear the arguments." His face was red and he swung to face the fire.

Oh, why had she pushed him so? Her husband rarely raised his voice.

Rebecca's shoulders slumped. "So it will go to trial then?" She sounded defeated.

The judge took several long, deep breaths and they all watched. His voice was much softer when he spoke. "I'm afraid so."

"Judge Ashbury?" Rebecca knocked on the door of his study. Mark was still in the parlor with Marvella, and she'd excused herself to speak to the older gentleman about work.

The door opened and his bushy eyebrows formed a singular line in the deep crease of his expression. "Miss Whitman?"

"May I speak to you in private?"

"Of course." He moved to allow her entry and then shut the door behind her. "How may I help you?"

"Your words in the parlor got me to thinking. And I don't want to overstep, but I need some clarification."

He gestured toward a chair. "Please, sit."

She did and clasped her hands in her lap. "I have deep respect for you as a judge. I love learning about the law and justice and appreciate your comments about not discussing the case. It hadn't occurred to me that you would have to keep an unbiased attitude—as much as possible— for any case you hear. Especially since you know the accused."

He sat in his big leather chair and leaned back. "The American Bar Association has had many discussions of late on conflict of interest. They are working to create a standard of professional ethics for everyone involved. It is more difficult than you realize."

She could envision the weight of this trial weighing on his shoulders. "Is it wrong for me to be interested in the facts of the case?" She bit her lip. Hopefully he wouldn't dash her hopes of studying the case on her own.

"Not at all, but *you* must remain unbiased as well. Every word in that courtroom *must* be correctly documented. Your facial expressions and body language cannot—by any degree of imagination—be seen as leaning to one side or another."

She grimaced and scrunched up her nose.

"Like that." He pointed at her with a slight smile.

"I will work on that, sir." For the umpteenth time, she wished for a book on controlling one's features. If there was one, she'd demand Mark go to the library with her so she could check it out tonight.

"Don't jeopardize this case by not doing your part, my dear. We all must do our very best. Not only for the glory of God, but for the judicial system. *Joe* needs us to do our very best."

"Yes, sir." She made her way out of his office with slow steps. All these years, she'd wanted to see justice done. Always felt a bit of kinship with the underdog, so to speak. But seeing the conviction on the judge's face and listening to his words made her think twice about her own thoughts and behavior. Justice was supposed to be blind. Hearing all sides of the case. All the evidence. All the testimony.

Could she live up to the same standard?

SATURDAY, FEBRUARY 20, 1904

The library was quiet this morning. Mark had done every chore he could think of around the building, so he sat down with the paper and a cup of coffee. Everyone was predicting a blizzard and the skies outside did give that indication.

Kate had sent a message that morning telling him they were preparing for the storm, but asked for prayer since they were still in the middle of calving season.

He unfolded the newspaper. The headline—of course— was about the murder, but this article was different than all the others had been. Apparently, the city marshal and chief of police had asked the paper to get the word out that they were looking for anyone who might have known—no matter how short a time—the late Horace Bradstreet.

Details were given about the man: height, weight, muscular build. That seemed to imply that he had been a hardworking man. He was forty years old, but no one knew where he came from or any next of kin.

A reward was being offered for any information about Mr. Bradstreet, his associates, or if any additional witnesses to the crime came forward.

Mark set the paper down. The witness who identified Joe wished to remain anonymous, but why? Why should it matter? Eventually it would become a part of the court records. Surely the witness couldn't remain anonymous forever. And, if someone had indeed witnessed the whole thing . . . did that mean that Joe Cameron was capable of murder? And why? What was his motive?

Mark didn't believe the supposed motive. Theft? But Joe

had steady work and made a good wage. Of course, he could have a gambling or drinking problem that ate away at his money. Something like that could cause a man to become desperate.

The bell above the front door jangled. He'd just installed it yesterday so he would know when a new patron arrived. Since he spent a good deal of time reshelving the books people had returned or helping others to find the exact tome they needed, the bell would come in handy to help him greet new arrivals.

He headed to the entry.

"Good morning, Mark." Rebecca's cheery voice greeted him as she brushed snow from her coat. "It's beginning to come down out there."

"Good morning to you." He offered to take her coat. "When did it start? I've been so engrossed in the paper that I hadn't noticed."

"Oh, just a minute or so ago. When I left my apartment, it wasn't snowing."

"What are you up to today? Need another mystery or two to get you through the snowstorm?" He wiggled his eyebrows at her.

With a laugh, she patted his arm. Warmth shot up to his shoulder at her touch. "You do know me well, but I would like to ask if you have any books by Charles Spurgeon or Matthew Henry? The judge mentioned yesterday at the courthouse that he loved reading the works of those two preachers. I know nothing about them other than their names, so I was hoping that you would be able to help me."

"Of course. We do have several here at the library. Follow me." He waved toward the room on the right. "I must say, the judge has good recommendations. I love reading both Spurgeon and Henry."

"Are there others you recommend?"

If only more people in town had the same yearning for knowledge. "Scofield and Moody are two of my favorites. Scofield's pamphlet *Rightly Dividing the Word of Truth* is one I read each year."

"May I check out several books from each of them? Is that allowed?" The eagerness on her face rivaled the growing eagerness in his heart to know more about this woman.

"Of course. I think that can be arranged." He went to build a stack of books for her.

By the time they made it back to the main desk, the number of books had grown to a sizable stack of fifteen.

"Oh my." She pointed to the window. "I better get home. I still need to get to the grocers in case they shut down because of the snow."

With a glance, his eyes widened. While not a blizzard, it *was* snowing heavily.

He scribbled furiously in the log and on a slip for her. Then made a note for the front door. "Grab your things. I'll lock up and carry these books for you. I can come back in a little bit, but I have a feeling I will end up closing early anyway. Especially if the storm worsens."

"Thank you." She touched his arm again. A habit he hoped she would continue. "But please don't take any chances. Promise me you won't stay out too long in this."

"I promise."

She raised her eyebrows and gave him a stern look. "I will be coming to knock on your apartment door later today, Mr. Andrews. I'm quite serious."

"I promised and I will abide by it."

"Good." The gaze she leveled at him enticed him to be on his best behavior. "I might even invite you to partake of some hot chocolate with me if you follow through."

They bundled up, he placed the sign on the door saying he would be back shortly, and they headed out.

The snow was now huge flakes—probably the largest he'd ever seen—and within seconds, they were both covered in a layer of white.

Rebecca crinkled up her nose and poked him in the shoulder. "It's a bit reckless, but I don't wish for the books to get wet, so should we make a dash for it?"

Looking down at the stack in his arms, he had to agree. "I think it's best."

She lifted her skirts an inch or two and with that, she was off. Leaving him behind before he could even position the books into a safer position.

By the time she reached the apartment building, she was laughing and the melodic sound floated toward him. A second or two later, he caught up to her. She waited for him on the bottom step.

Out of breath, he handed her the stack of books. "I better get back. But I do hope you will consider me for that hot chocolate invitation later."

"You honor your promise, Mark Andrews, and it will be forthcoming."

"Enjoy your reading."

"Thank you."

He waved at her and headed back toward the library.

"Be careful! It's getting slick. A light rain fell first and I fear the dropping temperatures may have iced the walkway under the snow."

"Duly noted."

Two steps later, his feet shot out from under him.

Rebecca opened the building door balancing the stack of books. She couldn't wait to dive in and get lost in reading. It was the perfect day for it.

"Ahhh!"

The shout, followed by a thud, made her glance back outside. Uh-oh.

Mark.

In a flurry, she set the books on the floor then dashed back outside to help him. "Are you hurt?"

"I don't think so, at least not physically." His feet slid back and forth as he pulled himself back up to stand.

"Here, let me help you." Rebecca went down the steps. "I had a feeling—" But before she could finish, the icy pavement claimed another victim. She landed in a pile at Mark's feet.

"Rebecca! Are you all right?"

She started laughing. "I'm fine." She barely managed to sputter out the words. "I . . . I . . . oh mercy." She tried to get up, but by now the snow had been swept aside by their backsides so there was nothing to give her any purchase. "How did we both manage to find the patch of ice?"

"It's a wonder we kept our balance when we first arrived." Mark moved toward a space where there was more snow coverage. "I think the snow helps with a foothold. Try to move to the side where the snow hasn't been disturbed."

Rebecca nodded and scooted across the ice to where the snow still covered the walkway. She got on her hands and knees and glanced up to see Mark was finally standing.

"There. Nothing to i—" Down he went again.

Peals of laughter escaped her. She couldn't help herself. It was too funny. She used her hands to steady herself as she attempted again to get on her feet, but it seemed the minute her boot soles made contact with the icy sidewalk, that was the end of being upright. She sprawled out with hands and feet going in four different directions. This made her laugh even more and by now tears streamed down her face.

He moved toward her, crawling atop the ice, his laughter causing another round of giggles from her. "Here. Use me for support. Let's scoot closer to the steps and then maybe you can move up them by scooting up on your . . . uh . . . well . . . backward."

Rebecca could hardly breathe she was laughing so hard. She did as he suggested and was at last able to get into a sitting position on the top step. She looked down at him. "Now what are *you* going to do?"

"It would seem I'm meant to make camp here." His amusement at their situation was clear as his eyes twinkled. "But I'm determined to have my own way. I *will* master this ice."

"Well, beyond the sidewalk is that patch of grass. Maybe the ice won't be so slick there."

"That's right. Let me try it." He made his way on hands and knees. "All of this just to get back and shut down the library."

Rebecca glanced around her and could hardly see the building across the street. "You did post a sign. Perhaps you needn't go back. It might be best to just come inside for that hot chocolate. After all, others are sure to have the same trouble we're having."

Mark turned around and sat down. "You know, you're right. We're now in a blizzard. There's no sense in my going all the way back to the library."

She smiled and dusted off the heavy snow from her shoulders. "I am determined to make it inside. Come along, Mr. Andrews." She started to laugh again. "I'm certain that together . . . one friend to another . . . we can see this through."

His head pounded from the previous evening of drinking. Since so many calves had been born the past couple days, he'd stashed a bottle in the barn. Not likely he'd make it into town any time soon. Normally, he kept his drinking to a minimum so he could keep his head straight, but the winter here wouldn't end! This was the longest he'd stayed *anywhere*.

Kate had been none the wiser since he'd sent her to bed earlier, telling her he would handle the calving for the night. After all, he said, she'd been working too hard and needed to rest.

He was such an attentive husband.

He'd gotten a little too happy with the bottle after that. Woke up with his face in the hay, an empty bottle, and a cow licking his face. Six new calves lay content with their mamas. Must not have been a bad night.

He hid the bottle, got cleaned up, and was doing chores when Kate greeted him with a kiss and sent him to bed.

Sleeping hadn't helped. In fact, the headache he woke up with at noon was hideous.

Not that he could tell her that.

So he'd gone back out and worked in the barn like a good, loving husband should do.

The snow had been coming down for hours, but they could still see the house from the barn. Which was good. Harvey drew the line at risking his life in a blizzard. He'd have to put his foot down if she insisted on staying out in this.

"Darling . . . how are you?"

His wife's voice took his attention from the manure he'd been shoveling.

She wrapped her arms around him and snuggled in.

"Better now that you're here." He dropped the shovel and relished her body up against his. This was the best part of his scheme.

"I'm sorry things have been so busy lately. I've missed our time together." She kissed his chin. "Kimball told me he's got some sandwiches waiting for us inside. Will you join me?"

"Of course."

Hand in hand they walked back to the house. Once inside, they discarded their snowy things and headed to the kitchen.

Angus sat at the small table with a cup of coffee and a paper.

The headline that faced outward almost screamed off the page: "Police in Search of Murder Victim's Acquaintances."

He took a moment to swallow.

"Sandwich, darling?" Kate touched his elbow.

"Yes, sorry . . . thank you."

"You're awfully pale. Are you not feeling well?"

It was a shame that such a beautiful woman wouldn't survive his plan.

"My head is pounding." Not that he could tell her why, but now his stomach was nauseated. "I'll be fine."

"Oh dear." Kate's plate clattered to the table as her gaze shifted to the window. "I fear we're in for an all-out blizzard. I can't see the barn anymore. I thought we had more time." She raced to the kitchen door. "I need to get the rest of the expectant mamas into the barn. Will you help me, Harvey?"

At that moment his stomach decided to revolt and he dashed out the back door and retched. He wiped his mouth and came back in, practically falling into a chair. "Sorry."

"I'll go." Angus got up from his seat.

"No, Dad. You've been sick. I don't think that's such a good idea—"

"Don't argue with me. It needs to be done."

Kate clamped her mouth shut, but crossed her arms over her middle.

The old man walked to the door. "I'm weak, but I'll be fine for a bit. Harvey looks dead on his feet. Can't have him losing the contents of his stomach every few steps. Neither one of us is strong enough to haul him back."

Harvey's head spun, but he started toward her. Had to put on a good show of gentlemanly duty. "I don't want to put your father at ris—"

Falling to the floor wasn't a show. He heaved some more.

Kate crouched next to him. "Oh, honey. Are you all right?"

He swiped at his mouth with his sleeve. "You better go without me. Before the storm gets worse." Maybe luck would play in his favor and the storm would take them both.

"I still don't like it." Kate rushed for her winter gear. "At least it shouldn't take too long. I brought them up from the pasture and into the holding pens earlier this morning."

Angus nodded and started layering up.

Kate sent Harvey a sympathetic look. "Go lie down. I'll come check on you as soon as I'm done."

Father and daughter headed out into the storm, clinging to the rope tied from the house to the barn. Harvey watched out the window until they disappeared into the wall of white.

"Harvey! Harvey, wake up!" Kate's voice broke through the fog in his brain. She was shaking his shoulders.

"Huh? What's going on?" He sat up in the bed, which made the pounding in his head worse. It had been sheer stupidity to drink that entire bottle.

"It's Dad. I can't find him."

"What do you mean, you can't find him?" More than anything, he wanted her to go away so he could shove a pillow over his head and block out the world.

"We were moving all the expectant cows into the barn. I lost sight of him. Then he didn't respond when I called to him."

He groaned and swiped a hand down his face. "I'm sure he's close by. We'll find him." Good. At least he sounded supportive and encouraging. "I'll help you look." Even though the thought of heading out into the storm made him want to finish all of this right here and now.

"Thank you, darling. I know you're not feeling well, but I couldn't bear it if anything happened to him. Kimball and

Rodney are out there looking too. This is all my fault. . . ." She sniffed. "He was just trying to help."

Well, maybe this blizzard was doing him a favor and taking care of the old man.

Harvey inhaled and stood up from the bed, willing his stomach contents to stay down. Not that there was anything left.

In minutes, they were outside and the blizzard hit him square in the face. The sting of the pelting snow took his mind off the piercing pain in his head. At least for a moment.

Keeping one hand on the rope, he followed his wife toward the barn as she shouted into the wind and snow, calling her father's name.

Thirty minutes later, Harvey was about to quit. This was for the birds. They were frozen and no one could see a thing.

"Over here!" Kimball's shout. "By the old outhouse!"

He and Kate trudged through the snow until they ran into the cook.

"He's half frozen and unconscious, but at least he's still breathing." Kimball slapped Harvey's shoulder. "Help me lift him. These old bones aren't as strong as they used to be."

"I can get him. You take Kate back to the house. I'll be right behind you."

The roar of the storm covered up any replies.

Harvey leaned down and dragged his father-in-law up out of the snow and hoisted him over his shoulder. He grabbed hold of the rope and headed back to what he hoped was the house, not the barn.

Of course, the longer he spent out here, the worse for the old man, right? And how bad would that be?

But he didn't want to risk his own life any more than he already had.

He'd just let nature take its course.

Surely the old man wouldn't survive this.

Each step closer to the house made his smile stretch a little wider.

Soon enough this would all be his.

12

WEDNESDAY, FEBRUARY 24, 1904

The blizzard shut down Kalispell for several days, but it had been a wonderful respite for Rebecca. She'd read books, taken notes, rested, and even tried her hand at a bit of baking.

Of course, if she was honest with herself, the best part had been Mark. They'd met in the common sitting area in the foyer downstairs and talked. Several of the other occupants of the building had joined them during their time shut in.

Mark's intellect and company were more than enjoyable. Mr. and Mrs. Abernathy from apartment one were much older and had the tendency to fall asleep at any given moment while they talked about their favorite topic: the blizzard of '63. While Mr. Smuckers in apartment three had become quite a chatterbox during the storm. In fact, he'd chattered on about the weather while Mr. and Mrs. Abernathy snored in their chairs.

The time with Mark had been educational. Fun. She

loved his way of looking at things. He reasoned and thought through things, and he wasn't afraid of her intellect. Unlike Samuel Tuttle. Not that Sam would ever admit a woman could be smarter than he, but he was put off by it all the same.

Mark encouraged her inquisitive nature and sought her wisdom and opinions on many subjects. His appreciation for her thoughts seemed sincere, which gave her even more confidence to speak her mind with him. They talked at length about the ranch and his father. About his dreams for the library, and her dreams of seeing justice prevail. Once again, he encouraged her to consider becoming a lawyer.

Through the course of the storm she'd come to respect him even more and found herself . . . comfortable with him. Like she'd never been with anyone else.

"All rise." The bailiff's booming voice made her jolt. The time for reminiscing and daydreaming was over.

Court was now in session.

Rebecca's pencil flew over her paper as she kept up with all that was said. All morning she'd prayed about her heart and attitude.

The judge's reaction the other night when Mark brought up the case had challenged her. It was her duty to listen and accurately record what was said, no matter what feelings this case stirred in her. That didn't mean in her off time that she wasn't allowed to form an opinion. At least, she hoped that wasn't the case. For now, she was doing well to focus on the job in front of her.

Joseph Cameron was being arraigned for the trial. The prosecuting district attorney charged him with murder. A crime punishable by death.

Judge Ashbury set a hefty sum for bail after the DA presented that they indeed had a witness who would testify. The town had been speculating about the anonymous person, but the person's identity would remain unknown for now.

Court was adjourned and Joseph Cameron was taken away in cuffs back to the jailhouse.

The trial would start in one week.

Rebecca slipped back to her desk to transcribe her notes. The entire time, she'd had to fight with her mind to stay unbiased. Unopinionated. Focused on only what was presented.

Once she was done with the transcripts, it was time to bring them to the judge. As she got up from her desk, she allowed herself to recall the details. The prosecution's case was weak at best. At least in her mind. Of course, the prosecutor wasn't about to lay all the evidence out at the arraignment. Only enough to give the charges weight with the judge as he set bail.

She stopped off and filed one set of the notes. Then walked down the hall toward the judge's chambers.

The attorney appointed to Mr. Cameron had barely said a word. Why was that? Wasn't it his job to defend his client?

The more she thought about today in court, the more the incident from her childhood reared its ugly head. The thought of another innocent man going to jail for a crime he didn't commit made her sick to her stomach. The thought of another innocent man *dying* for it was . . .

Horrific.

If she were Joe's lawyer, she'd have spoken up. It had seemed so far-fetched to her for a woman of her status to be a lawyer. Not so much, anymore. Not with Mark's encouragement.

The closer she came to the judge's chambers, the more she thought about the possibility.

What would it take for her to become a lawyer? Now that she made a good living, she might be able to afford more schooling.

At the judge's door, she bolstered herself and knocked.

"Come in."

Rebecca opened the door and gave him one set of her transcribed notes.

"Miss Whitman"—a smile stretched across his face—"how may I help you?"

Rather than going into detail about what this new trial had initiated in her, she took a different approach. "Sir, might I have a moment of your time?"

"Of course." He removed his spectacles and laid them on his desk.

Folding her hands in front of her, she stood straight and tall. "I would like to inquire about what . . . what might be required . . . or rather what it would entail for me to become a lawyer."

"Ah, you are fascinated with the law, are you?" The twinkle in his eyes grew. "I had a feeling."

"Yes, sir. In fact that's why I became a court stenographer in the first place. I witnessed a crime when I was a little girl."

"Do tell."

After she'd relayed the whole story, she stepped closer to his desk. "You see, sir, I knew that being able to work in the legal system would be greatly fulfilling. But the more

I think on it, the more I would like to pursue becoming a lawyer. If you think that's acceptable, Judge."

He stood up and came to the other side of the desk. With his hand, he motioned for her to sit and he took a chair next to her. "I think it's more than acceptable. I think it's highly commendable, my dear. Ella Knowles is the first woman to practice law in Montana. She's been at it a good many years now and lives in Butte, where she's been practicing cases for the mining industry. My wife and Ella are quite good friends since Miss Knowles is heavily involved in the women's suffrage movement. Perhaps we can invite her to town for a visit and the two of you could chat."

"Really?" She clasped her hands at her heart. "You would do that?"

"Yes, my dear." He stood and patted her knee. "Studying the law isn't easy and will take a good deal of time, but with all the books I've seen you poring over, I doubt it will be too difficult for you."

She stood as well, the thrill of his words spreading through her with each beat of her heart. "Thank you so much. You've encouraged me more than I can say." The judge believed in her. Mark believed in her.

It was almost too much to fathom.

He waggled his bushy eyebrows. "Won't Marvella love to hear this news? I do say, she'll be making a new campaign today to make you a lawyer as soon as possible."

It was so nice to be back in the library. Even though the time away had been more than enjoyable.

Normally, Mark didn't mind the winter storms because it

gave him a chance to catch up on his reading. But this time was different. He hadn't finished a single book.

Rebecca asked him to have tea or hot chocolate with her once a day. And he thought of her more and more often. It was quite distracting.

It had been lovely to spend time together. In fact . . .

He enjoyed it a bit too much.

She'd been adamant about only wanting a friendship. If he was honest with himself, he wanted more.

The common sitting area downstairs had afforded them space without compromising her reputation. Several other tenants joined them in the evenings for lively conversations and a game or two.

But the more time he spent with Rebecca Whitman, the more he liked her. The more he could see falling in love with her—

Mark! Stop! Here he was again, thinking about her. He shook his head and focused on the blank sheet of paper on his desk. What was he doing?

Oh, yes. Making a list of all he wanted to accomplish this week. He dipped his pen into the ink and wrote until he had filled the page.

All right, maybe the list was a bit ambitious, but a good bit of hard work should keep his mind occupied until he could shake this little crush of his.

That was all it was. She wasn't interested, so he shouldn't be.

If he chose to pursue a woman, she probably needed to be a willing participant.

He'd never really thought of himself as being ready to settle down. But maybe he was.

Yes. Perhaps it was time to think along those lines.

Good heavens. Better not let Marvella get wind of his thoughts, or he'd never hear the end of it. He chuckled and double-checked his list.

The bell over the front door jangled and he glanced up.

Rodney stomped the snow from his boots and took off his hat.

The look on the man's face told a tale Mark didn't want to hear. He dashed out of the office area. "What's happened?"

"It's your father, Mark. You sister sent me to fetch you."

"Is he . . .?" No, please, no.

"No, sir. But Mrs. Kate thinks he's near death."

Mark scrambled back to his desk and wrote a large sign for the door. "I'll close up. Do you have a horse for me?"

"I do."

Bless Kate! She thought of everything.

"Good." He raced around. Taped the sign to the door. Turned off all the lights. "Can you do me a favor, Rodney?"

"Sure. Anything." The man hadn't moved. His hat still in his hands.

"Would you please go to the home of Judge Ashbury and inform Mrs. Ashbury of what has occurred? She can inform the town council and the Ladies Library Association. In case someone else wants to open the library while I'm gone."

"How long do you think you'll be away?"

That stopped Mark in his tracks. "I . . . I don't know. Tell her probably a few days."

"I'll head over there right now."

"Thank you."

Rodney headed out the door and Mark checked to make sure he had what he needed. He closed up the library and headed down the steps toward the waiting horse. He should go to his apartment and get a few things. Just in case.

Mark made quick work getting home, packing a bag, and then getting back out on the road toward the ranch. Dad had always read to him and Kate when they were sick—something their mother started, although Mark's memories of that time with her were fading.

He'd grabbed three different books that he knew Dad would enjoy. The least he could do was read to his father. It might compensate for the lack of communication between them. Or at least keep them from arguing.

Tears stung his eyes even more than the cold against his skin. He didn't want the past and all his father's disappointments in him to be the last thing Dad remembered of him.

Had he been wrong to give up ranching? To go to college?

God, help me. I don't know if I've failed my father. Have I honored him? Or have I been completely selfish in all this? Please don't allow my stubborn pride to get in the way. And if it is Your will, Father God, I ask that You spare him. I don't wish for him to suffer, but I would love to have more time with him.

The horse couldn't go too fast because there was still so much snow on the road. It gave Mark the time to calm down, breathe, and pray.

Almighty God held all of them in His strong and capable hands. And according to Scripture, He knew the numbers of their days. Mark would rest in that fact.

Dad knew the Lord.

That was the most important thing right now.

When Mark finally reached the ranch, he rode up to the front porch, dismounted, and tied up the horse. He could take care of the animal later. He didn't even bother with his things, which were rolled up and tied behind the saddle.

He raced inside and Kate met him in the hallway outside their father's room.

"How is he?"

"The doctor fears pneumonia is setting in." She sniffled and wiped her face with a hankie, but her shoulders were stiff. "But he's strong. He'll pull through. I'm sure of it."

"What happened?" Mark pulled her toward the parlor so they could talk.

"We had a lot of calves born the past week. The day the blizzard came, Harvey had stayed up all night so I could sleep, and then I went out to relieve him. We came in for lunch but the blizzard began to rage."

For a moment, Mark thought she might cry, but she dabbed at her face with a hankie and lifted her chin. "Poor Harvey hadn't been feeling well and retched, so Dad offered to help me get the rest of the mamas inside the barn. I'd already gathered them up from the pasture, but Dad and I lost sight of each other in the storm." The last words were choked.

Mark grabbed her hand and squeezed. "It was quite the storm."

Her head bobbed up and down for several seconds, then she glanced at him. Her tear-filled eyes filled with pain. Fear. "Once I had all the cows inside, I called out for him over and over, but I couldn't find him. I came back to the house and fetched Kimball, Rodney, and Harvey so they could help me search. By the time we found him, I fear he'd been collapsed in the snow for over an hour."

Mark dipped his head in a brief nod. He hugged his sister.

"It'll be all right. Thank you for what you did. We'll just pray that he has the strength to get through this. I'd like to see him now"—he headed toward Dad's room—"and sis?"

"Yeah?"

"Go get some rest. I'll stay with him until you are awake again."

Her lips formed a thin line, a sure sign she couldn't speak. Tears streamed down her cheeks. Then his strong, ranch-loving sister fled the room.

Mark faced the hallway. Could it be true? Was his time with his father coming to an end? Why was it that people never understood how short their time was until it was too late?

Life had gotten busy.

It was always that way, to be honest. People found more and more ways to stay busy and occupied. They'd lost the time to spend with loved ones. The art of deep conversations that spanned an entire evening. And traded it in for what?

Entertainment?

He'd been just as guilty of it. Trying to keep Dad, the ranch, Kate—all of it—at arm's length so he could pursue his own dreams. Diving into his books for escape.

And now . . . his dad might be dying.

He'd used the excuse of education and knowledge. But what was that compared to his family? His own father?

Had he wasted precious time he could have spent with him? *Should* have spent with him?

There were so many more conversations he wanted to have with Dad. Questions he wanted to ask. No. He couldn't lose Dad. He couldn't.

God, give me another chance . . . please. . . .

The prayer seemed selfish. Maybe it was. But it was what kept pouring from his heart.

Surely God would understand.

Opening the door to his father's bedroom, he studied the man who'd raised him.

Dad's red hair and blue eyes had often made him look fierce and stern, but there had been times when they shared laughter. Back when Mother was still alive.

The seriousness of raising two kids on his own had made Dad's fierceness come to the forefront. Smiles and laughter were scarce.

Grief could do that to a man.

He'd filled the roles of both mother and father. Made sure Mark and Kate were educated and well-rounded. Ready to serve the Lord with their gifts.

Dad had endured a lot of loss over the years. He always said that it was only because of God's gifts that he'd been able to make it through.

And his eyes always lit up whenever he spoke of Mother.

Funny, Mark never wondered why Dad didn't remarry. His love for Susannah Andrews had been a love for a lifetime. Mark and Kate never considered him unhappy. Simply . . .

Driven.

To provide for them. To train them up right in the ways of the Lord. To leave them a legacy.

All of which he did.

Mark pushed away any thoughts of Dad's temper. Right now, he would focus on all the good things. His father's amazing qualities.

The sacrifices.

The love.

He stepped toward the bed. "I'm here, Dad." Settling into the chair Kate must have occupied the past few days, Mark laid a hand over his father's and let the tears fall.

13

The library had been closed for three days.

Rebecca's thoughts went back to Mark. Marvella had informed her about him needing to leave because of his father, but no more news had come. Did that mean the worst? How was Mark handling it?

If she knew her way out to the ranch and had a horse, she'd be out there in a split second.

Where had that thought come from? Standing on the steps of the library, she pondered all these feelings. Mark had come to mean a great deal to her. Of course, he was her friend. A very dear friend. Nothing more.

What a bunch of hokum.

She walked down the steps and stopped again. No. She and Mark were just friends.

So if he started courting a lady in town, she wouldn't have a problem with it . . . would she?

Oh, she hated how her mind worked. Of *course* she would

have a problem with it. Mark was the most handsome, the most intriguing, the most intelligent man she'd ever met.

And she cared about him.

Admitting it—even in her mind—made butterflies flutter in her middle.

No. She couldn't think of him that way.

She frowned and straightened her shoulders. This was ridiculous.

Mark Andrews was her friend.

Period.

End of thought.

With a deep breath, she stomped across the street. There. Argument over.

But it wasn't.

Deep down, Mark held a piece of her heart. A piece no one had ever had access to before.

It was perfectly natural for her to be worried for him. Concerned at what would happen if he lost his father before they had a chance to mend all their grievances.

Men could be so stubborn sometimes.

The thought made her wince and then laugh. Women were just as bad, if not worse. Look at her. And Marvella Ashbury.

Now *there* was a stubborn woman. She definitely ruled her roost, and made certain everyone knew her hand in things. Of course, the woman had a heart of gold. One Rebecca would never wish to hurt. But she was a force to be reckoned with.

Like a hurricane.

She covered her mouth.

"Miss Whitman."

As if she'd conjured up the woman with her thoughts, Marvella Ashbury sat atop her carriage directly in front of Rebecca.

She took the time to catalog her surroundings. Wait. She hadn't gone very far from the library. "Yes, forgive me, Marvella."

The older woman laughed so hard, the carriage shook and the horses sidestepped. The look on her driver's face as he kept them under control was comical indeed. "Oh, my dear. If only you could have been privy to what I just witnessed. Come. Sit up here with me and I can give you a ride wherever you need to go."

The driver set the brake and hopped down, then assisted Rebecca up into the carriage.

"Thank you." She sent him what she hoped was an apologetic smile for the disturbance. Then shifted in her seat to face Marvella. "Pray tell, what did you just witness?"

The carriage jostled into motion.

"You should be on the stage, truly you should."

Oh boy. "Why would you say that?" She gulped over the lump forming in her throat.

"Without saying a word, your face appeared to go through all the motions of having an argument. With yourself, mind you. One moment your face was jubilant, the next you were frowning, the next you were almost angry—as if you were giving yourself a scolding—and then you went into uncontrollable laughter. My dear, it was quite entertaining."

"Oh dear." Exactly what she feared.

"Now, you simply must tell me what was going through that pretty little head of yours." Marvella patted her knee. "Is there a man in your life? You know I am the soul of discretion and would be honored to carry your secret for you."

She bit her lip. Goodness gracious, how was she to get out of this one? "I want to be a lawyer."

She just blurted it out. Maybe not the smartest of moves. But it worked.

Marvella's face lit up like the fireworks on New Year's Eve. "Oh my stars, that is the best news!" She clapped her hands together. "And you were hoping to go to the library to research this, weren't you?"

"Um, yes. Exactly." It wasn't a lie. She had hoped to look up Ms. Ella Knowles. More than that, she'd wanted to see Mark. Which had then caused her rampage of thoughts, which had led to her facial expressions, which led Marvella Ashbury to inquire.

Before she became a lawyer, she should devise a way to tame her features and write a book about it. She couldn't be the only one who struggled with an expressive face. And keeping her thoughts in check.

Her self-appointed mentor was talking. She better pay attention.

" . . . the judge refused to give you the afternoon off so you could attend the Women's Club meeting. Of course, I gave him quite a piece of my mind over that one, but he insisted. And in the end, he was right, my dear. You are a working woman—rights for which we have fought for decades—and he couldn't just give you the afternoon off so you could attend the gathering." The woman barely took a breath before continuing. "At first, he'd called it a silly women's thing until I reminded him that this silly women's thing had been responsible for many improvements in the city, as he would do well to remember. Why, we have been fighting to keep the railroad from being moved. You know what it did to Demersville. It killed it. Poor town."

Rebecca shook her head. "I didn't know."

"Well never mind, we will *not* allow that to happen to Kalispell. At all costs, we will fight having the main line moved." She stiffened and lifted her chin. "The judge, good man that he is, realized his faux pas and apologized. It was a major mistake to suggest our club work was anything but phenomenal. He said so himself. But then he also had to share that you *still* could not have the afternoon off."

At that moment, a yip from the floor of the carriage brought Rebecca's attention down. "Sir Theophilus!" She leaned over and lifted the tiny dog out from the blanket nestled with hot bricks. "How good to see you, my friend. I didn't realize you were down there."

The dog licked her face and it made her laugh out loud. "Well, what did I miss from the meeting?" She cuddled the dog against her chest so he would stay warm.

"That's the beautiful thing, my dear." Marvella's chin stuck out. "Not one thing. I moved the meeting to tomorrow afternoon. That way you can join us."

"I would be delighted." Might help her to get her mind off of Mark. It would also give her a chance to wear the new navy walking suit she'd just purchased.

"Good, good." The carriage stopped in front of the apartments. "I'll have Jim here pick you up so you don't have to slog through all this snow."

"That is very thoughtful of you, Mrs. Ashbury, but I can certainly walk. It's not far."

"Not another word. I insist."

Mr. Wilkes assisted Rebecca from the carriage and she curtsied toward her hostess then looked back at him. "Thank you."

"You are most welcome, miss. I shall fetch you tomorrow."

The carriage pulled away and Marvella waved. "Don't forget to wear that new smart suit to-mor-row!" The last word was sung in typical Marvella fashion.

As Rebecca walked up to the building's door, she pulled out her key—

Wait a minute. How did the woman know about her suit?

Rebecca placed her hands on her hips and watched the carriage as it traveled down the street.

The woman was a wonder.

As the sun set, Mark watched it descend. The large window in his father's bedroom gave him an almost panoramic view. The sky held so many colors tonight. Reflected off the clouds, the pinks and oranges tinged purple and a deeper burnt orange. Then the sun was below the mountains' horizon and streaks crossed the sky in shafts of light. Soon stars began to twinkle as the sky darkened to its midnight blue. After a quarter of an hour, it was a velvety night sky above the snow-covered peaks.

The moon shone bright as it rose opposite the sun.

If only he had someone to share these moments with.

More and more often of late, he'd longed for a family.

Especially after seeing Kate married. And after the past few days when, during the brief times Dad had been awake, he'd talked of their mother, their marriage, and all the wonderful memories he carried.

Dad admitted that if it was his time to go home, he wouldn't argue with God. Many times in the past, he would have. But not now.

He'd made his peace.

"Son?"

"I'm here, Dad."

"Thanks for coming out."

"I'm glad I could be here."

A tap at the door brought Mark's head around. "Oh, good evening, Doc. Good to see you." They'd been waiting for the man to make his rounds and his way back to the River View.

"Mind giving me a few minutes with your father?" Doc Hart lifted his medical bag.

"Not at all." Mark squeezed his dad's shoulder. "I'll be back." Closing the door as he left the room, he walked to the kitchen for another cup of coffee.

Kate sat at the table with her Bible in front of her. "Hi."

"Hi."

"All the calving is done."

"That's good." He ran a hand through his hair. It was time for a haircut, but he doubted that would happen anytime soon, not with Dad's future uncertain. Inconsequential things like haircuts didn't matter.

He poured himself a fresh cup of coffee, then leaned against the sink. Words weren't necessary at a time like this. They were both too tired anyway.

Mark had to give his brother-in-law credit. The man had taken care of so much around the ranch the past few days. Harvey was a hard worker.

He closed his eyes and sipped the dark brew, inhaling its

enticing aroma. Prayerfully, the doc would give them a bit of good news. That's all they needed. Just a tiny bit of hope.

Several minutes passed and Doc Hart came into the kitchen followed by Harvey. "All right, you two." He aimed his words at the siblings. "Your father is getting older and the healing process simply takes longer. He needs complete rest. If he could let go of all his worrying—especially for things here at the ranch—that would be best. So maybe you need to discuss how you can help him do that. I do believe there's a chance he will be able to recover from this."

Mark reached for the man's hand and shook it. "Thanks, Doc."

"You're welcome, Cowboy." The older man smiled. "Sorry. It slipped out. But I guess you herd books now, so the title still works."

Kate laughed. A sound Mark hadn't heard since he'd come on Wednesday.

Harvey plopped into a chair.

"I'll see myself out." The doctor took his bag and shoved his hat back on his head.

"Well, that's good news." Kate reached for Harvey's hand.

He scooted his chair closer and wrapped an arm around her shoulders. "I think it's wonderful. But remember that he's still weak. I just don't want you getting your hopes up. People grow old and die, honey. Your dad has lived a long life. He's ready for this, you heard him yourself. He's prepared for it, and he has you two as his heirs. You can manage the ranch just fine, even if your dad dies."

She sat up straight and swiped at her eyes. "I know you're trying to help, but you're wrong." Fire tinged her words.

Mark knew better than to stay and intrude. Harvey

would have to learn soon enough how to handle Kate. Besides, he'd dug the hole.

Truth was, Mark hadn't much appreciated the words either. In fact, he found his brother-in-law's attitude disturbing. But there were plenty of people that looked at life that way.

Mark returned to his dad's room to find his father sitting up a bit, propped up by a number of pillows. "Will you continue to read to me, son?"

"Of course." He picked up the Bible off the table beside the bed. They'd been reading through the New Testament when Dad was awake. They were in Second Timothy.

"'Paul, an apostle of Jesus Christ by the will of God, according to the promise of life which is in Christ Jesus, to Timothy, my dearly beloved son: Grace, mercy, and peace, from God the Father and Christ Jesus our Lord. I thank God, whom I serve from my forefathers with pure conscience, that without ceasing I have remembrance of thee in my prayers night and day; Greatly desiring to see thee, being mindful of thy tears, that I may be filled with joy; When I call to remembrance the unfeigned faith that is in thee, which dwelt first in thy grandmother Lois, and thy mother Eunice; and I am persuaded that in thee also. Wherefore I put thee in remembrance that thou stir up the gift of God, which is in thee by the putting on of my hands. For God hath not given us the spirit of fear; but of power, and of love, and of a sound mind.'"

His throat clogged with emotion. Things he'd longed to say. "Dad . . ."

"I know, son. I know. Just remember that He hasn't given us a spirit of fear. I'm not afraid. Even if it is my time."

Mark gripped his father's outstretched hand. "Thank you, Dad. For everything you gave me . . . everything you taught me. . . ."

"Pass it on, Mark. My greatest joy would be to see you have a family of your own. I hear there's a pretty young court reporter who's been spending a lot of time at the library. . . ."

How in the world had his father found that out? He nodded. "You met her at the Ashburys' home when we had lunch with them. Remember?"

"I do. She was a sweet thing. Smart too. You could do a lot worse."

For the first time in a long while, he wanted to share everything with his father. "I think I'm in love with her. She fills my thoughts constantly. We were determined to only be friends, but I think somehow our feelings got away from us. At least mine did."

His father chuckled, which led to a fit of coughing. Mark helped him sit up and pounded on his back as his father struggled to clear his lungs.

"I should let you rest," Mark said as the coughing subsided.

"No. Wait. I want to say something."

Mark helped him ease back against the pillows. "What is it, Dad?"

"I was . . . wrong."

He swallowed and fought against tears. "Wrong about what?" Dad rarely owned that he was wrong about anything.

"I shouldn't have made such an ordeal about the ranch. I know you love your work at the library. I know that Kate is the one who loves the ranch, but I want you to inherit equally. I did all of this for you two. It was my only thought. Create something . . . something I could leave to my children. Something they could leave to their children. It's never been about controlling you . . . like you thought. But . . . you're all I've got."

He gripped his father's hands. "I'm sorry, Dad. I suppose I never tried to see it through your eyes. Rebecca told me that by rejecting the ranch, you probably felt I was rejecting you."

Dad coughed a bit then wiped his mouth with a handkerchief. "Smart gal you've got."

"I never meant it that way. I love you, and I've always admired what you did here. Making a ranch out of nothing but a few Texas cows. I've tried to want it for myself, but my heart is in the library work."

"I know that, and I've come to understand it's not your rejection of me, although it seemed that way for a time. No matter what happens . . . I love you and always will. I'd never disown you."

The heartfelt words from his father overwhelmed him. "I know that, but thank you for saying it."

Dad smiled. "Now, what are we gonna do about that little gal of yours? You probably ought to propose before some other fella gets the notion."

"Propose?" Mark swallowed a growing lump in his throat. Was he ready to make that kind of a move? Propose to his good friend?

"Bring me that small wooden box on my dresser," Dad requested.

Mark did as his father asked and handed him the box.

He waited as Dad opened the lid and moved the contents around until he found what he wanted. He pulled out a ring and held it up to Mark.

"I want you to take this for your little gal. It was one of your mother's favorite rings. The last one I bought her. Got it after selling off that prized bull we had. The one that won the blue ribbon at the State Fair, remember?"

"I'm afraid I don't. I was only five when Mother died."

His father nodded and brought the ring closer to his face. "Of course. I forgot. You never had a chance to really know her. It isn't right for a boy to not know his mother."

"You kept her memory alive. Sometimes the stories you told about her made me feel that I was right there. I don't know how I can have a memory of those things, but your stories did that for me."

"Well maybe this will do it for you again. I bought her this ring because when we wed we were poor as poor could be. I managed to get her a gold band, but it wasn't much. I told her one day I'd get her a ring with a diamond, and this is it. She said she didn't need a diamond—that her little gold band was more than enough, but I know secretly she loved it. She loved pretty things, even though she was the hardest-working ranch woman around." He turned the ring to catch the light. "She wore it with her gold band." He held it out to Mark. "I want you to have it. You'll need it for proposing."

Mark took the ring and examined it closely. A small diamond nestled between two tiny rubies. He didn't remember much, but he remembered his mother loving the color red. Imagining his father giving it to his mother made him smile.

"Thank you, Dad. I'll cherish it, and if and when I do get around to proposing . . . I'll be proud to offer it."

His father smiled and closed his eyes. "I think you ought to go do it right away. This is a small town, but it's filled with mostly men. Single men looking for a wife. Don't let her get away from you, son. Life can be so much shorter than we think, and you don't always get the time you'd hoped for."

His father's words ran through his mind that night as he dozed off to sleep in his old room at the ranch. Kate had asked him to stay for several days because they were all worried about Dad passing. Even with the encouraging words from the doc, Dad just didn't look well. Kate wasn't at all encouraged by his lack of interest in food or drink. None of them knew how much time he had left.

Time.

Dad had said you don't always get the time you'd hoped for.

Time.

James chapter four, verse fourteen came to mind.

"'Whereas ye know not what shall be on the morrow. For what is your life? It is even a vapour, that appeareth for a little time, and then vanisheth away.'" His whispered words hung on the air.

A loud knock on the door brought Mark flying up out of bed. He opened the door to find Kate standing there in her robe.

"Come quick. I don't think Dad's got much longer."

14

Ladies, I'm so pleased you could join us today and meet our very special guest. When our own Rebecca Whitman mentioned wanting to train and become a lawyer, I knew it was imperative that she meet my friend Ms. Ella Knowles, Montana's first female lawyer." Pride filled Marvella's bosom. Oh, the things she did for the people of this town. What a privilege and honor it was. With a glance to Ella, she nodded.

The petite, forty-something woman smiled in return.

One glance at Rebecca showed her excitement at meeting Ella. Why, she appeared ready to jump out of her seat at any moment.

"For those of you unfamiliar with Ms. Knowles, I will better acquaint you," Marvella continued. "To pursue her dream of becoming a lawyer, Ms. Knowles first had the monumental task of changing Montana law as it was illegal for women to practice law in this state. But never fear, she put her hand to the plow and tilled the way. She was the first American woman to address a state legislature and proceeded to get the law changed in 1889, allowing women to practice law. She took the bar examination and passed—doing better than some of the men, I might add." The ladies chuckled.

"She became one of only fifty women able to practice law in these United States of America." Marvella gave a little clap of her hands and the women followed suit. Miss Whitman's eyes were full of admiration.

Oh, but she was only getting warmed up. "In 1892, Ms. Knowles was nominated by the Populist Party to run for Attorney General of Montana. She was only the second woman in the history of America to be nominated for that position. She lost, but only because we women couldn't vote for her. However, the winner, Mr. Henri Haskell, appointed her his Assistant Attorney General.

"Her list of accomplishments goes on and on, but since she is here, I will let her tell the rest of her story." Marvella paused while the ladies clapped again. "We'll get to that in just a moment, but first I need to remind you ladies that we have a very important event planned in May. We will go to Helena to march with other suffragettes from around the state. If you haven't already spoken to someone on the planning committee to let them know if you will be attending, you must do that today. We must plan for the trip and the hotel."

She nodded to Rebecca. "We definitely hope you will be able to join us. I know that you will be an asset to our group and our most famous chapter member. For those of you who weren't here for our last meeting, I have taken Miss Rebecca Whitman under my wing as my personal protégé. I am most certain it will simply be a matter of time until she joins the ranks of Ella Knowles as a full-fledged lawyer."

Marvella again clapped her hands and the others joined in.

Armed by the encouragement of the women, Rebecca sat a little straighter in her chair and suppressed the urge to sneeze. Now was not the time to catch a cold. Not only had she donned a winning outfit, but these women believed that she could become a lawyer.

Wouldn't that be something? Her. A lawyer.

To have *the* Ella Knowles travel all the way from Butte was quite a thing. Marvella and the judge must truly have faith in her potential.

Marvella returned to raving about Ms. Knowles, regaling them with stories from the years they'd known one another. Then she pulled out a piece of paper. "Before Ms. Knowles speaks to us today, I would like to share some glowing words that have been shared about her." She cleared her throat and took a long sip of water. "Ms. Knowles has been described by the world-renowned paper the *Atlanta Constitution* as being 'the most successful female lawyer in the United States.'"

All the ladies clapped and nodded.

"That same paper declared that she is 'one of the most remarkable women in the world.'"

More clapping.

"The *Los Angeles Herald* said that the 1902 International Mining Congress convention 'was nearly thrown into a panic' by her efforts." She leaned toward Ella. "I know you lost, dear, but bravo."

A bit more clapping. Lots of whispering.

"And in *Progressive Men of Montana*—gracious, see the irony?—they published a three-page feature on this amazing woman."

Sir Theophilus yipped from at her feet.

Rebecca lifted the tiny dog. "Shh. We have to be attentive. Ms. Knowles is about to speak."

He licked her face.

At the gasp of the woman next to her, Rebecca cringed and set the small pup in her lap, petting his head. Perhaps she needed to read up on etiquette with pets at social gatherings next time she was at the library.

Marvella was sing-songing her way to a finale of her second—or was she on the third now?—introduction. "If only women were judges, we'd have the country set to rights in a jiffy. Wouldn't we, ladies? The world needs women to take a stand and do important jobs. Without further ado, I give you"—she held out an arm in a dramatic pause—"Ms. Ella Knowles."

The room erupted in a standing ovation.

Something warm spread its way across her lap. Oh, no! She couldn't stand now. What in the world was the etiquette for a dog relieving himself on her brand-new expensive walking suit?

"Oh dear!" Marvella rushed across the room and grabbed Rebecca's arm. Dragging her out of the parlor, she called out, "Mi-mi!" The woman's voice rang throughout the vaulted ceiling of the marbled hall.

Rebecca darted a glance over her shoulder and saw Ms. Knowles had stood up and was speaking to the women's club.

Of course, she would have to miss the very person who

came to speak to the group because *she* wanted to be a lawyer. How did this happen?

"Don't you worry one bit, my dear. She can keep an audience captive for hours, and we shall have a private dinner with her later. Right now, we have to get that stain out of your suit before it sets."

Out of the corner of her eye, she spied Clarence who, whilst Marvella continued to drag her, successfully captured the wriggling dog out of her arms.

Mimi also met them mid-drag and rushed to do her mistress's bidding.

None of which Rebecca heard. Partly because she wasn't listening, and partly because the liquid had seeped through her bloomers and irritated her skin.

This was *not* what she'd planned. Not at all.

Marvella plopped Rebecca on the side of a large tub in a lavish bathing chamber, and Mimi prepared a bath for her. A wave of dizziness caused her to close her eyes for a moment. The excitement had likely been a bit much. Marvella said something and left. Surely to return to give her directions on whatever else must occur.

At that moment, exhaustion hit. Rebecca didn't care about the meeting happening downstairs. Didn't care about her new walking suit. But the bath sounded heavenly.

Within minutes, she found herself undressed and soaking in a bubble bath that would rival all of her best memories. She leaned her neck against the edge and closed her eyes.

A face danced in her mind.

Mark.

She let out a long sigh. Poor man. She prayed for his

father. Prayed for Mark. Hoped she'd get to see him again soon. In fact, that was what she wanted most. To see Mark.

"Miss?"

Rebecca jolted upright in the water. It was now quite cool. She shivered. "Goodness. I must have fallen asleep."

"It couldn't have been for long. Don't worry. I've got the stain out of your dress and have it drying in front of the fire as we speak." Mimi held up a large, fluffy towel and a thick robe. "Why don't you dry off and put this on, and I've set up the guest room next door for you. There's several books for you to choose from if you'd like to read, and a nice hot cup of tea. Not to worry, the meeting will last for hours, I'm sure."

Never in her life had she been treated so wonderfully. "Thank you, Mimi."

The maid left the bathing chamber and shut the door.

Maybe she should allow the dog to relieve himself on her more often.

She shook away the thought and laughed.

After climbing out of the tub, she used the softest and fluffiest towel she'd ever touched to dry off. Once ensconced in the robe, she headed toward the guest room, where the roaring fire made everything cozy and warm. She climbed into the bed, sat up against the mahogany headboard, picked up a book on gardening, and began to read.

"Miss?"

For the second time that day, she jolted awake to the maid's voice. "Mimi. I am so sorry. I don't know what's wrong with me." Other than a raging headache and stuffy nose. Ugh. No wonder she fell asleep.

"Miss, I'm so sorry, but Ms. Knowles had an emergency

and had to catch the last train back to Butte. She was planning to stay overnight, but I believe a client needed her as soon as possible."

She should be disappointed, but at the moment, she didn't care. At least she'd had the opportunity to meet the woman. "That's all right. It's been quite a day, hasn't it?"

Mimi chuckled and laid out Rebecca's clothes on the bed. "Your things are dry and pressed. Mrs. Ashbury is downstairs waiting for you."

"Thank you." After the maid left once again, Rebecca dressed, but her head swam. She just needed some rest. And more tea. Oh, how she hated these head colds in the winter.

As she made her way down the stairs, the judge was at the bottom waiting for her. "My dear, you look awfully peaked. Are you feeling ill?"

"My nose is all stuffed and my head hurts, but I can't blame Sir Theophilus for that." Her attempt at humor at least made the man laugh.

"Allow me to call for the carriage. You should get home and rest. I'll have Mrs. O'Neill make up a batch of soup and we will bring it to you later."

"That would be so nice. Thank you."

He called for Clarence.

Marvella appeared. "I'm sorry dear, but he's driving the carriage with Ms. Knowles to the train depot."

The judge frowned. "What about Jim?"

"He's taken the other carriage with Sir Theophilus to the veterinarian."

"Whatever for, my dear?"

As the judge's wife explained that the small dog had never had an accident before, Rebecca couldn't wait any longer.

"You know, I think I'll walk home. It's not far." She headed for the door, unwilling to argue with either of the people who had become so dear to her.

"I'll send soup," the judge called out to her.

She waved a hand, but didn't say anything.

She heard Marvella call to their housekeeper about soup and Rebecca wanted to laugh at the antics of the older couple, but all that came out was a rasp. Why was her throat so sore?

With her coat bundled around her, she walked as fast as she could to her apartment. But the cold seeped in and made her feel worse. Now the aches were settling in and all she wanted was her bed.

"Miss Whitman!" A familiar voice called her name. A voice that she liked.

Very much.

But everything was a bit foggy.

"Miss Whitman!"

Oh, how she wanted to get home. Who was calling her? Was she imagining things? Oh, please don't be that annoying Mr. Tuttle.

"Rebecca!"

Oh, that was just Mark. He was her friend. A friend she liked a lot. Especially his smile.

"Rebecca!"

All of a sudden a wall was in her way.

She bounced off of it and couldn't get her balance. Why was the world spinning? "Ow!" She put one hand to her forehead and the other out in front of her in case there was another rogue wall where it didn't belong.

But instead of a wall, the snow-covered ground greeted her with a thud.

15

Sitting by the massive bed at the Ashbury mansion, Mark read from one of a dozen serial mysteries he'd brought.

Rebecca had fallen asleep several minutes ago, but he kept reading aloud simply because he wasn't ready to leave her. Last night, he hadn't meant to startle her like he did. He'd simply tried to gain her attention. But when she walked straight into the wall, his heart had threatened to jump out of his chest.

He finished the chapter and set the small book in his lap.

Her cheeks were quite flushed, but the doctor said it was simply a cold and a sprained wrist, thanks to her fall. Her winter hat had kept the knot on her head from being a more serious injury.

Watching her walk straight into that wall last night had been horrifying. He'd hoped to tell her of his father nearly dying in the night, but after he and Kate and some of the servants had gathered round to pray for his father, Dad had suddenly taken a turn for the better. After a long and tiring night, Dad's breathing improved and his fever lowered.

The doctor came out around nine and was most impressed with the changes in his patient. He gave guarded encouragement that Dad appeared to have turned a corner and was now on his way to recovery. Mark fell asleep almost immediately after the doctor left but woke a short time later feeling the need to return to town. He had thought it was due to the library, but now he understood it must have been Rebecca's need of him.

"Mark?" The judge's voice from the doorway took his attention away from Rebecca.

"Good afternoon, Judge."

"How's our patient?" He took slow steps toward the bed and put a hand on Mark's shoulder and squeezed.

The affectionate gesture was a balm to Mark's heart. He'd struggled with leaving his dad back at the ranch, but Kate had promised to keep Mark informed every day. "I think she's doing well. You heard what the doctor said, right?" He winced. Why hadn't he paid attention to who was in the room when Doc Hart gave his diagnosis?

"I did. Just wanted to check on her."

The care etched on the man's face touched Mark.

"She's only been in our lives a month, but she's quickly become like a daughter to me. At least, what I imagine it would be like." His voice was wistful.

"I know she cares for you a great deal, Judge."

"I know that as well." The man smiled down at Mark and stepped to the side of the bed. There he bent over and kissed Rebecca's forehead. "The good Lord never blessed us with children of our own, but He's blessed us mightily with others' children." He stared at Mark and winked. "You . . . and Miss Whitman here."

"I'll adopt you." Rebecca's hoarse voice came from the bed.

The judge turned and grabbed her extended hand. "I would love that, my dear."

"Me too." She struggled to sit up a bit.

The older man propped up a couple more pillows behind her. "How's that?"

"Perfect." She gave them a weak smile. "Please sit. I am loving all these handsome gentlemen waiting on me hand and foot."

The judge's cheeks pinked and Mark grinned. He offered his chair to the judge and went to fetch another. By the time he came back, they were laughing about Sir Theophilus's latest escapade: digging in the manure of Marvella's rosebushes.

"No. He didn't." Rebecca had tears streaming down her face.

"I'm afraid so, my dear. A little white dog. Black manure. Roses with thorns. You can do the math, I'm sure."

After the laughter subsided, Rebecca shifted her gaze to Mark. "How is your father? I've been praying and praying."

"He's quite ill with pneumonia. We thought we'd lost him, but we gathered around him and prayed and God gave us a miracle. Doc is hopeful that Dad can recover over time if he can let go of his worry about everything on the ranch and commit himself to complete rest. But we all know how difficult that is for Angus Andrews."

The judge crossed his arms over his chest. "It would take a miracle."

"Don't we all know it." Mark shook his head. "With so much happening around the ranch, he can hardly stay abed.

He'll no doubt sneak out to the corrals to see for himself how things are going."

But Rebecca held up a hand. "Wait a minute. What if you hired a nurse to stay at your apartment with your dad and you brought him here? Into town? Wouldn't that take away some of the stress of worrying about the ranch? Out of sight, out of mind?"

"Huh. That's not a bad idea." Thoughts tumbled around in his brain. "At the ranch, there's only the housekeeper and Kimball to check on Dad from time to time because Kate and Harvey are out running the ranch. If he had constant care—someone completely focused on him healing and resting—he might make a lot of progress."

Rebecca bit her lip and scrunched up her nose. "It might cost a good deal though. I just thought of that."

"That's all right. My dad has plenty of funds and I have saved quite a bit if he balks at the idea. I have room in my apartment for him. The nurse would only need to be there during the day when I'm at work. I could be there in the evenings and at night."

This could be the perfect solution!

The judge considered him. "But, son, you might want to have the nurse all the time. You won't be able to get much work done if your dad needs you in the middle of the night and you don't get your rest."

He hadn't thought of that. "You may be right. It's definitely something to consider."

"And don't worry about the cost. Marvella and I will take care of everything."

Mark's head shook back and forth. "No, sir. I couldn't allow you to do that."

"You can argue with me about it later. For now, you go take care of what needs to be done to get your father moved to your place. I'll stay here with our other patient." He grinned at Rebecca.

Mark stood. The love he saw between these two people who he loved made his heart soar.

Wait. *What?*

"Mark, what is it?" Rebecca frowned up at him. "You look like you've swallowed your tongue."

He blinked several times. Did he really just admit that he loved Rebecca? No denying it. It was true. From the bottom of his feet to the top of his head, he knew it. But what would she think about this? Now definitely wasn't the time to spring that on the poor woman. She was bedridden, after all.

If he wanted to work up to proposing like Dad suggested, he should probably prepare the girl. Make sure she wanted more than a friendship. There would be plenty of time to sort through his feelings later. "Nothing." He pasted on a smile and backstepped his way to the door. "I'll come check on you in the morning before I head to the library."

She waved a hand at him. "Oh, I'll be fine. I'm sure I'll be right as rain tomorrow and back to work."

"Oh, no you won't, young lady." Good for the judge. He nipped that in the bud right away. "Doc's orders are for you to stay right here, in bed, until Tuesday."

"But we have so much work to do to prepare for the trial." Her voice squeaked.

"You're going to stay put. Trial doesn't start until Wednesday."

Mark watched the two face off.

Rebecca finally leaned her head back on the pillows with a huff. "Fine. You win. This time."

"Good girl." The judge picked up the book Mark had been reading. "Now, where were we?"

Mark sent her a wave as the judge started at the beginning.

She waved back.

It didn't matter if the older man was rereading the book. From the look on Rebecca's face, it was clear she was enamored.

And so was Mark.

WEDNESDAY, MARCH 2, 1904
KALISPELL COURTHOUSE

Rebecca had spent every spare moment that morning praying for the Lord to guide her heart, mind, and hands as the trial for Joseph Cameron's life was about to begin.

Deep in her heart, she was convinced the man was innocent. She had no proof. But she had a plan. She would make an extra copy of her notes every day so she could go over them later. After her duties were done in the courtroom, she would head to the library and start reading up on law and the investigation processes. Then she would search for other murder trials. Anything and everything that could help her understand and "rightly divide the truth," just like the Bible said.

"All rise," the bailiff called. "Court is now in session."

Rebecca took her seat and started jotting in shorthand every word. She wasn't about to miss a single thing.

The prosecutor was the district attorney. He stood up and straightened his jacket, then began his opening statement. "Gentlemen of the jury, today you will hear testimony that will leave no doubt in your mind that Mr. Joseph Cameron did indeed murder Mr. Horace Bradstreet, with a knife, in the middle of the street, on the night of February eleventh. All over a simple wallet. I thank you for your service to our country and your willingness to serve on this jury. Mr. Joseph Cameron is guilty of murder." He tapped the railing in front of them and then returned to his seat.

Mr. Cameron's lawyer stood and approached the jury. "Gentlemen of the jury, I too thank you for your service to this court, but the prosecution is trying to convince you to convict an innocent man. Mr. Joseph Cameron arrived on the scene after Mr. Bradstreet had been stabbed and was only trying to save the man's life. Mr. Cameron is innocent. Thank you." He took his seat.

The district attorney called the officer who was first on the scene to the witness stand. He asked him to run through every detail of the night.

"I happened on the scene, it was sleeting and snowing, and I saw that man—Joseph Cameron—with blood all over his hands, bent over another man's chest. He was crying for help and police.

"Then there was another man—the witness, Harvey Monroe— who pointed to Mr. Cameron, calling him a murderer. He showed me the weapon. A knife, its sheath, blood all over both."

Harvey Monroe. So he was the man who wanted to remain anonymous. But . . .

Why?

The DA held up a bloody knife. "Was it this knife right here?"

Rebecca jarred and forced herself to focus on her shorthand.

"Yes, sir. That's the knife."

"Then what happened?"

The officer folded his hands in his lap. "Then we—other officers had arrived on the scene—took the two men down to the station, separated them, and recorded their statements. I interviewed Mr. Cameron first. He explained that he was walking home, saw what he thought was another man robbing the man on the ground—Mr. Bradstreet—and went to help. He found Bradstreet lying there with a knife in the middle of his chest. Joe said he squatted down to see if the man was still alive and saw his eyes open. He thought the man was still breathing, so he pulled the knife from his chest."

The DA angled a look at the man. "And why, exactly, did he say he did this?"

"Because he thought it would help stop the bleeding and ease the man's pain."

Murmurs were heard throughout the court.

Judge Ashbury pounded the gavel. "There will be order in the court or I will be forced to ask all of you to leave."

Quiet settled in once again.

The officer finished telling about Cameron's testimony and then dove into his interview of Mr. Harvey Monroe. "Mr. Monroe told us that he saw Cameron approach Mr. Bradstreet with a knife drawn. Cameron demanded Bradstreet's wallet and when he refused, Cameron stabbed him. By the time Monroe reached the two men, Cameron had thrown something into the alley and Monroe took the knife away from Cameron and then we were there for the rest."

The officer started to say something else, but the DA cut in. "Did you find Mr. Bradstreet's wallet on his person?"

"No, sir."

"It is quite safe for all of us here—the jury—to deduct that Mr. Bradstreet's wallet was stolen."

"I can't say that for sure, sir, but we do know that the wallet was not with Mr. Bradstreet when he was dead."

"That will be all, officer."

The DA sat down and Joseph Cameron's lawyer stood. "Officer Jones, did you find Mr. Bradstreet's wallet on Joseph Cameron's person?"

"No sir, we did not."

Several gasps were heard in the gallery. Then everyone hushed.

Very interesting. They didn't find the wallet, which they were trying to connect as motive for the murder.

"You said there was blood on Mr. Cameron?" The defense attorney held the officer's gaze.

Rebecca scribbled her shorthand as fast as she could. Focus was important. Especially when they spoke fast.

"On his hands and the sleeves of his coat."

"But Mr. Cameron readily admitted that he pulled the knife out and covered the wound with his hands, so that would account for the blood, correct?"

The officer took a moment, then nodded. "Yes, that is correct."

"Was there blood found on anyone else at the scene?"

"Yes, sir. Blood was found on Mr. Monroe's hands and on the front of his coat."

More gasps from the courtroom.

"How do you account for that, Officer Jones?"

"Mr. Monroe stated that he wrestled the knife away from Mr. Cameron."

"Did anyone see this?"

"No, sir."

The gallery filled with murmuring.

"Order!" Judge Ashbury pounded the gavel.

The room quieted.

"Thank you." The lawyer took his seat.

Whispers erupted once more. Judge Ashbury tapped his gavel and sent a glaring look out to the audience.

"Redirect, your honor."

Judge Ashbury nodded to the DA. "Go ahead."

"Officer Jones, according to the eyewitness, Mr. Cameron tossed something away."

"Yes, sir. That is what Mr. Monroe stated."

"But you didn't take his statement until you were at the police office."

"Yes, sir."

"So did you send someone out to check the alley after that testimony?" The DA's voice rose in volume.

"Yes, sir."

"Was anything found?" Even louder.

"No, sir."

"How much time had passed?" Quite a dramatic volume now.

"About an hour, sir."

"So!" The DA smacked the wooden railing with his hand and turned toward the jury. "It is totally feasible that Mr. Cameron stole the wallet, and when he saw he was caught, he threw it in the alley. Where it was likely picked up by another thief while the police were gathering testimony."

"Yes, sir." The officer shifted in his seat, looked down at his hands, and then shrugged. "That is feasible."

Rebecca kept her features neutral, but couldn't believe Cameron's lawyer didn't say anything! Why didn't he object?

Everything moved on. The DA called Harvey Monroe to the stand. He was sworn in and then gave his testimony, almost exactly like Officer Jones had said.

"Mr. Monroe, you asked to be anonymous until the trial, why was that?"

"I'm a part of a prominent family—the Andrews family. I am married to Kate Andrews, Angus Andrews's daughter. I didn't wish to bring unwelcome attention or potential harm to the family. Especially during one of the busiest seasons on the ranch."

"I see. Completely understandable." The DA inclined his head. "The court is grateful that you have taken time out during such an important season to help us with this case."

Monroe smiled and looked toward the jury. "Of course. It's my duty."

Rebecca didn't know what to think. This man was Mark's brother-in-law. Did Mark know Harvey had witnessed the murder? He never mentioned anything.

Then there was the fact that every expression Harvey made, every word he said—it all seemed a bit too . . . rehearsed. The jury seemed to appreciate the man and his social status. By the way they smiled and nodded, it reminded Rebecca of one of those men's clubs where the members were all sworn to secrecy and spoke only to each other. She'd heard plenty about them in Chicago.

Rebecca pushed the thought away. Harvey Monroe was neither an actor nor a man guarding secrets.

But what if he is?

The nagging thought wouldn't go away. Still, what did a man like that stand to gain by seeing Joe convicted of murder?

After Harvey was excused—once again with only one question by Joe's lawyer—the DA then called the coroner.

Rebecca braced herself for what was to come. The part she despised. The man went into gory detail about how Horace Bradstreet died. How the knife cut through him. What it did to his insides. The fact that he lost so much blood in a matter of minutes that it cost him his life.

After she was done writing down the testimony, she gave a little shiver.

She stole a glance at the jury—they looked a bit queasy as well.

But then she spotted Joe's wife. Tears streamed down her face as she sat behind her husband. Marvella had her arm around the woman's shoulders.

Just then the judge called a recess.

For several moments, it was almost as if she were frozen to her chair as she watched the crowd disperse.

What would happen to Mr. Cameron if he was convicted? What would happen to his wife? Things didn't look good for him. Even if the evidence against him *was* all circumstantial, the jury probably found it easier to believe the prosecutor's side to everything since Joe's lawyer had hardly done his job.

No. That wasn't fair of her. She stood and gathered her things. Prayerfully, Joe's lawyer was just waiting for the defense's turn.

As for Joe, he looked like he could fall apart at any moment.

Couldn't the jury just look at him and see the truth? All Rebecca knew for certain was that if Joseph Cameron was convicted, innocent or guilty, he could be hanged for the crime.

16

I t had taken much longer than Mark would have liked, but he was finally headed out to the ranch with a wagon. Once Doc Hart had approved the plan, Mark rearranged his apartment and got everything the good doctor had instructed him to have on hand.

A nurse was at his apartment now, waiting for him to return with his father.

One of the ladies of the library association volunteered to be at the library this morning, and the rest of the town was engrossed with the murder trial, so it was the perfect time. Should be smooth and quiet for Dad.

The only hurdle he had left was his sister. Would Kate balk at him moving Dad?

For that matter, would Dad refuse?

Okay, so maybe two hurdles.

When the ranch was in view, he put his doubts behind him. This was the right thing to do and he was going to follow through.

Besides, after the idea had settled into his heart and mind, he'd begun to look forward to some time with his father again. Sure, they still had their differences, but they'd made great strides in healing old wounds.

He pulled the wagon up to the front door of the sprawling family home and set the brake.

Kate came over from the barn. "Mark! It's so good to see you. What's brought you out here? And with a wagon?"

"Let's go inside and I'll explain."

"All right."

In the parlor, Mark gripped his hat in his hands. "I want to move Dad to live with me for a while. I've talked to Doc Hart, who thinks it's a good idea. Just until Dad gets his strength back. If he's with me, he won't be tempted to help with the ranch or stress over how things are progressing. I've hired a nurse to stay with him around the clock."

Kate exhaled and let her shoulders drop. "Oh, Mark. That would be wonderful. I've been so worried about him and feel like he's just not getting well here. I began to worry that what the doc said was true . . . that the stress of being here and worrying about the ranch was hindering his recovery."

"I know. That's exactly why I started praying about it." Mark hugged his sister. "You've done an amazing job, Kate. Allow me to take this one thing off your plate for right now."

"I'm so thankful that you moved back here. It truly has been a gift for all of us. Dad loves seeing you, I bet he will be happy to get to spend some more time with you."

Mark grimaced. "We can hope, but he may not like being moved away from the ranch."

"Being closer to the doctor and hospital will be good for him. And having a nurse with him all the time? That will surely help him to heal faster. At least it will keep him on his best behavior."

Mark tipped his head toward Dad's room. "Would you help me pack up his things? I'd like to get back in time to relieve Mrs. Limon at the library this afternoon."

"Oh, I'm so sorry, Mark. I didn't even think of you having to rearrange your schedule to do this." She scurried toward their father's room.

Dad slept soundly as they moved around the room. It only took them an hour to pack up everything they could think of that he might need while at Mark's apartment in town. It was probably too much, but they both wanted him to feel comfortable and at home.

Then they prepared the wagon. Layers of blankets covered the bottom. Several pillows and blankets were ready to cover Dad once he was in, and then Rodney helped Mark fashion a canvas cover for the wagon bed, so Dad wouldn't have to be in the elements. Kate had ten bricks heating in the fireplace so they could surround Dad with them and keep him warm.

Mark rubbed his hands together and glanced at his sister once they were back in the parlor. "All right then, I think we're ready."

"What's all this?" Harvey marched through the front door all dressed up in a suit. "And what's with the wagon out front?"

Mark studied him. Why was he all decked out? "Where have you been this morning?"

The man puffed his chest out. "If you must know, I was a witness to a crime and had to give my testimony in court this morning. Now please answer *my* questions."

It rankled Mark that his brother-in-law just waltzed in and took command. But he would be nice. This was about his father. "We're moving Dad to my apartment for a while. I've hired a nurse and that way you guys don't have to worry about him, and he won't have to worry about the ranch." Mark patted his brother-in-law on the shoulder. He needed to get to know the man better. This awkwardness between them made things difficult.

"That's ridiculous. The old man loves the ranch and would want to live and die here. It's cruel to move him." Harvey put his hands on his hips.

"Now, darling." Kate sidled up to him. "I think this is the best thing for Dad right now. And for us. It's been hard to watch him decline."

Wait a minute. The only case at the court was the murder trial. Harvey was a witness? Mark opened his mouth—

"I don't like it. I think your father should stay right here." Harvey emphasized it by pointing to the floor.

Enough. "No offense, Harvey, but you don't have a say in the matter. Kate and I have already made the decision."

His brother-in-law narrowed his eyes. "Well, what does your father have to say about it?"

"He's asleep. And I would appreciate you not disturbing him. Tell me about this testimony you gave this morning. This is for the murder trial?" Mark did his best to keep his voice in check.

"That's of no consequence to you." Harvey sneered at him. "I don't think it's wise to move your father."

Kate put a hand on her husband's chest. "I appreciate your protectiveness of Dad, but we've already made the decision. Mark has gone to a great deal of trouble to make sure that everything is taken care of. Now I'm going to go get Rodney and Kimball to help us move him." With her chin held high, she walked away.

Mark followed, more than a little concerned about the anger he saw on Harvey Monroe's face.

The rest of the afternoon in court had been taken up with the testimony of each police officer at the scene—there had been three—and they repeated the same evidence against Joe.

He had blood on his hands.

He'd been found kneeling over the body.

The wallet was missing.

But even as the DA went on and on and on about the same things with each officer, Rebecca had to fight to not frown. How could the testimony of one eyewitness and the small amount of evidence make everyone believe that Joe did it?

No one—other than Harvey—ever heard Joe threaten Horace Bradstreet, with or without a knife. The wallet was missing. Joe and Harvey had both been covered in Joe's blood. In fact, Harvey was the one the police saw holding the knife. Not that she wanted to blame another man just to prove Joe Cameron's innocence, but somebody had to be thinking it.

After she submitted all her notes from the day's session, she put on her coat and headed out. Perhaps a long walk in the cool air would help her think.

"Rebecca, my dear!"

Marvella's voice brought her attention up. "Good afternoon, Marvella." She smiled at the woman in the carriage.

"You look positively dreary."

"Oh, it's just the trial." Rebecca frowned. "Too many things bother me about it. I was just taking a walk to clear my head."

Marvella patted the seat next to her. "Join me a few minutes. You can surely get back to your walk in a bit."

"Yes, ma'am." She grinned. The woman wasn't told no very often and Rebecca wasn't about to start today.

"I am truly devastated by this case. What they are doing to poor Joe. But Judge won't allow us to even speak about it at home, he says it would be ethically wrong since he is presiding over the case." She harrumphed. "I even suggested that we hire Mr. Cameron a better lawyer since the one appointed to him seems to care more about his cat than his client's life—which *is* on the line, mind you—but the judge shot that down as well. We couldn't help one side or the other."

"That makes sense, Marvella. I don't like it, but I appreciate that the judge is honorable in these things. Gives me confidence in our legal system." She bit her lip. But hadn't she had the same thoughts? Mr. Cameron's lawyer wasn't helping much at all. But what could they do?

"I don't have to tell you how upsetting all of this is to me." Marvella put a hankie to her mouth. "Sitting in the courtroom with dear Mrs. Cameron, watching what is happening with Joe's no-good lawyer." She lifted her chin. "Forgive me for talking ill of the man. I don't even know him."

"I understand. It has been difficult for me to record every word. Over and over again the DA keeps pounding the same issue about Joe being over the man when the police arrived. About him having blood on his hands. About the wallet missing. And what Mr. Monroe saw."

"I don't believe that man." Marvella shifted in her seat. "Not one bit. I think he's lying."

Down in her heart, Rebecca did too. But how could they prove it?

If only someone had found the wallet.

But then, there was the knife. And the blood.

Wait a minute. The police said Harvey had blood on the front of his coat and on his hands. While Joe only had blood on his hands and on his coat sleeves.

"Stop the carriage!" She laid a hand on Marvella's arm as the rig jolted to a stop. "I have an idea. I don't want to say anything until I know more, but please pray. I have a feeling the truth will come out!" Excitement bubbled up. She could do this. She could help set a man free.

She dashed from the carriage toward the library, running for all she was worth. She didn't care what anyone thought. This was more important than social conventions.

She raced up the steps and darted in the doors. Now where was Mark?

Out of breath, she put a hand to her chest and gazed around.

Mark popped his head around a shelf of books. "Everything all right?"

She jumped. "Gracious! Yes. No. I need your help."

Concern filled his eyes. "Of course. What can I do?" He set down a stack of books, took her hand, and led her to his chair behind the circulation desk.

Rebecca gave him the short version of everything she'd heard in court. "So now, I'm thinking of trying a little experiment. Will you help me?"

"You can count me in." He rubbed his hands together.

"I've always loved trying to solve a mystery. When do you want to try your little experiment?"

"Tomorrow night? After I've gathered the supplies?"

"Sounds good."

"Mark . . ." She bit her lip.

"Yes?"

"Did you know that your brother-in-law witnessed the murder?"

He leaned up against the desk and crossed his arms over his chest. "Nope. In fact, I didn't know until I was out at the ranch today—by the way, I moved my father to my apartment, but I'll get back to that in a minute—and Harvey arrived all dressed up in his Sunday best and he told us that he had given his testimony in court."

How could she say what was on her mind without insinuating that his sister's husband was guilty of something?

"You didn't believe him, did you?" There wasn't any accusation in his voice, which helped her feel better about asking him to help her . . . but what if she was right?

She winced. She didn't want to lie to him. "Let's see what happens with my little experiment. Now tell me about your dad. Is he all right?"

Mark filled her in on the move of his father, the nurse, the doctor's advice, and his excitement to have his dad with him for a while.

"I tell you what. Why don't I make some of my special cinnamon cookies? When my father was sick, he always asked for them—said they even had healing powers. I'll need to go to the grocers, so maybe I can have them ready for tomorrow."

"That sounds good. Say, why don't you join us for dinner

241

tonight? Marvella is sending over food this evening and I'm sure it will be enough to feed a small army." He raised his eyebrows and smiled. "What do you say?"

"Sounds wonderful. I'll be there."

"Perfect."

The bell jangled over the door and Mark sprang from his perch and darted to the front to help whoever it was.

Rebecca couldn't help but smile.

Tonight, she'd have dinner with Mark and his father. It sent little tingles up and down her spine.

And then?

She just might solve the mystery of who *actually* killed Horace Bradstreet.

It was an odd sensation, having his father in his apartment. Taking care of him and all. But Mark couldn't wait to hear what he thought of Rebecca.

"It's nice to see you again, Mr. Andrews." She sat down next to his father at the table.

"No more of that, young lady. I insist you call me Angus."

Mark had been hesitant to bring his father out to the table. Dad had been exhausted after the move and the nurse said he slept most of the afternoon. But now he seemed to perk up and was all smiles for the court stenographer.

They chatted about her job while Mark fixed their plates.

"What is this I hear about Harvey being a witness today in court?" His father turned to Mark. "You know anything about this?"

"Not until today." He set a plate in front of Rebecca and

then one in front of his father. "Dinner is served. Thanks to Marvella, of course."

His father's eyes widened. "Looks delicious. Even though I don't have much of an appetite. I'll do my best."

Laughter rounded the table during dinner as Rebecca and Dad hit it off like nothing Mark had ever seen before. Where had this congenial man come from? Or had he encountered some sort of light-from-heaven moment when they thought they were going to lose him?

Whatever it was, Mark was enjoying it. "Would you like more of the Charlotte Russe, Dad?"

"No. No. I've had plenty to eat. I think I'd be better off to rest a bit."

Mark helped his father up from the chair. Dad leaned on him heavily. Maybe it hadn't been such a good idea to get him up.

Of course, Dad had insisted. After all, he said, he'd been sleeping all day and the doctor said he could sit up if he felt like it. He probably just wanted to spend time with Rebecca. And Mark couldn't blame him for wanting that, but it seemed to cost Dad a good deal.

The steps to the bedroom were slow as his father—a man who had always been larger than life—struggled to shuffle forward.

"I'll gather up the dishes." Rebecca's cheery voice washed over them.

"Thank you, dear. It was a pleasure to see you again." Dad was out of breath, talking and walking at the same time.

Lord, please help him to heal here. It was heartbreaking to see his father in such a weakened condition.

"I'm so glad you could join us for dinner, Angus." Dishes clinked.

It was a good thing the apartment was small. The distance to the table was a mere twenty steps or so, but it wore his father out like he'd run a marathon. Mark eased him onto the edge of the bed.

His dad huffed and his shoulders slumped as he worked to catch his breath. "She's a gem, Mark. Don't let her get away."

"I don't plan to. For now, however, I want to focus on you getting well. I'm so glad you're here. Just don't worry about anything."

"I'm not worried. You know, me and the good Lord have had quite a few discussions on my tendency to worry. And to get angry. He doesn't want me to do it anymore."

Mark chuckled. "Neither do I."

"It hasn't served me well, that's for sure."

Tucking the blanket around his father, Mark could see that his dad's color was better than it had been earlier in the day. He was definitely making progress toward recovery. Hopefully that would come even faster now with a change of scenery and a full-time nurse to keep him on his toes.

"Go on now and get back to that pretty gal of yours." Dad closed his eyes. "I'm done for and plan to sleep."

"Good night, Dad."

"Good night."

Mark left his father and rejoined Rebecca. She was already elbow-deep in soapy suds and had quite a few dishes washed.

"I'll dry." Mark picked up one of the plates she'd put in the rinse water and grabbed a towel. "Your nose is scrunched up like you're thinking hard. Want to talk about it?"

"It's the trial. Joe's not guilty. I feel it deep in my heart. He's telling the truth and no one will listen to him. I know how that feels and it's terrifying and frustrating and overwhelming." With a huff, she lowered another dish into the sudsy water.

"It must have been hard on you as a child to have known the truth and not be heard." It was beyond what he could fathom, but he saw how it weighed on her.

"It was. It still is. I mean, I don't have people doubting me like that now, but whenever there's the slightest question about something I've said or done, it comes back to haunt me. Now, with Joe stating his innocence, I can't help but remember every detail of the day when I witnessed that man being attacked. I can well imagine Joe just happening upon him. Joe's the exact kind of guy who would stop to help someone in need." Scrubbing the plate in her hands with the rag, she stiffened.

"Hopefully his lawyer can get that across to the jury."

Rebecca shook her head. "That's the thing. I don't think his lawyer even cares. I know that's an awful thing to say, but he rarely objects and the DA is horrible about leading the witnesses. Judge Ashbury even asked him at one point if he'd like to get up in the witness box himself. The entire courtroom laughed, but, Mark, this is no laughing matter. This is a man's life. If he's convicted of murder, Joe will hang."

17

Mark unlocked his apartment door while he balanced a stack of books on his knee. Now that Dad was doing a little better, maybe they could read and discuss some of his favorite books. Dad did love a good story.

Wiggling his way inside his apartment, Mark dropped the books in a chair, closed the door with his foot, and then headed to his bedroom.

"Nurse Chambers, it's me, Mark." Didn't want to alarm the woman at the sound of someone just walking in.

When he rounded the corner, he stopped. Dad was sitting up again! Mark had been certain that yesterday had wiped his father out, so he had prepared himself to find Dad in bed. Especially after Dad moaned so much last night once he was back in bed. But he looked wonderful now.

"Wow. You must be feeling better."

The nurse smiled at Mark and patted Dad's shoulder.

"He's doing great. I'll be back in a few minutes, Angus." She gave Mark a nod. "He's had a good day."

"I'm glad to hear it."

The nurse smiled. "I'll give you two some time together."

His father shifted and offered a slight grin. "Good to see you, son."

"You too. Looks like you've had a nice day?"

"Better than most. I haven't felt this alive in a while. And Nurse Chambers is quite the woman. Great company and conversationalist."

"That's wonderful news." Mark sat on the bed beside him. "Marvella is sending dinner over again in a few minutes, and I brought home a huge stack of books to read. I thought we could do that in the evenings together."

"Sounds like a plan to me." This time, Dad gave him a fuller smile. "You know, we haven't played checkers in a while."

Mark leaned back. "Hey, if you're up for it, I'm sure I could scrounge up a board and some checkers."

Dad's fingers thrummed on the coverlet beside him. "Thanks for bringing me here. I know it's a big imposition."

"Not a bit. It's good to have you."

"Did Doc have to twist your arm? Was he worried I would try and go out in the middle of a blizzard again?"

"No one twisted my arm, Dad. As soon as I had everything in place, I drove out to the ranch and told Kate. She agreed with me and here you are. You were sick, you know—you almost died."

Dad's eyes grew wide. Then he looked down. Fidgeted with a thread on the covers. "Well, I'm thankful you did it. Gives Kate a well-earned rest. I knew it was bad. I was ready to go. Thought about giving up a couple of times when the pain was intense and I couldn't draw a decent breath. But I guess God has me here for a bit longer." He shifted his eyes up and smiled. "Bringing me here—it was the right thing to do."

"Glad you think so." He patted his father's leg. "I'm going to go find that checkerboard and bring the books in here for you to look over. Miss Whitman is joining us for dinner again and she's bringing you a surprise, so be on your best behavior, all right?" He got up from the bed and headed out to the parlor to the wonderful sound of his dad's deep laughter.

Rebecca showed up exactly at a quarter of six. She smelled of vanilla and cinnamon.

Delightful.

She offered up a plate of cookies. "Delivered as promised."

"They look delicious." He took a big whiff. "And smell even better."

"Thank you."

"Did you get what you needed for our experiment to prove Joe's innocence?"

"I did."

"Good. Supper just arrived so I'll get Dad. If you want to put the food on the table that would be a great help."

"I'd be happy to do it." She turned toward the kitchen. "I'll just save these to surprise your dad later."

And later that was exactly what she did. After dinner, Rebecca presented the plate of cookies to his father. "Here you are, Mr. Andrews—sorry, *Angus*. And if you don't want to share them with Mark, that's totally fine. I made these for *you.*" She curtsied and winked. Mark had already settled his dad back in bed and Rebecca placed the plate on the mattress beside him.

"Well, aren't you the sweetest lass." Dad lifted a cookie off the plate and took a bite. "These melt in the mouth. They are delicious. Reminds me of something my mother used to make. Oh, Mark, I wish you'd known your grandmother. Baked like nobody else could, and these cookies taste just like her cinnamon shortbread."

Mark reached forward to grab one.

Dad pulled the plate closer to his chest. "No. I mean they're horrible. You wouldn't want any of them. I'll have to eat them all."

Laughter filled the room and Mark's heart overflowed.

Nurse Chambers walked to Dad's side. "All right, everyone. I'm going to have to insist that Mr. Andrews get his rest."

"Aw"—Dad sounded like a whining child—"but I wanted to play another game of checkers with Miss Whitman."

The nurse shook her head.

"I'll come back tomorrow and play a game or two with you." Rebecca headed for the bedroom door. "Besides, I'll need the rest of the evening to practice so that I have a chance of beating you tomorrow."

"Sounds like a challenge. All right then, I'll see you to-morrow, Miss Whitman."

"I'll be in later, Dad." Mark followed Rebecca to the door.

"We still need to finish that book about Captain Ahab and the big white whale."

"That we do, Dad. But now you need to rest." Mark pulled the door closed and stepped to the kitchen, where

Rebecca had started cleaning up. "Let me do that. You're my guest."

"How about we do it together, like yesterday? That way we'll get done faster."

"I like how your mind works."

Together they washed and dried the dishes and put them all away in the cupboards. Her wavy hair was coming out of its confines as she scrubbed down the tiny kitchen counter. He liked it a lot.

When she met his gaze, she tipped her head. "What? Is something on my face?" She swiped at it.

"No. You look just fine."

"Then why are you looking at me like that?"

He shrugged but couldn't keep the smile from his face. "Why don't you tell me about your experiment?"

She bit her lip. A charming habit that always meant she was thinking through something.

Then she dove into the details of the trial that day.

The more he heard, the more he disliked what he heard. What on earth did Harvey have to do with all this?

"So this is what I'm thinking." She handed him an apron. "I brought everything we'd need. Put it on. Wait, get rid of your coat and tie first."

Several blinks later, he lifted his eyebrows. "An apron? What does this have to do with the trial?"

"Oh, just do what I ask." She grabbed another apron and slipped it over her neck then tied the strings in the back.

Mark licked his lips and narrowed his eyes. "Fine. But I can't help but notice that you handed me the one with the ruffles." He put on the apron.

She giggled and then put her hands on her hips. "Now we just need something that will be like blood."

"What?"

"Oh! I've got it." She filled a cup with coffee from the percolator and then added flour to it. She stirred it and looked down into the cup, then held it up for his inspection. "There. What do you think? Is it about as thick as blood?"

"Um, I guess." Where was she going with this?

"Good. Wait. I forgot something." She ran out of his apartment and he heard her steps on the stairs. Must be getting something out of her own apartment. Footsteps again, then she was back. "I asked Marvella to bring over an old piece of canvas from their stables."

She spread out the canvas so that it covered the floor. Then she grabbed a knife from his kitchen. Holding it up in the air, she picked up the cup of coffee. "All right. This is what we're going to do. We're going to reenact what happened."

He held up his hands. "So am I stabbing you, or are you stabbing me?"

"Oh, stop it." She sent him a glower.

Then they both broke into a fit of laughter.

The nurse came out of the bedroom with a scowl on her face. "Shhh!" She surveyed the floor, gave them another look, and then shook her head.

Mark pinched his lips together and straightened.

Rebecca did the same. "Sorry!" she whispered across the room.

Once the nurse was back in the bedroom, Rebecca let out a long sigh. "Whew. That was close."

"You almost got us in trouble." Mark wagged a finger at her.

She slapped a hand over her mouth as her shoulders shook. "Stop making me laugh. Now be serious. This is important."

"Sorry." He pasted on the most serious face he could muster. Then counted to ten to make sure he could hold it. "All right. I'm ready."

"Okay. Here's the plan. I'm going to pour this thick coffee all over the knife. I'll be Joe. You be Harvey."

"What if *I* wanted to be Joe?"

Shaking her head, she pointed the knife at him, the struggle to keep a straight face clear on her face. "Mark Andrews, if you don't stop misbehaving, I'm just going to have to find someone else to help me."

"Sorry. I'll be helpful. I promise. Even if I have to play Harvey." He sucked his lips into his mouth.

"Once I get the blood—well, coffee—on the knife, I'm going to pretend I've just pulled it out of Horace's chest. Then you take it from me, all right?"

He nodded. "I can do that."

She poured the coffee and the knife was covered. She got down on the floor.

Mark approached her and whispered, "Hey! Stop, murderer!" He took the knife from her.

As they both stood up, Mark studied his hands. The only coffee was on his hand.

Same for Rebecca. Their coffee—fake blood—was only on her hand.

Huh. That didn't line up with the actual crime scene at all.

She seemed to be thinking the same thing. "Harvey did say he had to wrestle it away from Joe. So this time, let's try it with a bit of resistance."

They started over and this time pretended to struggle. Rebecca got a tiny bit of coffee on her sleeve. Mark remained clean.

She placed her hands on her hips. "All right, let's try it one more time. Just to be certain. Make sure you really fight me for it."

"Yes, ma'am." He put on his most menacing expression.

She giggled. "Let me get back in position."

Once more, they did their best to reenact the scene from the testimony. The knife also slipped out of their hands and fell to the floor.

This time, Rebecca had the thick coffee on her sleeves and hands, but Mark had it on his hands and that was it.

"I think this proves it."

"Proves what exactly?" Mark bent to pick up the knife.

"I think Harvey's lying." She scrunched up her nose. "I know he's your brother-in-law and I'm sorry, but I don't see any other logical explanation. There was no reason for him to have so much blood on the front of his coat. Even if he had to struggle to get the knife away from Joe, it wouldn't have left so much blood on the front of him."

Mark took the knife to the sink and cleaned it up. When he turned back around, she was waiting for him to respond. Harvey wasn't his favorite person, so it was easy to believe that the man had lied.

Mark shook that thought away. *Examine the facts. . . .*

Judge Ashbury had drilled into them about remaining unbiased. But no matter which way he looked at it, things didn't add up.

Mark nodded to Rebecca. "I think you're right. As much as I hate to say it, I'm pretty sure Harvey is hiding something."

Friday, March 4, 1904

Rebecca paced in her apartment, chewing on her thumbnail. Would the judge give her a moment of his time this morning? Was she even allowed to approach him about what she'd done?

This type of thing had not been covered in her stenography classes. And she hadn't studied enough of the law to know yet what she could and couldn't do.

It didn't matter. She simply *had* to speak to him this morning. He usually arrived quite early. So she would too. Then she'd just need enough gumption to go knock on his door and make her case.

Putting on her coat, she braced herself for what was to come. Today could be life changing. She grabbed her things and headed out the door. Once she'd locked her apartment and headed down the stairs, she snuck a glance toward Mark's apartment. Last night had been wonderful. At least she knew she had his support.

And of course, Marvella's.

But the judge wouldn't appreciate that.

No. She had to do this on her own two feet.

Rebecca stomped out of the building, willing herself to stay strong in her resolve.

God, I hope I'm doing the right thing. If I'm not, please show me the way. I just can't abide another innocent man dying when I could do something about it.

Over and over in her mind, she rattled off the words she'd prepared. She made it to the courthouse in record time and scurried up the steps. Without even taking off her coat or setting her personal belongings down at her desk, she headed straight for the judge's chambers and knocked on the door.

"Come in."

All right. Now was the time. She could do this.

Opening the door, she swallowed. "Judge Ashbury?"

"Miss Whitman." He normally greeted her with a smile. But today, his face was serious. "How can I help you?"

Where had her rehearsed words gone? "Sir, I . . . I did an experiment last night with Mr. Andrews's assistance."

"Oh?"

The story tumbled out and the more he frowned, the faster she talked. "So, if you can see, sir, I don't believe the evidence backs up Mr. Monroe's testimony."

Judge Ashbury pointed to a chair. "Sit."

She obeyed.

Then he stood, his lips pinched together. The usual twinkle in his eyes gone. "Miss Whitman, while I admire your passion for the law and justice, I must remind you that you are not an attorney for the defense. Nor are you an attorney for the prosecution. Neither are you an investigator of any kind."

"But sir, there's—"

"I won't hear any more, Miss Whitman. You are the court stenographer. A very prestigious position. It isn't your job to decide whether the man is innocent or guilty. That's the jury's job."

"I know that, sir. But what do we do when there's testimony or evidence that doesn't line up?"

"Miss Whitman. I cannot listen to any more. It's for the attorneys to do the best thing for their clients. Justice must be blind. Unbiased. Now I need to ask you to return to your desk and prepare for court today. Do your job to the best of your ability, understood?"

"Yes, sir." Her shoulders sagged. Every inch of her felt the defeat as she stood and headed toward the door.

"Miss Whitman?"

With her hand on the doorknob, she looked over her shoulder. "Yes, sir?"

"Your fervor for the law and defending the innocent is commendable. You will make a fine lawyer one day."

If only that could help Joe Cameron. But she appreciated the judge's words. "Thank you, sir."

She closed the door to the judge's chambers behind her, then leaned up against it. Was that it?

"I can't let an innocent man hang."

The steps she took back to her desk were like slogging through mud compared to the vigor with which she'd entered the building. The very thought of another day in that courtroom with the knowledge she now carried made her want to weep.

At her desk, she laid out her things, and hung up her coat. But her mind wouldn't stop whirling. There had to be something she could do.

The courthouse was still empty except for her and the judge. At least that's how it seemed. Maybe there were others preparing for the day as well.

"Wait a minute." She glanced at the clock. Seven o'clock. That meant she had some time. "Why didn't I think of this before? I'll simply write a letter to Mr. Cameron's attorney." Realizing she'd spoken her thoughts aloud, she darted her gaze around the room. Whew. No one had heard her talking to herself. She didn't want anyone thinking she was a bit loony.

She took out a piece of paper and penned the note quickly. There wasn't any time to waste.

"Ah, Miss Whitman. How lovely you look today." Sam Tuttle walked into the room.

"Good morning, Mr. Tuttle. I'm sorry but I'm very busy." She focused again on the paper.

"I've been thinking about us."

That jarred her from her thoughts. She glanced up. "There *is* no us, Mr. Tuttle."

He smiled. "Only because you have not allowed for us to have time to get acquainted. I'm convinced that once you do, you would share my thoughts that we would make a perfect couple."

How on earth did that man think they would make a perfect couple? Had he not heard a word she had said to him? "No, Mr. Tuttle, I would not."

He chuckled. "Usually when one is so adamant about something, it's because they know the truth of it. I think you are playing hard to get, as many a young lady does."

"Maybe the young ladies are playing hard to get, Mr. Tuttle, because they don't wish to be with you. Now please leave me alone. I need to finish this letter." Never in all her years had she spoken to anyone in such a manner. But the man was clearly out of his mind.

"Well, I have taken the liberty to go over your head."

Sam's words once again brought her to a stop. "You . . . went over my head?"

"Yes, to obtain another's opinion and permission to court you."

Rebecca straightened at this. "Exactly whom did you go to for this permission?" Good heavens. Had the man gone to the judge to seek his agreement?

"I wrote to your father two weeks ago. I anticipate a reply almost any time."

"My *father*? You wrote to *my father*?" Her raised voice was bound to bring the judge to see what was wrong, but she didn't care. If someone didn't stop her, she just might put her fist in Sam Tuttle's smug face.

He nodded. "I am a take-charge kind of man, Miss Whitman."

She got to her feet, ready to take a little charge herself. "How *dare* you!"

"Good grief, what is going on in here?" Judge Ashbury appeared in the doorway. "I could hear you through my closed door."

Rebecca turned and glared at the judge. "I was just about to punch Mr. Tuttle in the face."

"See," Sam began, "this is exactly why women shouldn't hold job positions. It gets them too worked up."

Rebecca crossed the space between them in a flash and raised her arm to hit Sam. Judge Ashbury moved just as quickly and gripped her arm.

"I do understand why you wish to hit the man, my dear. I'm sure he's been quite obnoxious in regard to your position and choices. However, I need you and cannot afford to have you taken off to jail."

Sam sputtered and turned red. "I find this appalling, Judge Ashbury."

"As do we, Mr. Tuttle." The judge raised one eyebrow. "And since it's far easier for me to get another secretary than it is to get a stenographer, I'm going to have to let you go. Unless you feel you can work with Miss Whitman and keep your offensive behavior to yourself."

"Well! I never!" Sam opened his desk drawer and took out several things. "These are my personal possessions." He slammed the drawer shut. "I will not stay here to be further insulted." He marched to the coat tree and took his coat and hat. "I need no further proof that women in the workplace are not only uncalled for, but dangerous!"

"Sam"—the judge pinned him with a hard look—"my arm is getting weak."

Rebecca wanted to burst into laughter but hid her face so that Sam would think she was still a threat.

He hurried to the door without another word.

Once he was gone, the judge let go of Rebecca. She started laughing and the judge joined in.

"Thank you, sir."

"You are most welcome, my dear. I must say, until you arrived, I'd never witnessed Mr. Tuttle's behavior toward women. I apologize on behalf of all men."

She scrunched up her nose as the depth of what the judge just sacrificed hit her. "What will you do without a secretary?"

"I've managed many times without one, I'm sure I can make do for a while. In fact, I might just give Mrs. Ashbury the privilege of selecting my next one. That should keep her busy for a bit and there won't be any chance of me hiring a cad, now will there?" His mustache wiggled with his lips as he released a hearty chuckle.

"Leave it to Marvella, and I'm sure you will have the most astounding secretary ever to be found." All the weight of their previous discussion fell away as the relief of the moment took her mind off the sorry state of affairs in the courtroom. It was like a breath of fresh air filled the room with Mr. Tuttle's exit.

So the little tart thought she was smarter than he was?

Harvey paced inside the men's restroom. Good thing he'd decided to sneak into the courthouse this morning. He'd overheard everything. He'd been hoping to leave a threatening note on that sniveling secretary's desk. There had to be a way for him to sway the jury and that fellow seemed to be the one to help him. But now Tuttle was gone.

No matter. Listening outside the judge's chambers had given him some interesting insights.

Miss Whitman—as the judge had called her—was the one who was taking notes for the court. Obviously, she suspected his testimony wasn't true. The problem was, she was going to send something to Mr. Cameron's attorney.

Which he couldn't allow.

So what were his options? Watch her? Follow her to find out how she planned to get a letter to the lawyer? If he hired someone to do something about it, that could lead back to him. If he did it himself, someone might see him, and now that he was recognizable as the witness in the case, that could spell disaster as well.

But what choice did he have?

Miss Whitman couldn't be allowed to communicate with the lawyer.

He pulled out his pocket watch. What a mess.

Kate would wonder where he was if he wasn't around the ranch all day, but it couldn't be helped.

Plain and simple, he only had one choice.

Miss Whitman had to be stopped.

For good.

18

For an hour, Rebecca had scribbled out what she wanted to say. Over and over. Trying to make it as clear as possible. Giving the illustration of her experiment. Asking lots of questions. But she also had to ensure that no one could trace the information back to her.

Because it could put her job on the line. Not that she wasn't willing to risk her job, but she also wanted to handle things the best that she could.

The defense attorney just needed the information, then he could have his own forensic analysis done.

Today, the prosecution would finish presenting their case. Would the judge want the defense to present their case today? She'd have to wait and see.

Even if the defense did start today, surely he wouldn't finish up in one day . . . would he? Of course, the man hadn't proven to be all that on top of things.

She tucked the notes into her handbag. *Lord, show me what to do.*

It was time to head into the courtroom. If the case didn't conclude today, she could go to the library this evening and do some research. If by some chance everything got wrapped up and was headed to the jury, well . . . she'd just have to do something drastic. She bit her lip. Probably not the best of ideas, but what choice did she have?

The courtroom bustled with activity as people in the gallery chattered. Several members of the press had gathered. More than yesterday. Why was this case getting so much publicity? It didn't make sense. The victim wasn't famous. The accused wasn't famous. Their local paper, she could understand. But why all the others?

Then a reporter who Rebecca didn't care for one bit cornered the district attorney. "We've gotten word that you are running for governor of Montana."

The man held up a hand as his audience waited with notepads and pencils held ready to write down whatever spewed out of his mouth. "The issue right now is seeing justice done for poor Mr. Horace Bradstreet. I will give a statement about any political interests later."

Huh. Later. Of course. Very ambiguous. Which meant everyone had to stick around and watch the show. No wonder the man had been so dramatic yesterday. He wanted the audience and the reporters watching. Not just the jury.

Rebecca seethed, but she closed her eyes. This was not the time to allow anyone to see her emotions. She simply had to learn to control her features. Especially if she wanted to be a lawyer someday.

One of the articles she'd read stressed that a good lawyer had to develop a good "poker face," whatever that meant.

Probably meant not giving away what was in one's hand. Which made sense.

Well, she had quite a hand to play. And she intended to use it.

Court went back in session and Rebecca recorded every word. Every reaction. Every motion.

Why Judge Ashbury allowed the district attorney to hash and rehash the same points he'd covered the last few days was beyond her, but then again, she didn't yet know the law.

Not only did the DA say the same thing over and over, but he did it with different testimony on the stand. He'd found people in town who had served Bradstreet. People who all testified that yes, indeed, Horace Bradstreet was carrying a wallet.

The judge called a recess and Rebecca scrambled to the ladies' restroom. She was hesitant to leave, but couldn't wait any longer and wanted to make sure she was prepared for the rest of the session.

The courtroom was in a bit of chaos when she returned and she had to push her way back in.

That was when she felt something on her hip. But she was surrounded by people. She moved quickly to her place up by the judge and took her seat.

Something poked her in her right thigh.

Rebecca frowned and reached in her right pocket. There was a stiff piece of paper. Where did that come from?

Studying the crowd, she checked the room, but no one watched her. She pulled out the paper and read the neat and bold script:

If you know what's good for you, stop snooping

Her heart jumped up into her throat and beat like she'd been running a race. She shoved the paper back in her pocket and checked the room again. But everyone seemed focused on conversations. Not her.

Who could have put the note there? Racking her brain, she tried to recollect the faces she'd seen as she pushed her way back into the courtroom. But she hadn't been focused on that.

"All rise."

This was no time for her to fall apart. Nothing could happen to her in the middle of the courtroom. And afterward, she'd simply have to take the note to the judge.

The court was back in session and the DA held up a piece of paper and approached the bench. "Your Honor, I would like to enter this in as a piece of evidence." He showed it to the judge.

Judge Ashbury inclined his head. "So noted."

The DA swung to the jury. "Allow me to read this to the court."

"Proceed." The judge didn't sound happy.

Oh boy. Rebecca hated to even think what was in the slimy, politically hungry district attorney's hands.

"This is a newspaper clipping from Kansas City dated July 9, 1892. In it, the arrest of one Joseph Cameron for armed robbery is listed."

The room erupted in chatter and gasps.

The judge pounded his gavel. "Order!"

The gallery was quick to respond. No one wanted to miss whatever happened next.

The lawyer went back to his table and picked up another piece of paper. "Your Honor, I'd like to present this additional piece of evidence."

"Bring forth the exhibit." Judge Ashbury held out an arm.

The DA handed him the paper.

The judge read it and then handed it back. "I presume this has been verified?"

"The telegraph operator is here to testify to that effect."

"Proceed."

The district attorney lifted the telegram. "This is a telegram from the sheriff in Kansas City, who has been the sheriff since 1890." He cleared his throat. "'Joseph Cameron is a common thief who used a *knife* to threaten his prey.'"

Mrs. Cameron began to cry.

Joseph's head drooped.

The gallery stared.

"Read the rest, counselor."

At the judge's command, the district attorney paused, then lifted the note and read in a much softer voice. "'He served his time and was released into the care of a Pastor Rawlings, who put him to work for the Baptist Church.'"

Whispers traveled throughout the courtroom.

The district attorney sat down.

"Order." The gavel hit the desk several times. "Does the prosecution have anything else?"

"No, Your Honor."

Judge Ashbury looked at the clock and down at his desk. "The court will adjourn for today. The defense may call their first witness Monday morning at nine a.m. sharp. Court is adjourned."

Praise God the judge was willing to adjourn today. That meant she should have time to get to the library, do some research, and then write up something for the defense attorney. If she had it delivered to him this evening, he would have time to read it and prepare for Monday.

Rebecca rushed back to her desk to transcribe all her notes.

Hope sprang up within her. She *could* do something about this grave injustice. Because now she knew for certain . . .

Joe Cameron was innocent.

Once she finished up with her transcriptions, Rebecca remembered the note. While fear was still prevalent, she had something else she wished to speak to the judge about. And if she told him about the note, he might not allow her to even continue in her job.

Worry and curiosity battled. But her drive to discover the truth won out.

At his chambers, she knocked on the door and braced herself.

"Come in."

With a bit more confidence than she felt, she prepared her speech. "Judge Ashbury?"

"Yes, Miss Whitman?" His tone was resigned as he took off his spectacles.

"I'm sorry to disturb you, sir. But here are my transcriptions and I did have a request."

"Miss Whitman, you know my stance—"

"Forgive me for interrupting." Instead of her usual furrowed brow when she was inquisitive, she'd determined to smile and look the innocent student. "I don't wish to be rude, but I'm not here about that. You've taught me well that justice needs to be blind. I am also learning how important research is to the law. I know that I have a lot to learn if I want to become a lawyer. In fact, I'm headed to the library now to begin my studies, which brings me to my question. Would it be possible for me to see the police reports submitted from the investigation into Mr. Cameron? I think it would be highly educational to see how the investigative process works."

His eyebrows raised. "That is commendable of you, Miss Whitman, to further your education." Several seconds ticked by as he studied her.

Could he see her thoughts on her face? Was there any chance he knew why she *really* wanted to see the reports?

"I will grant your request, and not just because I have a soft spot for you, my dear. They are of public record and have already been submitted for the trial. Far be it from me to quench the fire for the law that I see in your eyes." He stood. "Follow me. But they must—and I can't emphasize this enough—they *must* be back on my desk before court resumes. Understood?"

"Yes, sir. Thank you for the opportunity."

Several minutes later, armed with the reports, Rebecca made a dash for the library. When she entered the building, she hung up her coat and took her things to the circulation desk.

"Rebecca. How lovely to see you. How's the trial going? Any new developments?"

The eagerness in Mark's eyes to see her was a balm to her dry and thirsty spirit. "Good evening. That's why I'm here. First, I need to see books on the laws of Montana pertaining to jury trials. Specifically murder trials."

"Hm . . . you're stretching my librarian brainpower." His

face scrunched up as he pondered her request. "I know we have a section on the law, but I'm not sure about the specifics contained within." He pointed to the clock on the wall. "When I close up in thirty minutes, I need to get home to Dad, but perhaps you could bring whatever we find to my apartment. Dad and I would love to help you search through all of it. I'm assuming it's needed quickly?"

"Yes, very." She leaned closer, checked to make sure no one else was around, and whispered. "In fact, it's imperative that I get something off to Mr. Cameron's lawyer tonight as soon as possible."

"I see. Then I guess we better get to work."

"Indeed. A man's life is on the line."

19

M ark unlocked his apartment door and opened it for Rebecca to enter. "Here you go."

He went to his bedroom while she settled into the parlor. "Dad?" he called through the open doorway.

"Hello there, son." His father was sitting up all the way. Not just propped up with pillows. And there was pink in his cheeks.

Mark tried not to look surprised, but it obviously didn't work.

"Don't look so shocked." Dad put his hands in his lap.

Nurse Chambers grinned. "Your father has been reading to *me* today. *Moby Dick*, I think it is?"

"You got it." Angus Andrews practically beamed. "And I think she might like it."

Mark stepped closer to the bed. "Dad, wow. You look great. You must be feeling a good deal better."

"I am. Almost miraculous, I'd say. I don't know if it's the change of scenery, or the nurse here, or getting to spend time with my son . . . but it's working."

The nurse nodded. "He has improved steadily all day long. Even walked himself to the water closet earlier without any assistance."

He couldn't quite believe it. *Thank You, God!* Mark held up a finger. "You know, I'm going to use the hall telephone to call Doc. I bet he'll want to see this."

His dad nodded.

Nurse Chambers called out, "Mrs. Ashbury delivered dinner again. It's in the kitchen."

Turning to the parlor, he ran smack-dab into Rebecca. "Oh, I'm so sorry." He caught her arms. "I didn't realize you were there."

"That's all right, but I heard your father's voice and he sounds so much better. I had to come see my checkers rival." She grinned and went into the bedroom.

"I'll be right back." Mark didn't think it mattered if anyone heard. They were fine without him anyway.

Running, he made it to the phone just in time to see Mrs. Simmons finishing up a call.

"It's all yours, Mark dear." She hung up the phone.

"Thank you!" He put the earpiece to his ear and clicked. "Operator."

"Doc Hart, please."

"One moment."

The line was silent for a second.

Mark shifted his weight.

"Hello?"

"Doc Hart. This is Mark Andrews. You won't believe it, but Dad is sitting up for long periods and he walked by himself today."

"Land's sakes. I'll be right over."

"Thanks, Doc. I had a feeling you would say that."

Mark hung up the phone and hurried back to his apartment, where he heard the joyous sounds of laughter and his dad's strong voice.

He wasn't sure what God was up to, but boy, oh boy, he was grateful.

He glanced at the table and took in all the dinner dishes that Marvella brought over.

That woman. She was eccentric. Over-the-top in so many ways. But she had a heart that was pure gold. She loved to serve those she loved. And what a blessing it was.

He didn't have a lot of fancy dishes, but he brought out the mismatched set that he had and served everyone a plate of delectable goodies from Mrs. O'Neil's kitchen.

"If you'll all sit at the table, I'll bring the food. Doc is on his way, so Nurse Chambers, you should just join us. I'm thinking Doc will want to talk to you and get your report. Besides, there is more than enough food."

Rebecca offered her arm to Dad. It made Mark smile the way she'd just become a part of the family.

Whoa, now. Slow down those thoughts.

That was the smart thing to do, of course. But as soon as he'd allowed himself to admit that he cared for her, well, his heart was taking off without him. Good heavens, part of his family? They hadn't even courted yet!

One by one, he brought everyone a plate then offered a prayer of thanks for Dad's continued recovery and for the food.

Dad shared stories about ranch life when he was younger and learning how to take care of cattle. He had them all roaring with laughter thinking of the great big, strong Angus

Andrews being a scrawny kid, hanging on to the horns of a bull for dear life.

"Knock knock!" Doc's voice caused them all to turn toward the doorway. "I let myself in. Hope that's all right."

"Of course, of course." Mark jumped to his feet. "Would you like a plate of food? Marvella sent enough for about ten."

"No, thanks. I already had my supper." The doc's eyes were wide. "But ain't this a sight." His head slowly shook back and forth. "I don't ever think I've seen a patient recover so fast." He set his bag down and placed his hands on his hips. "When Mark said you had been to the table for dinner, I just about fell off my chair. Thought for sure maybe you'd overdone it. But now look at you."

"I'm feeling pretty good, Doc." Dad patted his chest. "There's still a bit of a cough, but I feel like I can breathe just fine. Not only that, but that malaise I was feeling and lack of appetite . . . it's gone."

The doctor leaned over and listened to his father's chest. "Let's go to the bedroom where I can give you a complete exam." The two men left the table and Mark couldn't help but smile. Dad was moving slow, but it seemed like he was nearly his old self again.

Doc Hart came out and chuckled. "I've never seen anything like it."

"So this isn't just a fluke? He has improved?" Mark hated to be skeptical, but he'd heard plenty of cases of people rallying and then going into a rapid decline.

"I wasn't sure what to think at first, but his lungs are almost clear. Which is nothing short of a miracle. I think the stomach illness he was having made the pneumonia that much worse because he felt bad and wasn't getting out of bed. When you stay abed too long it can make pneumonia progress rapidly, as everything settles in the lungs."

"Stomach illness?"

"Yeah, he didn't tell you? He'd been having bad spells every week or so. It got particularly bad right before he caught pneumonia out in the blizzard. But that seems to have passed. In fact, if he continues to improve, you could move him back to the ranch this weekend." Doc picked up his bag, coat, and hat. "If you'll excuse me, I'm going to head on home to my wife now." He grinned and walked to the door.

"Thank you, Doc. I appreciate it."

"You've done a good job, Mark, taking care of your father. I know it hasn't been long, but he recognizes the care and concern. He's appreciative. Even if he doesn't say it in words."

Doc's words did a world of good to Mark's heart. Maybe he and Dad could get to a good place where they didn't rub each other the wrong way every time they talked about the ranch. Wouldn't that be wonderful?

"Nurse Chambers, I have my buggy. May I give you a lift home? I don't think Mark will be needing your assistance at night anymore."

"That would be delightful." She was already putting on her coat. "I'll see you in the morning, Mark."

He closed the door behind the doctor and stepped over to where Rebecca sat on the settee in the parlor. She already had numerous tomes open in front of her, but she'd tucked her feet up under her skirt and was engrossed in some papers.

He sat next to her. "What has you so mesmerized?"

"Let me finish reading." She held up a finger.

Mark got back up and checked on his dad. He was already asleep. The day of activity and good news had apparently worn him out. Mark shut off the light and quietly closed the door.

When he went back to the settee, he took his place next to Rebecca again.

She clicked her tongue. "You're not going to believe this."

"What?"

"These are the police investigation reports from the Bradstreet murder case. Judge Ashbury allowed me to take them so I could learn more about the law." Leaning toward him, she tapped the page. "Look at this. It hasn't been brought up in the trial at all."

"I'm afraid I don't know what I'm looking at. Footprints?"

"Yes. They found footprints that matched Horace and Joe. We know that. But there was another set of footprints that were much larger than Joe's."

"Right. We know that Harvey was there." He raised his eyebrows. "Tell me what you're thinking, because I'm afraid I don't think like a lawyer or an investigator."

"Okay, so on the north side of the victim, the mud and snow was all a mess and smeared together, presumably because of the struggle between Harvey and Joe, right?"

"Makes sense."

"But there were footprints on the *south* side of the victim. The side where Joe was leaning over the body. One set was Joe's. The other set didn't match Joe's." Her face lit up like she'd solved the case. "Don't you see?"

Even after all the mysteries he'd read, he wasn't putting

two and two together. Either because of the beautiful woman next to him, who distracted him with every move she made, or because he wasn't enough of a sleuth. What was she thinking? "No. Sorry, I'm still not understanding. How does this prove Joe's innocence?"

"Because in Harvey's testimony, he said that he was never on the south side of the victim. The side where Horace was presumably stabbed. The side where *Joe* presumably stabbed him."

An awful dread made his stomach curdle. "Do you think that Harvey . . . ?" He couldn't finish the question. No. His sister's husband seemed to be a decent man. Kate was an incredible judge of character. So was his father.

Rebecca's face had paled considerably and a new sadness filled her eyes. "No. Maybe. I don't know. We can't jump to conclusions and accuse another man who might be innocent, but Harvey hasn't been honest. We know that much. We have no idea what his motive was. Whether he had something against Joe or if he was paid to lie . . . now, you can tell I've read too many mysteries. None of it makes sense. But right now, the fact remains that there's nothing in the reports about Harvey's footprints. Why didn't this get mentioned in court? Because it wasn't helpful to the prosecution's case. It would cast doubt. And the jury can only convict . . ."

"Beyond a reasonable doubt."

"Beyond a reasonable doubt."

They both said it at the same time as they nodded.

Her face lit up again. "This is it! This combined with my experiment from last night should give the defense attorney enough for his case! Thank you, Mark, thank you *so* much!" Rebecca let out a little squeal and then practically jumped into his arms. She squeezed his neck so tight, he couldn't breathe.

Tapping her arm, he wheezed, "You're welcome."

Immediately she released him. "Sorry! Sometimes I do get a bit overzealous when I'm excited." She bit her lip.

Her face was only about a foot away from his. And as their gazes connected, Mark was drawn like a magnet to her lips. "I enjoy watching you as inspiration hits."

They studied each other for several seconds.

Then she licked her lips and he blinked. Everything in that moment made him wish he *wasn't* a gentleman.

Easing himself back a few inches, he took a long breath. "I know you wanted to write something up for Mr. Cameron's lawyer before it got too late. Is there anything I can do to help?"

Her head jerked back to the papers. "Oh, yes. Let me get started on a letter. Do you know how we can have it delivered in such a way that it can remain anonymous?" She tucked some stray curls behind her ear, and her cheeks flushed.

So she'd felt it too.

That made his heart soar. Maybe, once all of the hubbub was past, he could speak to her about being a bit *more* than friends.

Wait. She'd asked him a question. "Um . . . I can go down to the corner by the mercantile. There's usually a paperboy or two willing to run errands for a few cents. At least until around eight." He glanced at his watch. "It's seven thirty now. I'll run down and see if I can fetch one."

"Thank you."

She gave him a smile, but this one was different from all the other times she'd smiled at him.

It sent his heart into overdrive.

She shook her head, as though to clear it. "I'll write as fast as I can."

Pulling on his coat and hat, Mark made his way out into the evening with a new bounce in his step.

Harvey followed the kid through the streets of Kalispell. He'd watched Mark give the kid an envelope outside Miss Whitman's apartment building. This must be it. It had been far too long of a day attempting to figure out what Miss Whitman would try. Now he would find out.

At least he'd had the foresight to wear his good suit into town today. That made him look respectable. Which he would need right now if his instincts were correct.

The kid jogged and Harvey had a tough time keeping up with him and staying hidden at the same time. But then he saw the small boy look at the envelope and slow down. He approached a nice little home with a picket fence out front.

Harvey read the mailbox.

Perfect.

The defense lawyer's name.

He caught up to the kid and tapped him on the shoulder. "Good evening, young man. Out to run an errand?"

"Yessir. To the lawyer man here."

"Well, isn't that Providence. I'm headed to visit him right now." He held out a nickel. "Why don't you allow me to take it in for you."

"Wow, mister. Thanks!" The boy slapped the envelope in Harvey's hands and then ran off toward the mercantile.

For several moments, he stood and observed everything around him to make sure no one was watching out of the neighbor windows. Out of the lawyer's house.

Nope. No one had seen a thing.

Harvey tucked the envelope into his pocket and headed home.

Now to think up a story to tell Kate.

20

Rebecca wrote with lightning speed on her pad. The defense attorney had called Joe to the stand and he was giving his testimony.

She knew everything that he said. Had heard the story enough times. Read the police investigation reports.

When would the attorney bring up the blood spatter on Mr. Monroe? The shoe prints. It was difficult to keep her seat as she waited for the moment of truth.

"Mr. Cameron, is there anything else you would like to say to the court?" The lawyer was soft-spoken. Nothing like the dramatic beast of a DA.

Joseph Cameron turned to the jury and made eye contact with each one of them. "I did not kill Mr. Horace Bradstreet. I did not steal from him. I know it's hard to believe since I once was a thief. But that was a long time ago. I have been an honorable citizen ever since."

"Amen!" Marvella's voice cut through the silence from

the gallery and Rebecca had to work to keep from smiling or laughing.

"Order!" Judge Ashbury called down.

Several people chuckled.

Joe continued. "I am asking you to believe me. I went to help the man. I had seen another man hovering over him before I got there. *That* man must've stabbed him. Not me." Tears streamed down Joe's face.

Rebecca fought tears herself, but kept writing. How could they not believe that heartfelt testimony?

The judge opened the floor for closing arguments.

Wait. Why hadn't the defense attorney brought up anything else? She blinked hard and stared at the man. But he didn't appear to be preparing anything else.

With everything in her, she wanted to yell out for everything to stop. But she couldn't. She'd lose her job. The judge would throw her out of the courtroom. Nothing would be admissible and the trial would have to start all over again.

So she swallowed and took notes.

The DA pontificated for almost twenty minutes.

The defense attorney said one simple sentence. "Joe Cameron is innocent."

And then they sat down. By this point, Rebecca wanted to run from the room screaming. It couldn't be over. It couldn't!

The judge spoke to the jury. Gracious, she had to write all of it down.

He gave instructions. They were dismissed to a room to deliberate.

Everyone else sat and waited.

The judge went to his chambers.

Rebecca stood up on shaky legs and walked to her desk.

Her mind swirled with options, but all of them included breaking her vow to the judge and the court. If she talked to Marvella about what she knew. If she spoke to the defense attorney.

She'd read enough in those law books late last night to know that she had no choice. If she wanted to be a lawyer one day, she couldn't cross the line now. Especially as a woman. They'd never allow her to practice law.

Oh, if only Mark was here. He was the only one who knew everything she did. But she couldn't leave the courthouse. The jury could come back any minute with a ruling.

At this point, her only option was to pray. And pray hard.

I don't even know what to say. But God . . . he's innocent, isn't he? I can't bear to see another innocent man go to prison. . . .

Everything from that experience as a child came roaring back. Her mind was flooded with the memories. Everything she'd tried to do.

It wasn't your fault.

The words washed over her. She opened her eyes and stared at her trembling hands. It wasn't her fault no one believed the testimony of a ten-year-old girl. It wasn't her fault that the man died in prison.

As much as she'd wanted to change everything, there was nothing she could have done different. She'd done her best.

Just like now.

It was so hard to trust anyone but herself, and yet . . .

Who better to trust than the Creator of the Universe? *She* couldn't fix this. But He could.

God knew what was happening. Surely, He wouldn't allow an innocent man to be convicted.

Marvella was on a mission.

She marched back to her husband's chambers, lifted her hand, and gave the door a hearty knock.

"Come in."

Opening the door with a flourish, she got ready to give the judge her famous stare. The one that always put him in his place. But when she saw his face, her heart plummeted. "Oh, my dear." She closed the door and rushed to his side.

"I don't know what to do." He shook his head. "I never thought it would come to this point. I have lectured everyone around about how wonderful and trustworthy our legal system is and today, I feel we have failed. What if the jury convicts Joe?"

If her husband was this broken . . . willing to talk about the trial and how he felt about it when the verdict hadn't even been given, things were dire indeed. "Rebecca left the courtroom in a rush. Positively pale. I think this has taken its toll on her as well."

"I've failed her too. Told her not to get involved because the legal system worked. Cameron's lawyer would surely do his job. But the prosecutor had bigger fish in his sights with this one. I don't know why I didn't see it."

Placing her hand on her chest, she dipped her chin. "What do you mean?"

"The district attorney is about to announce that he's running for governor."

She gasped. "No!" Why that sleazy, slimy little worm.

She never did like him. No wonder he paraded around the courtroom the way he did.

And the press. They had newspapers from all over the state in the courtroom.

"My dear, I am so sorry for how I've treated you during all this. You know that I think you are the most honorable of all men, don't you?"

"Yes, my dear." He smiled up at her. "I know. But it is nice to hear." He gripped her hand. "You are just like Rebecca, you hate to see injustice done."

"Well, as I see it, the best thing we can do with our time right now is to bring it to Almighty God and lay it at His feet."

"Once again, my dear. You are correct."

"I know."

Lunch had passed. And then several hours more.

Rebecca sat at her desk, reading the law books she'd borrowed from the library. After pouring out her heart to God, then having a nice long cry, then a bit more praying, she'd forced herself to sit down in her chair and make good use of the time.

In the last four hours, she'd filled up twenty-five sheets of paper with notes.

She would make an excellent law student, if she did say so herself.

"Miss Whitman." The bailiff called to her from the doorway. "The judge has requested everyone's presence in the courtroom."

"Thank you." Swallowing back the bile that threatened to creep up her throat, she stood. Picked up her stenographer's notebook and a couple of pencils, then headed to the courtroom.

The room was quiet. Quieter than she'd ever heard it.

"All rise."

Judge Ashbury entered and took his seat.

Everyone else sat.

A pin could drop and she would probably hear it.

Taking a deep breath, she held it.

"The jury has not been able to come to a decision."

Oh no. More waiting. But at least there was more time . . . for someone to *do* something. She wanted to melt into a puddle right then and there, but she blinked and did her best to keep a straight face.

The judge continued. "Court is adjourned until tomorrow morning when they will continue their deliberations until a verdict is reached." He pounded the gavel, stood up, and left the courtroom.

Rebecca took her notes back to her desk. She'd already transcribed everything from earlier today. All she needed to do was finish up what just happened and then she could escape this place.

And, God willing, the cry within her heart screaming that she'd failed.

Again.

21

MONDAY, MARCH 7, 1904

The bell over the door jangled and Mark looked up in time to see Rebecca rush into the library, tears streaming down her cheeks.

With quick steps, he went around the circulation desk.

She walked straight into his arms and sobbed against his shoulder.

He let her cry, and when she pulled back, he offered her his handkerchief. "Did they convict Joe?"

She shook her head and mopped up her face. "No. Not yet. The jury couldn't come to a decision. That means there are men who think he did it."

"Why don't you come sit with me for a few minutes? There are several ladies looking for books right now, but when they need help, they can come find me."

"Okay."

He took her hand in his and walked her to his desk. They'd never touched like that, but after she cried in his arms, he took the chance that things could be different between them. He sat her in the chair, and then he lowered himself to the corner of the desk. "Are you allowed to tell me what happened?"

For the next several minutes, she shared the events of the trial. How devastated she was that the defense attorney didn't use any of the information she'd sent to him. "Maybe he thought whoever wrote it was a fraud since it was sent anonymously. Maybe he didn't take the time to investigate. Whatever the reason . . . I failed. If Joe gets convicted, I don't know what I'll do. I can't go through this again."

Mark squeezed her shoulder. "Have you told the judge about what you witnessed as a child?"

She nodded. "He knows that's the main reason I became a court stenographer."

"I'm glad you told him. I bet this is killing him inside."

"You wouldn't know by the way he's made all of us not talk about it." The bitterness in her voice was unlike her.

"But that's his job. Wouldn't you want a judge to be unbiased?"

With a huff, she rolled her eyes at him. "You always have to point out the obvious, don't you?"

The bell jangled over the door again. "Look, I've got quite a bit of work to do here and it's nearly time to close up. Why don't you go over to my apartment? Help my dad eat up all that yummy food that Marvella keeps sending over and play some checkers with him. He'll love it. And it will probably help you feel better too. After that you can ride with us to the ranch. I'm taking Dad home."

"Taking him home. Already?"

"He's more than ready to go. Look, it'll probably be dark before we get back and I wouldn't want to do anything to risk your reputation, but Dad would enjoy your company. Plus, I'd like to introduce you to my sister."

"I'm not worried about my reputation. Mr. Tuttle seems to think it's already ruined since I work a job outside of the home. I'll be happy to ride along. Anything to get my mind off of the trial." She gave him a half smile and stood.

Since she was above him now, he had to look up at her.

She put her hand on his cheek. "Thank you. I'll see you later?"

"I'll be there as soon as I can."

Arms loaded down with books, Rebecca made her way out to the wagon. Angus was raring to go back to the ranch.

Not that he wanted to leave Mark. He'd made sure to re-iterate that time and again. But he balked at having a nurse hover over him. Complained about the cost. And he wanted to get back to his own room with his special view. Especially now that he was feeling so much better. All he could talk about was helping Kate prepare the ranch for the spring and summer. It was his favorite time to plan for the year and dream big.

Rebecca had done her best to keep her thoughts on Angus and not on the fact that Harvey lived on the ranch as well. Why was Mark so calm about bringing his father home if he suspected Harvey as well? At the very least, the man had lied. Right? Hadn't they proven that?

But as she watched Mark, she couldn't deny him the joy of seeing his father on the mend. If he wasn't worried about Harvey, then she shouldn't be.

That was easier said than done. She adored Angus and didn't want to see him suffer, but it was all too easy for her to blame Harvey for everything. It was the only thing that made sense.

As Rebecca made it to the wagon, she heaved the books into the bed and purposed to keep her thoughts light and happy. "Think this will be enough for him?"

Mark laughed. "For about a week, maybe. He's determined to read all my favorite books so that we'll have something to discuss and won't fight about the ranch."

It was good to see that sparkle back in Mark's eye. He wasn't worried about losing his dad anymore.

"Well, I think that was the last load."

Mark adjusted things in the bed of the wagon. "Why don't you tell Dad to come on down."

Angus had refused any help earlier, so Rebecca was sure this would be fun. Probably why Mark sent her rather than going himself.

After another trek up the stairs, she ran into Angus in the hallway. "A bit anxious to get home, are we?"

"Not anxious to leave you, lass." He winked. "You can come visit me as often as you like."

"Why? So you can wallop me at checkers every time?"

"No"—he made a face—"that wouldn't be the reason at all. You could bring those cookies with ya."

Oh, how he brought out the laughter in her, even in the midst of this horrible waiting with the trial. "I'll come as often as I can. The wagon's ready." She held out her arm as they started down the entry steps.

He studied it for a moment.

"It's not for you, Mr. Andrews. I'm quite certain you don't

need the help. It's for me. I've been up and down these stairs so many times, I'm afraid my poor legs might give out any moment."

He took her arm. "Bring that handsome son of mine along with you when you visit, please. It'll be good to see him more often."

"He loves spending time with you."

"I'm a-thinkin' that he loves spending time with *you*."

She patted his arm. "Oh, Mr. Andrews. We're just good friends."

"Not according to the blush in your cheeks."

Now she knew where Mark got his charm. And his smile. Roguish as it was. For the life of her, she couldn't think of a good response.

Her cheeks heated even more.

"Now what have you done to Miss Whitman, Dad? She's positively pink!" Mark stood behind the wagon, hands on his hips. Smiling.

Gracious, that smile.

"Not a thing, son. Not a thing." Angus released her and walked over to the side of the wagon.

"Here, let me give you a hand." Mark went to his father's side.

"Many thanks." He huffed as he made it onto the seat. "I'm not quite as strong as I'd like. Not yet."

Mark darted back over to Rebecca. "Let me help you up. Hope you don't mind sitting in the middle?"

"Not at all. It'll keep me warm."

He quirked an eyebrow.

She swatted his arm. "Because I'll be between you two. You'll block the wind. Oh, you know what I mean."

With his hands on her waist, he lifted her up into the wagon.

Warm indeed.

Harvey sat in the parlor listening to the family chatter. He gave an occasional smile and kept an arm around Kate's shoulders.

Blast this turn of events!

His plan was so simple. Get in, get married, get rid of the wife, get out. With all the money, of course. But this time had been more complicated from the beginning. Kate had been worth it, though. Fiery, beautiful, strong Kate.

He wouldn't mind keeping her if she wasn't such a church-going, goody-two-shoes.

But the greatest complication of all was Angus.

Harvey almost arranged good ol' Angus's demise by putting a little lye soap in his hot chocolate every night. It was working too . . . until they moved him to town. Angus's death would have put the ranch into Kate's hands and Mark's. And it hadn't taken much for him to come up with a plan to eliminate both of them.

But now, Angus was back and in decent health. To make matters worse, he was on good terms with Mark.

How could things have gone so wrong? He'd have to start all over with Angus. But this time, he'd gotten ahold of some thallium. Which would make things quicker and easier. And no one would be the wiser, because Angus had just been sick.

Good thing, too. He was ready for things to go his way. That cursed Horace Bradstreet had made a mess out of everything. Which necessitated he get out of town sooner rather than later.

Too many people had seen his handsome face this time. He wasn't a man who blended in. People would remember his good looks and his testimony in the murder trial.

So, by this time next week, he needed to be rid of the Andrews family and on his way.

Maybe to Mexico for a while. Until he ran out of money.

Then he'd have to go find wife number ten.

22

The morning had been the longest he'd ever endured. At least it felt that way. He must have glanced at the clock at least a hundred times. But it hadn't made it move any faster, and it hadn't brought anyone into the library.

The entire town was probably at the courthouse, waiting for the verdict.

Mark had prayed for Rebecca, knowing what a huge toll this was taking on her heart. But she was strong. It only made her fervor to become a lawyer stronger.

Funny, he wanted to cheer her on. Women working outside the home wasn't exactly the norm, as Sam Tuttle was happy to point out. But if anyone could do it, Rebecca could.

The world needed more people like Rebecca.

He needed Rebecca.

It was hard to believe that she'd only arrived a little more than a month ago. And oh, they'd clashed. But now . . .

He couldn't think of life without her.

It was probably time to send that letter to her father that he'd started over a week ago. Because he didn't know how long he'd be able to wait to tell her how he felt.

The bell over the door jangled and Mark stood up to see who it was. "Chief Crane. Good to see you."

"You too, Andrews."

"I figured you'd be at the courthouse."

"Marshal Shelton is there. I'm headed over now, but I needed to get these new wanted posters to you so you could get them posted on the bulletin board." He handed him a stack of papers, nodded, and headed back toward the door.

"Thanks, Chief." At least this would give him something to do for a few minutes. Each month, he was given a list of criminals who had been caught so he could remove the old posters and make room for the new ones. It seemed like each time, there were more and more. What was the world coming to?

The stack today was thicker than usual.

He started with the list of ones to take down. Once he had the dozen or so taken care of, he straightened up the ones on the board and then started placing the new ones. Hopefully there would be enough room.

Somehow, this always made him feel like he needed to wash his hands. Probably because of reading the horrible things these men did.

Ugh. Not his favorite part of the job, but a good public service. Many a criminal had been caught because a good citizen recognized him from one of the posters.

The board was almost full. He riffled through the last in the stack. Four more.

He shifted things a bit closer so he'd have enough room. Then placed another poster. Then anoth—

He froze.

David Morris. Wanted for murdering his wife with poison. All for her inheritance.

Mark swallowed. Stared.

His heart plummeted. No. It couldn't be.

But he couldn't deny the resemblance.

Shave off the beard and mustache in the picture, and David Morris was a dead ringer for Harvey Monroe.

Kate! If Harvey was this David Morris person, she . . . and Dad! They could be in serious danger.

And the trial! Harvey's testimony was all a lie. Exactly as Rebecca thought.

He had to get to the courthouse. Maybe he still had a chance to save Joe. But he also needed to get out to the ranch . . .

Before Harvey did something awful to his family.

"All rise." The call from the bailiff didn't make Rebecca feel any better. In fact, her stomach threatened to climb up her throat. But at least it would all be over soon.

She closed her eyes for a second and kept her pencil hovered over her notepad.

Judge Ashbury came in and everyone sat down. "Has the jury reached a verdict?"

The man at the end of the jury box stood. "We have, Your Honor."

"What have you decided?"

"The jury has decided that Joe Cameron is guilty of murder."

The court erupted.

Rebecca couldn't bear to look up. Couldn't imagine what Joe and his wife were thinking . . . feeling.

The gavel pounded over and over again until the crowd quieted.

The judge cleared his throat. "Court is adjourned for today. Tomorrow morning, I will give sentencing." He tossed the gavel down and walked out of the court.

Rebecca searched the crowd.

At the back, Harvey Monroe smiled at her.

Was he the one who'd shoved that note in her pocket? Oh, why hadn't she done anything about it? Brought it to the judge? Or the police?

All because of her silly pride. She hadn't wanted to get removed from the trial or lose her job. The very thought of proving Samuel Tuttle correct about women in the workplace made her want to scream.

But it had been wrong. *She'd* been wrong.

When she glanced back, Monroe was gone.

Her fists clenched. This wasn't over. It *couldn't* be over. Something had to be done.

Picking up her things, she marched toward the judge's chambers.

"Rebecca! *Rebecca!*"

Mark! She spun on her heel and searched the faces. He barreled toward her, his eyes wide, and shoved a wanted poster at her.

With a gasp, she covered her mouth. "That's Harvey, isn't it?"

He nodded, out of breath.

The man hadn't just lied about Joe. The gravity of the situation hit her . . . Angus!

Rebecca caught Marvella's eye. "Marvella." She waved at her to follow and tried to force her stomach to stay where it was.

When they reached the judge's chambers, she knocked. "Come in."

They'd all been leaning on the door so much they almost fell into the room. And then everyone started talking at once.

"Look at this wanted poster!" Rebecca held it out.

"Something has to be done about Joe. Can't we appeal?" Marvella's resonant voice.

"Sir, the verdict must be overturned!"

The judge held up a hand and took the poster.

He studied it for a moment and narrowed his eyes. "Where is Monroe?"

"He was in the courtroom just a few minutes ago. I saw him heading for the door after the verdict."

Mark frowned. "He's going back to the ranch. I have to go there!"

"It says here he poisoned his wife." The judge glanced again at the poster. "When your dad first got sick, Doc told me it reminded him of a person who'd gotten into poison. Do you suppose Monroe poisoned your father?"

Mark's frown deepened. "Dad started making marked improvement after I brought him to my apartment. If Harvey was poisoning him, Dad's rapid recovery would make sense. Once he was with me, Harvey couldn't poison him any longer."

The judge turned to Mark. "Go get the chief of police

and then take one of my horses and get out to the ranch. Who knows what this man is capable of if he suspects we're onto him."

"But he doesn't, right?" Rebecca squeaked the question.

Mark shook his head. "Let's pray not."

The judge looked at his wife. "Marvella, my dear, go get the driver and carriage. I need to head out to the ranch as well. I want to be there to see this man arrested." He turned to Rebecca. "Miss Whitman, please document everything we've uncovered in case anything goes awry. You and Marvella can keep each other company."

While she hated the thought of sitting on the side and waiting for justice to prevail, she respected the man too much to disagree with him. "Yes, sir."

The judge slammed his hand on his desk. "Let's go catch us a murderer."

"Here ya go, Angus." He handed his father-in-law a cup of hot chocolate. "Maybe this will help you feel better."

Angus's hands shook as he cupped them around the mug. "I don't know what's happened. I was feeling so good." His voice cracked.

"You probably did a bit too much. Nothing a little rest won't fix. Now drink up. I'll come check on you in a little bit." He kept his voice low. Smooth. Concerned.

Harvey closed the door behind him. Shouldn't take too long now. A day or two at most. He allowed the smile that he'd kept to himself to surface.

In the meantime, he could have a bit of fun with Kate. Might as well enjoy his last few days here.

"There you are, *darling*," his wife called to him from down the hall.

But . . .

Did her pet name for him hold a bit of venom?

He strode to her, fully intending to take her into his arms and whisk her off to the bedroom.

But she pulled a hand from behind her back and held something up.

Horace Bradstreet's wallet.

He studied the object and did his best to pretend he'd never seen it before. "What's that?"

"You know full well what it is. And it isn't yours." Kate tapped it against his chest and then stepped back. Her eyes narrowed. The fierceness that he'd admired was now on him full force.

"Where'd you find it?" Best to keep up his ruse. He might still be able to persuade her of his ignorance on the matter.

She took another step back. Her shoulders squared. "I can't believe you'd do something like this. I *believed* in you. *Loved* you."

While heartbreak was written all over her face, Kate wasn't a weak woman. A fact he understood all too well. It had been one of the reasons he was drawn to her. He'd wanted a challenge this time.

Looked like he had it. In spades.

He leaned against the wall and weighed his options. It would be too easy for her to call one of the men. They were nearby. And they would defend her to the death. "Why don't we go out to the barn so we can discuss this?"

"What is there to discuss?" Tears shimmered in her eyes. Along with white-hot fury.

Well, two could play at that game. Enough of the charade. He pulled himself to his full height and stepped toward her. She knew he could overpower her every day and twice on Sundays.

But then she whipped out a knife. "Don't come any closer."

So she wanted to play. Fine. His blood pumped through him. "You wouldn't stab me. Now come on, give me the knife." He lunged.

She was faster.

The blade sank into his shoulder as he grabbed her around the neck with his other hand and squeezed.

Her eyes grew wide and she sputtered.

He chuckled softly. "What's that, my darling wife? Nothing to say?" He spun her around and dragged her into the next room, keeping his hand around her throat until she passed out. Oh, to end her now. But no.

He needed her alive. For the moment.

Yanking the knife from his arm, he clamped his jaw and wrapped his arm in a bandana. Hopefully that would stop the bleeding.

He lifted Kate with his good arm and grit his teeth against the pain as he hefted her over his good shoulder and carried her out to the barn. He plopped her in the two-seater buggy and tied her hands. For good measure, he tied another bandana around her mouth.

Then he raced inside. "Hey, Kimball?"

"Yes, Mr. Monroe?" The man peered around the kitchen door.

Harvey kept his bad arm toward the door and smiled as big as he could. "I'm going to take Kate for a belated honeymoon. Can you make sure that Rodney takes care of things around the ranch?"

The man wiped his hands on a towel and studied him. His brow creased. "Sure." He shrugged.

"Angus is resting in his bedroom."

"All right."

"I'll see you in a few days." With a wave he headed back to gather up Kate. Angus, Mark, and Kate. The most casualties for one of his scams, but it would be worth it.

He'd even throw in Kimball and Rodney if he had to. Maybe even that cute little court stenographer.

His heart raced in pace with the throbbing in his shoulder.

Nothing could stop him now.

Nothing.

23

Mark burst into his father's ranch. Where was Dad? Kate?

"Dad?" He raced to his father's room and found him pale and unconscious.

Footsteps sounded behind him. "Mark. What's wrong?"

He looked at Kimball. "What's wrong with Dad? How long has he been like this?"

The man approached the bed. "He started feeling poorly again last night after you brought him home and took to his bed."

Harvey. He'd poisoned Dad again. He fisted his hands. "Where's Kate?"

"Harvey just left with her not more than thirty minutes ago."

"Left? *Where?*"

"He said he was taking her on a belated honeymoon."

For a moment, Mark thought he might throw up.

"Something's wrong. What is it?" Kimball gripped his arm.

"Harvey is a murderer. He most likely killed that man in town. And his last wife. Who knows who else." Mark

302

yanked the wanted poster out of his pocket and unfolded it. "With poison."

Kimball read it and sat down hard on the bed. "I should have seen this."

"What do you mean?"

"He's been asking to bring your dad's hot cocoa to him, so they can chat." Kimball shook his head. "It's all my fault. He's probably been slipping something in his drink."

Mark shook his head. "Harvey did this. Not you. Now I need you or Rodney to fetch Doc Hart as fast as you can. Tell him we think my father's been poisoned. It may be the only chance we have to save Dad."

"I'll go myself." Kimball raced out of the room.

Mark bent over his dad and kissed his forehead. "God, help him. Please." He stood back up. "Dad, I'm here. I'm going to do everything I can to make sure Kate is all right."

He left the room at a run and headed out to the barn. "Rodney!" It took several shouts, but the man came running.

After Mark filled him in, the judge's carriage raced up the lane. The older man jumped down. "What's happened?"

"Harvey took off with Kate. And I think he's poisoned my father. Kimball went for the doc."

Another carriage barreled toward them. Mark squinted. "What on earth?"

"Marvella." The judge groaned. "I should have known."

The carriage came closer. Rebecca was with her. Of course she was. "Looks like she's got company."

Marvella got down from the carriage and marched through the snow, her face full of fury. "Where is he? Did you catch him?"

"My dear, *you* are not supposed to be here."

She waved a hand at him. "As if anything could induce me to stay behind when there's a monster on the loose. That man is going to pay."

Rebecca was right behind her. She came up to Mark and hugged him. "I'm so sorry."

He relished the comfort. At this point, he didn't know what to do next. "Harvey has Kate."

She released him and tugged on his arm. "There's no time to waste. The police chief will be out here soon. And we need to make a plan."

He followed her inside. "I don't know how we're going to do that. We have no idea what he's up to."

"Oh, yes, we do." Rebecca entered the house and pointed to the table. "Sit."

Everyone did exactly that.

Except Rebecca. She paced around the table. "Harvey is all about the money, right? That's why he poisoned his previous wife?"

"Right." Mark pulled in a deep breath and put all his energy into focusing on Rebecca's words.

"Well, as far as he knows, he's gotten away with everything. If he's poisoned your dad, Mark, then he'll have to kill you and Kate next. To get his precious money."

"But if we all died unexpectedly, wouldn't the authorities be suspicious of him?"

"Yep. And he's going to think of that real soon, if he hasn't already. This man is not a first-time offender, remember. Your dad was sick because I think Harvey was trying to do this slowly. But Horace Bradstreet must have known Harvey and what he was up to. Harvey had to murder him. It's the only thing that makes sense. But if he had planned to do this slowly and then your dad got better while he was with you, he probably knows his time is running out. Which will make him speed up things. Which will make him more prone to mistakes. But he's not stupid.

"I just read a story similar to this. The villain married a woman for her inheritance, and slowly kills off everyone else. I think Harvey's going to do what Mr. Miller did in *The Lady of the House.*"

Mark had just recently given that one to Rebecca and remembered the plot well. Oh . . . "Which means Harvey is going to come for *me* next because he needs Kate to be the last one alive. And then, when she dies . . ."

Rebecca nodded. "He'll inherit."

"Kate, we could have had a lot of fun together."

Her eyes narrowed. If fire could shoot out of them, he was pretty sure she'd decimate him with that look. "You're disgusting."

He'd tied her to the bed in the line shack. With a shrug, he smirked. "Well, after I take care of your brother, I'm going to come here and burn the shack down. They'll find your burned body and figure that you must have fallen asleep with your lantern still burning."

He didn't miss the flicker of uncertainty that passed through those pretty eyes. But anger quickly replaced it. "Mark's too smart for you."

Foolish woman. "Oh, I doubt that. You have no idea what I've done."

Not even a flinch. "I know you killed that man. Why'd you do it?" She didn't seem the least bit afraid of him.

Impressive.

He licked his lips and shrugged. "Because he recognized me. Knew my modus operandi."

Her livid expression morphed as her mouth gaped open. "Modus what?"

"Modus operandi. My operating procedure. How I make my money. Horace knew about each crime . . . each marriage I made." He smiled at her. "And then terminated."

"How many have there been?" She pinched her lips together.

"You were number nine, my *darling*." He dragged a finger down her cheek. "And my favorite by far."

"Don't *touch* me." She jerked against her restraints.

"Oh, don't worry. I'll leave you alone for a bit while I take care of things. But rest assured, I'll be back." He headed for the door. There was more than one way to accomplish his goal. It all depended on if the old man had died yet.

She spat at him. "I'm glad I stabbed you. I hope it hurts."

With Dad safely in Doc's care, Mark sought out the judge. He didn't have time to consider that his father had almost been killed. *Again.* No. His sister's life was on the line, there was a murderer on the loose, and they had to stop him. Harvey was smart, but he couldn't know they were on to him. So how did they get Kate back without putting more people in danger?

"What do we do now?" He swiped a hand through his hair.

The judge's mouth was tight in a thin line under his mustache. "I was just discussing it with the chief. I think since

Monroe will need to know if he was successful in getting rid of Angus, he'll come back to check on things. But somehow, we've got to keep him in the dark. Keep him believing that he's succeeded so far. If he thinks Angus is dead, then he will most likely come after you next. We should use that to our advantage and trap him. It's the only way we know he'll keep Kate alive. He needs to save her for last."

"Why would he have to do that?" Mark rubbed the back of his neck.

The judge put a steadying hand on Mark's shoulder. "Because you both stand to inherit the ranch. Your dad has talked to me about his will. If either of you die before him, then everything goes to the surviving sibling. So if you die first, then Kate will inherit. And when she dies, it all goes to her husband. But if Kate dies first . . ."

"Harvey won't get anything." The pure evil of the man's plan was sickening. What Mark wouldn't give to get his hands on Harvey. . . .

The chief of police nodded. "We don't think he'll risk coming back here to the ranch to find out about your father. He told Kimball that he was taking Kate away for a few days. He'll go into town for news. Quietly. We can set it up so Monroe will think it'll be easy to catch you."

The chief stepped forward then, his hat in his hands, a frown creasing his face. "There's another scenario we have to discuss. We know he has Kate. That's his leverage. If he feels rushed . . ." He took a slow breath and gave Mark a pointed look. "He could use you as leverage against her and threaten to kill you as a way to manipulate her to clean out your father's accounts."

"And then kill her as soon as he's done with her." Mark

shook his head. Too many of these scenarios ended with Kate being killed.

God, please protect her!

The police chief met Mark's eyes. "I have a couple of men I could post at the bank, as customers, just to keep their eyes and ears open. We don't want Harvey to go that route, but we've got to be prepared for every possibility."

Mark couldn't take any more. He slumped into a chair. "So you're saying, he could still kill Kate before he comes after me?" It was easier thinking that he could be the bait and save his sister. He didn't like any of their scenarios. Not one bit.

The chief nodded again. "I'm sorry, son. But yes. That's why we need to be careful. Not spook him. When he comes into town, everything needs to appear normal."

Placing his elbows on his knees, Mark leaned forward. It was one thing to put his own life on the line, but his sister's? He placed his face in his hands. *God, please . . . help.* No other words would form, but the Lord understood the groanings of his heart.

He sat up straight and looked at the chief. "Tell me what you need me to do."

The chief and judge shared a glance. "Go back to town tomorrow. Open the library. Work as if it was any other day. We'll have word sent to you that your father has passed. You can put up a notice at the library then. I'm expecting Monroe will show up either there or at your apartment. Once he learns that he's succeeded, he'll know it's time to eliminate you. We're counting on him wanting to get this all over with so he can disappear while everyone is focused on the trial and sentencing and what he presumes will be the hanging of Joe Cameron."

"Are you sure about this?" Mark didn't like the thought of people thinking his father was dead. Just the ruse made him feel sick to his stomach.

"Monroe's got to be champing at the bit to get out of town. So let's use that against him. Something simple. That always works best." The chief's jaw clenched.

"I agree," the judge replied.

"Well, I for one don't agree." Rebecca stepped forward, hands on her hips. "Is it really wise to use Mark as bait? Can you keep him safe?"

The concern on her face touched Mark deep within his heart. But he reached out his hands to her and placed them on her shoulders. "I'll be fine. Kate is the one we should be worried about. We have to do whatever we can to catch Harvey. Let me do this."

The frown etched on her face didn't ease, but she studied him and he saw the reluctant agreement in her eyes. "All right. But please . . . be careful."

Dr. Hart appeared just then. "I've treated your father with charcoal. Now we'll just have to wait it out and see what happens. This first night is crucial. We can take turns sitting with him to make sure he doesn't go into any distress."

"Mark, if you want us to wait with you, we will." The judge laid a hand on Mark's shoulder.

Mark laid his hand over the old man's. "No. I'd feel better if you went back to town and prepared for whatever comes next. I'll be at the library tomorrow morning. Unless . . ." He couldn't swallow the thought that Harvey might have already won. If Dad died . . .

"Don't even allow that thought." Rebecca came to sit next to him. "I'll stay with you and your dad."

"I'm sure my wife will want to stay as well." The judge nodded to where Marvella slept, snoring softly, in a wingback chair.

Mark nodded and gripped Rebecca's hand. "Thank you."

The older man smiled. "Try not to worry."

"That's right." The chief put his hat on. "I'll post a few men out here to keep watch. Out of sight, of course. If Monroe tries to come back here, they'll get him before he can get to you or your father."

Mark stood and he pulled Rebecca with him. "Thank you all for coming." He clamped his lips shut. There wasn't anything else he could say without losing his composure. The room emptied except for him, Rebecca, and the still-asleep Marvella.

"Let's go sit with your father." Rebecca tugged on his hand and led him down the hall.

Thoughts swirled in his mind. Disturbing thoughts. About what he wanted to do to Harvey. He tamped them down the best he could, but when he saw Dad—ashen and taking shallow breaths—his fury returned.

If Monroe touched Kate, he would *kill* hi—

Rebecca went to the other side of the bed and prayed aloud for his father. As her words washed over him, Mark sensed the battle between the Holy Spirit working on his heart and the flesh telling him to give in to his murderous anger.

It was going to be a long night.

It was touch and go through the night with Mark's father. Rebecca refused to leave Mark's side as they waited and prayed. Mark left the room several times and she prayed even harder for him. His emotions had been hovering at the surface all night.

Dr. Hart came by in the early morning to examine Angus. Mark stood by the bedside, and she stood next to him. Finally the doctor turned to them. "Your father . . ."

Rebecca held her breath and put a hand on Mark's arm.

" . . . is just too stubborn to die, Mark. I believe he will make a full recovery."

Rebecca felt Mark's shuddering sigh and squeezed his arm as she thanked God.

The doctor slipped his stethoscope in his pocket. "I'm going to continue sitting with him, but things look good."

Mark collapsed into a chair and buried his face in his hands, his relief palpable.

Rebecca knelt beside him, her own tears stinging the corners of her eyes. "It's going to be all right. We'll soon have your brother-in-law behind bars and your sister will be safe . . . and you will be too." There was no way she could promise that, but deep in her heart, she had faith it was true.

"I don't know what I'll do if he kills her. He nearly killed Dad." Mark raised his head and met her gaze. His bloodshot eyes pleaded with her.

Rebecca offered a smile as she took both of his hands in hers. "But he didn't. God protected all of you and He will continue to do so. We have to have faith."

Mark ducked his head for several moments. When he lifted his chin, his eyes were a bit brighter. "Listen to you. You talk as though you've been at this faith thing a long time."

"Once I understood about Jesus, the rest came easy. I have

you to thank for that. You were the one that showed me it didn't need to be complicated." She squeezed his hands. "You want to take a walk? Get a cup of coffee?"

"That sounds good." He glanced at his father again. "As long as we're not gone long."

Doctor Hart nodded at him. "I'll let you know if anything happens."

Mark took her hand and led her out of the room. Emotions had run high and it had been a very stressful time, but she enjoyed the warmth of his hand and the connection she felt with him.

After filling their cups with the strong coffee Kimball had left on the stove, Mark stared at her. "You know, you've come to mean a lot to me."

"And you to me. I've enjoyed being your friend." But oh, how she longed for it to be more. After all the conversations they'd shared, the books they'd discussed, and the time with his family, Rebecca longed for him. Dare she even admit what she could no longer deny?

That she loved him?

He stepped closer. "I'd like for us to be more than friends, Rebecca."

The yearning in his eyes was almost desperate, but after the night they'd endured, she couldn't blame him. She opened her mouth, but just as she started to speak, Dr. Hart interrupted.

"Your father is awake, Mark. He's asking for you."

The town was abuzz with the news that Angus Andrews had died in the night.

Harvey smirked. Perfect.

The question was, how to proceed now?

He headed to the mercantile to see what other gossip and news he could gather.

Three women bolted out the door as he approached. Several others scurried out after them. Harvey entered and went to the counter. "What's going on?"

"The city marshal and chief of police have been called away to help with a manhunt of an escaped criminal from Bozeman." The clerk's eyebrows were arched. "Everyone is going home to lock up the best they can."

Huh. Wasn't that interesting? With law enforcement decreased, it might play into his hands to expedite his plans today. "Wasn't the sentencing supposed to happen this morning at the courthouse?" He definitely didn't want to run into any of the DA's news cronies.

"Nope. Judge Ashbury thought it prudent to delay with the manhunt underway. You know, to keep people safe."

"Very wise." Harvey tapped the counter. "I should get home myself."

The owner of the mercantile appeared. "Please accept our condolences, Mr. Monroe. Angus was a good man."

"That he was." He dipped his chin. "My wife is taking it hard. I haven't seen Mark yet, do you know if he's still in town?"

"He was at the library a few minutes ago, my wife was just there when he got the news."

This day couldn't go any better. "Thank you. I'll head over there and see if I can catch him."

Things couldn't be more perfect.

Harvey kept his smile to himself as he drove the buggy

over to the library and waited outside. Movement in the windows caught his attention. So Mark was still there. Good.

His brother-in-law came out, a black band on his coat sleeve, and posted a notice on the door. Harvey glanced around. The streets were quiet—everyone was probably cowering at home, hiding from the escaped criminal. Little did they know, there was more than one on the loose.

Things were falling into place nicely.

He kept the buggy on the corner and watched the streets. No one would be suspicious of him here. His father-in-law was dead and he was here to fetch his brother-in-law. What could be more natural?

As the lights in the library went out one by one, Harvey knew the moment was upon him. The street was completely void of traffic.

His shoulder ached, but he could deal with a little pain. Especially for this payout. His biggest yet.

Once he had Mark, he'd take him out to the line shack and kill him. Then everything would belong to Kate.

Kate's will, the one Harvey had forced her to write, named him as the one to inherit her share, but of late, Harvey had thought of a different plan. If he kept Kate alive for a time—at least until suspicions about him died down—then she could clean out the bank account before he killed her. Maybe even sell the ranch and hand over the proceeds. Then he'd be set for life. He'd seen the books. The ranch had a fortune in the bank. And there was even more value in the land.

He'd be fine with either one, but both would be so much better.

The door to the library opened and Mark walked out, closed it, and locked the door behind him.

Time to make his move.

Harvey jumped down from the buggy and strode up the sidewalk. He walked up to Mark, peering around to make sure no one was watching, and showed him the knife. "If you ever want to see your sister again, you'll come with me. If you try anything, I'll slit your throat."

Mark stared at the knife and then up at Harvey.

Well, well. Mr. Librarian looked like he wanted to kill him.

"What have you done to Kate?"

Harvey smiled. "She's fine. As long as you cooperate."

"Fine like my father?" Mark's bloodshot eyes betrayed his grief and exhaustion.

"Yeah, I heard the old man died. So sad. Rest assured, Kate's still alive. For now."

Mark's Adam's apple bobbed as he swallowed. "I'll do whatever you say."

"Good. Now we're going to take a leisurely stroll out to the buggy and you're going to get in."

"Fine."

They walked down the steps side by side.

"Yoohoo! Mark!"

It was that wretched Ashbury woman. Harvey took a tighter hold on Mark, pressing the knife into his side as they reached the last step. "Get rid of her."

"It's me, Marvella. I simply *must* get into the library." Her little dog began yipping as she moved ever closer to them—then broke loose and ran at them full speed.

The hairy nuisance seemed determined to circle them,

barking and yapping all the way. Its idiot owner wasn't much better.

"Sir Theophilus!" Marvella yelled from the edge of the street. "You come here right now!"

Instead, the little mutt snapped at Harvey's shoes. Harvey yanked Mark closer to his side, doing his best to avoid the mongrel's attack.

"Get him out of here!" Harvey kicked at the dog.

"Don't you *dare* kick my dog! He's just being friendly."

"Lady, get him away from me!"

The dog lunged for Harvey's leg, and Harvey twisted away—just as Mark drove an elbow into his arm. Harvey went off balance and the knife went skittering out across the sidewalk.

With a roar, Harvey straightened—then froze.

Something hard and cold pressed up against the back of his head.

"Don't move, Monroe. You're under arrest for murder."

Marvella beamed. She'd been instrumental in the arrest of that villain Harvey Monroe and couldn't have been more pleased with herself. For reasons still unknown to her, the chief of police had been delayed, so he and his men weren't available when Mark and Harvey came out of the library. It was her quick thinking and Milton's approval that allowed her to participate.

She regarded her dog and smiled. "You'll be famous, Sir Theophilus."

"You both will be."

Marvella glanced up to find Rebecca coming toward her.

After Harvey Monroe had been arrested, Marvella had invited everyone back to the house. Rebecca hadn't been there when they'd arrested Harvey. Milton had sent her to find out where the chief and his men were. Rebecca arrived shortly after the arrest, along with the officers. They had all been rather shocked to find out Marvella's distraction had worked, but no one said a word.

They knew better.

Mimi brought refreshments, and Marvella took a cup of tea and two macaroons in celebration. Just let someone suggest that women weren't capable of aiding in a crisis.

"Weren't you afraid?" Rebecca took the seat beside Marvella. Sir Theophilus immediately jumped up on her lap. She shook her index finger at him. "Let's not have a repeat of what happened last time." The dog lowered his head to her lap and looked up in a most forlorn manner.

"He wouldn't dare." Marvella sipped her tea. "He's a hero now and needs to act like one. But to answer your question, I was not afraid. I knew we'd capture that man."

The butler appeared. "Ma'am, the city marshal has come."

"Well, do let him in." Marvella motioned to Mimi. "Go let the judge know."

"Yes, ma'am."

The maid took off for the judge's study as the sheriff entered the parlor.

"Marshal Shelton, do come in."

"Thank you, ma'am. Is Mark Andrews here?"

"I am." Mark came into the room, with Milton behind him.

The sheriff turned to face Mark. "We found your sister. She's safe and in good shape. She's at the ranch now with your father. He's also doing well."

"Praise God! Thank you for letting me know." Mark rushed to the man and shook his hand then turned to Rebecca and Marvella. "God has been working extra hours tonight."

"Bah. God is always at work, Mark. It only seems that He's sometimes at rest. But He always knows just what we need and when." Marvella straightened and smiled. "And He gives us the courage we need for the job at hand whether it's attending to our daily duties or capturing deadly criminals. We have only to put our hope in Him and He will do the rest."

Sir Theophilus gave a resounding yip in agreement.

24

Rebecca held onto Mark's hand as they walked down the lane to the ranch house. This was right. Perfect. Their hands fit together like two pieces of a puzzle. But the silence had stretched for too long. What was he thinking? Oh, to get inside his head. "I'm so glad the marshal and his men were able to find Kate so quickly."

"Me too. That was pretty scary. Not knowing where Harvey had taken her. They're good at what they do." He squeezed her hand. "It seems like life can finally be set back in order. With Harvey arrested and Joe's conviction overturned, I know you're happy."

"Very. Justice has been done." Rebecca couldn't help but smile.

Mark stopped walking and pointed. "You see that mountain peak right there?"

"It's beautiful."

"That's my favorite. I even gave it a name when we first moved here." He pulled her to his side.

"Oh?"

"Yeah . . . Mark's Mountain." He shrugged. "I know,

creative, right? But I was a kid. It was the best I could do." Turning her toward him, he tipped her chin up with his fingers. "Everything has happened so fast, I'll understand if you need more time."

"I already told you I would court you, Mark. Don't try and talk me out of it." She swatted at his chest.

"Actually . . ." He got down on one knee.

Her heart thundered. "Oh my." Could this actually be happening?

"I was hoping you'd agree to marry me?" He rose to his feet and drew her into his arms.

She bit her lip. "But I promised my parents I wouldn't go off and marry the first man I met." She did her best to keep a straight face, but she couldn't. Giggles erupted and she buried her face in his chest. "Of course I'll marry you. I love you." She held up a finger. "But there's something you have to do."

"What is it?"

"Write to my father. After receiving that horrible letter from Mr. Tuttle, I don't want him to think that you are in any way similar to the likes of that backward-thinking man."

Mark's lips twitched. "I think I can handle that."

"Good."

His eyes searched hers. "I love you." He placed a kiss on the tip of her nose. Then time stood still as she breathed him in. Their lips met and she was overwhelmed by this man. Her heart had chosen wisely.

He released her and picked up her hand again as they walked back to the house.

"I couldn't have been the first man you met. Surely you

met men on the train. Perhaps someone handed you your luggage when you arrived?"

Their laughter joined together in the crisp air. "Once I met you, no other man could measure up."

"You're just feeding my ego now." He winked at her.

"Hey, it works in every book I've read."

He pulled her closer and kissed her lips. "Who am I to argue with that logic?"

Epilogue

Judge Ashbury walked into the room at the Ashbury mansion where Rebecca was preparing for the big day. "Are you ready, my dear?"

Her heart hadn't calmed down since she woke up. "I am. I only wish my folks could be here." The judge and his wife had offered to bring them out on the train, but Dad's job couldn't spare him and her mother was just recovering from a bout of flu. Rather than delay the wedding, she'd decided to move ahead.

"I know, your parents are wonderful people. They raised you, did they not?"

"Mark and I will go visit them soon. And even though I'll miss them, I have you and Marvella."

"We will always be here for you and Mark. In fact, before all the festivities begin, I have a wedding gift of sorts to give to you, Rebecca."

It was the first time he'd called her by her given name. It was usually 'my dear' or Miss Whitman. Tears pricked her eyes at the endearment. "Oh, sir, you didn't need to do anything else. You've already given me so much." She glanced down at the beautiful gown they'd purchased for her and smoothed the lines in her skirt.

"I know it is difficult for a woman to get into law school, and as a married woman, you would like to stay close to your new husband."

"Yes, sir. Mark and I were going to research it together. But maybe the good Lord is telling me it can wait." She bit her lip.

"Nonsense. Thus, my gift. There is a process called 'reading law,' where you study as an apprentice under an experienced lawyer. Since I am experienced, I am willing to take you under my wing. Granted, my tutelage will be tough and I will have extremely high expectations, but after a long period of study, you may take what is called a bar examination so that you may be a part of the American Bar Association of lawyers. It isn't required, but I believe you should take it because you will pass with flying colors and prove to any and all naysayers that you are more than qualified."

It was more than she could have ever imagined. She clutched her hands to her chest and couldn't help the escape of a few tears. "Oh, Judge . . ."

"Now, now. None of that. You are deserving of this and so much more, my dear." He took both of her hands in his. "Just look at you. You are simply stunning."

Tears pricked her eyes again and threatened to fall. "I don't know what I would have done without you inviting me here to work, sir."

"Oh, stuff and nonsense. You were well deserving of the job, and stop the waterworks while you're at it. No one—

and I mean *no one*—wants to see this old geezer cry at your wedding." He wiggled those bushy eyebrows of his until she laughed.

Releasing his hands, she reached for her hankie. "Hopefully I won't need this too much today, but I'm a sucker for a good love story."

"You and me both, my dear."

"And no doubt Marvella is congratulating herself on all that's come to pass."

The judge laughed. "You do realize that it wasn't Marvella's idea to try to match you two together"—he proudly tucked his thumbs into his waistcoat pockets and gave her a grin that would rival the Cheshire cat—"that was all *my* genius at work."

Her eyes widened. "No." She waved her hankie at him. "That's not true . . . is it?"

Walking toward the door, he threw over his shoulder, "I know the entire town *thinks* that Marvella is the mastermind behind everything, the one calling all the shots, the puppeteer. . . ." He let the comment hang as he left the room and closed the door behind him.

Her mind raced through everything that she'd witnessed. No. The man was surely pulling her leg.

Laughter filled her heart and mind. Not even six months ago, she'd been in Chicago sending applications, searching the country for her future.

And it had brought her here.

To the Flathead Valley, one of the most beautiful places on earth.

And to Mark. The most wonderful man in all the world. God's special gift to her.

To think that she'd had to travel across the country to truly understand God's grace. The simplicity of faith.

But oh, how wonderful that was. Each day, she'd come to know her Lord and Savior better. She'd read through the Bible two times now—the second time with Mark as they prepared for their wedding. They'd devoted two hours each evening to read to each other.

When Marvella first intimated that she and Mark would be a great match, oh how Rebecca had bucked like a green horse out on the River View Ranch. New to her surroundings, unwilling to listen to guidance. But how wrong she'd been.

No matter how much the woman liked to be in the middle of everything, Rebecca would be forever grateful.

She was, after all, Marvella's most prized protégé.

The thought made her giggle.

The clock chimed for 11:45.

A knock sounded at her door.

Rebecca's heart kicked into high gear as she went to answer it. She'd asked Mark to come see her before the wedding, bending the old wedding tradition, hoping it would help her nerves when she walked down the aisle.

It must be him. Right on time.

Her hand slipped on the knob. "Um, you better open it." Not wanting to wipe her sweaty palms on her dress, she dashed across the room and grabbed her hankie.

"I know marriage can be scary, but I didn't expect you to run away." Mark's voice oozed his charm.

As she turned, she knew exactly what she'd see.

Those teasing eyes. And that smile.

Oh, that smile.

For months, she'd tried to keep her thoughts in check about this handsome man. Guarding her heart and mind. Keeping herself pure for this day. Wanting to keep God first in her mind and in her heart.

It hadn't been easy. But now, looking into his blue eyes, she knew that she was his. That God had ordained this union.

He raised his eyebrows. Waited.

Wiping her hands on the hankie, she ran back to him and jumped into his arms.

Thankfully, he caught her.

"I take it you haven't changed your mind?" His breath feathered her neck. Then he kissed her there.

"Of course not."

His lips made a trail up to her cheek.

They'd only shared a few kisses here and there since they got engaged. But now. Oh goodness.

She pulled him closer.

His mouth captured her own. "I love you." He spoke against her lips. "I never understood this kind of love until God brought you into my life." He stepped back. Took a long deep breath as he stared at her.

"Me neither." She hadn't understood unconditional love until she came here. Oh, how she wanted to share that with her family and everyone she knew.

The smile he sent her made her knees go a bit weak. Marriage was going to be so much fun. She fanned herself with her hankie.

He chuckled and held out his arm. "Ready to get hitched?"

Oh yes. She was ready. "Let's go, Cowboy."

Note from the Authors

Thank you for taking this journey with us to Kalispell, Montana, and the Carnegie Museum. If you go to Kalispell today, you can still see the amazing building, but it's now the Hockaday Museum of Art.

The gorgeous wood floors, banisters, and trim are all still there. One difference that we discovered was the front steps. They've obviously been redone sometime in the last century because (probably for code issues) there were originally nine steps whereas today, there are eleven.

Since the law plays a big part in this story, we had to do a lot of research into the laws of the time period. Conflict of interest is something that we are all well acquainted with nowadays, but the ABA (American Bar Association) Canons of Professional Ethics weren't adopted until 1908 and, even then, they didn't provide much guidance to courts and enforcement authorities on conflict of interest.

We love Judge Ashbury and know that he would do his best to stay above reproach in his dealings, but we wanted you—the readers—to see and understand his struggle.

For some interesting information about the Carnegie Library, head over to my website for additional links and fascinating tidbits: kimberleywoodhouse.com

Another historical location that we used in *The Heart's Choice* was The Brewery Saloon—which became The Palm—and which had a sordid and notorious past.

And for all of you animal lovers out there, Sir Theophilus is based off of a friend's tiny dog. He is a hoot. His name came from a huge stuffed penguin—a precious gift from my son several years ago—who was lovingly dubbed Sir Theophilus. He stands guard over my office.

We hope you will join us for the rest of THE JEWELS OF KALISPELL series, where we adventure into the historic train depot and the McIntosh Opera House.

—Kimberley and Tracie

Acknowledgments

Loads of people help us with every one of our books. We'd like to give recognition to a few of them here.
In Kalispell we'd like to thank:

- Gordon Pirrie and Mark Pirrie (owners of Western Outdoor and the historic McIntosh Opera House above it)—Gordon sent loads of information after we visited and answered my phone calls and questions over and over. Mark was a gem and let me into the actual Opera House. Be watching for more details and pictures for the coming books.
- Brit Clark—museum director—Conrad Mansion Museum.
- Terri Mattson—museum admin—Northwest Montana History Museum.
- Vonnie Day—Kalispell Chamber of Commerce (which is located in the historic train depot)—she even took me down into the creepy basement.

- Alyssa Cordova—Hockaday Museum of Art (which is in the Carnegie Library) Executive Director.

At Bethany House we'd like to thank every member of the team there, from editing, to marketing, to design, to publicity—thank you all so much!

Jessica Sharpe, our lead editor, you are a joy to work with!

Karen Ball, our editor extraordinaire. You. Are. The. Best. Thank you. Thank you. Thank you.

And to all of our readers who make this possible: we love you and appreciate each one of you.

To God be the glory!

—Kimberley and Tracie

Tracie Peterson (www.traciepeterson.com) is the award-winning author of over one hundred novels, both historical and contemporary. Her avid research resonates in her many bestselling series. Tracie and her family make their home in Montana.

Kimberley Woodhouse (www.kimberleywoodhouse.com) is an award-winning, bestselling author of more than twenty-five fiction and nonfiction books. Kim and her incredible husband of thirty-plus years live in the Poconos, where they play golf together, spend time with their kids and grandbaby, and research all the history around them.

Sign Up for the Authors' Newsletters

Keep up to date with Tracie and Kimberley's news on book releases and events by signing up for their email lists at traciepeterson.com and kimberleywoodhouse.com.

FOLLOW TRACIE AND KIMBERLEY ON SOCIAL MEDIA!

Tracie Peterson

Kimberley Woodhouse

@authortraciepeterson

@kimberleywoodhouse

THE TREASURES OF NOME Series from Tracie Peterson and Kimberley Woodhouse

◆ BETHANYHOUSE